IF WE DON'T

IF WE DON'T
Jordie Cole

DEDICATION

I want to dedicate this book to all the people in my life that have joined me on this journey. Those who boarded on the cruise ship of my imagination, flew on a magic carpet through the crevices of my mind, leapt off the cliff only to be disappointed when I killed off their favorite characters, and especially to those who pretended to listen as I rambled on and on and on about the visions in my head that I wanted to scribe on paper.

To my mom, thank you for your unwavering and unconditional love. I would not be where I am in life today without you, and I am beyond blessed to be your daughter. I will always love you more!

To Marc, thank you for embracing my quirks. Your relentless taunts remind me that you are always there for me, but beware, paybacks are hell. Oh, and this time, it really is 'my movie'.

To my brother whose endless taunts and teasing, and brotherly love, has molded me into a stronger person. I truly appreciate your hard-headed, rebellious spirit which, alongside teaching me what *not* to do, has been a welcome guidepost for my success.

To my family and friends who are always there when I need a good laugh or a stiff drink, who show me what it is to be a strong person, and who are always there to lend a helping hand or shoulder to cry on.

To Jon, thank you for 'volunteering' to leave the room when I need silence to write. Thank you for your encouragement, support, and patience.

And a special shoutout to my high school classmates who were the first to encourage my passion for writing. I finally did it, guys!

And thank you, God, for giving me a wonderful support system who encourages me to be my best. And for giving me the opportunity, and platform, to reach others. To God be the Glory!

"How cool is it that the same God that created mountains and oceans and galaxies thought the world needed one of you, too." – Unknown

"You are free to choose, but you are not free from the consequences of your choice." – Unknown

PLAYLIST:

I'm Coming Home – Skylar Grey
Mansion – NF
Someone You Loved – Lewis Capaldi
Remember the Name – Fort Minor
The Great Escape – Boys Like Girls
Almost Heaven – Jeremiah Lloyd Harmon
Flashlight – Jessie J
Shallow – Lady Gaga & Bradley Cooper
You Are the Reason – Calum Scott
I just Need You – TobyMac
Headstrong – Trapt
In the End – Linkin Park
Who You Say I Am – Hillsong
Oceans – Hillsong
Unbreakable – Sutton Foster (Gilmore Girls)

PART 1

CHAPTER 1

TWELVE YEARS OLD

His grandmother would have called the sound obtuse; his sister would have called it bleak, but to Issa, the sound that bounced off the walls was simply flat. It was a sound that hit deep down in the pit of his stomach, a sound that stopped the movement of the world around him so that even the slightest spec of debris halted mid-air during its turbulent flight to the ground. And yet, it didn't keep him from pressing the cord again, closing his eyes as he fought to keep his internal war from rising to the surface, his face a mask of indifference.

This wasn't the first time he'd sat at one of the noise machines or put his fingers on the cracked finger-like sticks, but this was the first since he had lost Bethany. Meeting in rooms like this always made him think of her, but until now, he couldn't bring himself to face the memories of his older sister and the melodies she would create.

3

'I did it', he thought as he keyed the note again. 'I did it', he repeated, anger rising as his knuckles pounded the keyboard. 'I did it, I did it…' he repeated the mantra, his hands slamming again and again until the words fell out of him in an angry roar that pushed him out of his seat and his hands fighting harder against the keys.

His breath hitched when the tune stopped humming and his chest rose and fell as he gained his bearings.

"Issa," he heard over his com, the muffled sound of Malik's taught voice centering him, "is it clear?"

Issa hesitated, not ready for his comrades to pile in, still reeling from his defeat against the wooden music box. The room he was in was well-fortified except for the gaping hole that tore through the ceiling. The clouds chose that moment to part, ever so slightly, allowing a single ray of light to bounce magnificent colors throughout the room. Issa searched around in confusion until he found the one window that remained intact. Pieced together with black lines, the colors bound together in a mural surrounding two clear lines that intersected at a perfect 90-degree angle. Instinctively, he reached for his neck and traced the edges of the perpendicular gold sticks, holding the emblem up to the glass; the shape was a match.

"Issa," Malik's voice pierced the silence and the cold metal slapped against his chest as he turned. Malik was one of the few Revival members that Issa genuinely liked and trusted, which was lucky considering Malik was the Revival's First-in-Command. One of the few men around with dark brown hair relatively clean and trimmed added to Malik's controlled and confident demeanor, unlike so many of the disheveled hooligans running around in their clan. Given his family circumstances, it was a miracle Malik was here at all. It is not uncommon for neighborhood families to be broken, but to have lost your entire family before you could even learn to say their names, it was heartbreaking. Most of the orphan children grow up reckless and unclean since they don't have anyone looking out for them and they're forced into the life of labor early on. In fact, looking at him now, you'd almost think that Malik and Issa's lives were swapped. Not old enough to sprout a beard, the dirt on Issa's skin clung to his face like a five o'clock shadow, instantly adding five years to his youth and helping him camouflage in with his fellow Revival members. And perhaps that's why Malik favored Issa, because he saw a bit of himself in the boy, or at least saw an image of who he could have been.

While other orphans ran around the streets, barely waking up in time for chores and work, Malik would sneak away to a nearby lake to ensure his clothes and body were clean. He governed his days, altering between attending his school teachings and joining the hunts for food, pacing his meals so that he would not go hungry between feedings. And when he reached the golden age of thirteen and was offered a chance to join the Revival, Malik took the opportunity with stride, practicing his drills in the evenings before bed and passing his entrance exam with flying colors. He was promoted to Third-In-Command at sixteen years of age and he quietly listened and watched his predecessors until they both stepped down to start families, leaving Malik to lead the Revival and the ripe age of eighteen years old. Now twenty-two, Malik had one of the longest reigning tenures as First-In-Command in the neighborhood's history, and he had no intention of leaving.

Standing taller than 6 feet, he was a stark contrast to Issa who, while he supported a similarly strong and lean build, was barely taller than 5 and a half feet tall. Issa, who couldn't recall the last time he had a decent bath, nonetheless attempted to calm the dark wavy locks that now reaches beyond his shoulders. His family was a solid unit consisting of a strong father who, at least on the outside, worked as one of the neighborhood's most able healers. His mother serving as a nurturer, responsible for guiding young women into motherhood and serving as an aide to orphans needing guidance and assistance as they learned to provide for themselves, all while Issa and his sister endured their educational and physical studies.

"What are you doing"? Malik prodded as he examined Issa. Issa panicked, knowing he had not fulfilled his role as a scout. This was his first real mission and he needed to prove his capabilities. His confidence faltering, he couldn't meet Malik's gaze as he approached. "If you forgot protocol…"

"I didn't," Issa interjected, his dad's voice scolding him for his rude manners. "I thought I saw something," he lied, hoping he sounded convincing enough to fool his commander, but the skeptical look on Malik's face worried him. He knew Malik had gone to battle for him, pushing the elders and Revival to accept Issa into their tribe. An internal rage consumed Issa. There were reasons the Revival had rules, there was a purpose to the entrance exam and tests, but those rules were bent for Issa's sake and he was not fulfilling his promise.

"Where?" Malik questioned, surveying the room, his left hand instinctively reaching for his gun.

"I was wrong, just a rat," Issa rattled, instinctively reaching for his curly locks again and Malik cringed internally as he registered Issa's tell. Malik relaxed and his posture settled as he sized up the space. His eyes stopped briefly as he caught sight of the music box, the soft dust clearly interrupted in waves of distress.

Scout days were always hard on Malik, but this had to be one of the worst. He liked Issa, he even put his own neck on the line for him, but he had to admit that there was a heightened fear allowing a juvie to run lead at scout. But he was the one that pushed the elders to give Issa a fair chance, and Malik was determined to provide it, knowing a single mistake could mean imminent harm not only for the Revival, but for their entire neighborhood.

A cursory overview of the room told Malik that they were still at risk. The dust that enveloped the room was even and settled with the exception of Issa's footpath that led to the piano, but that's where it stopped. He'd noticed the open interior doorway immediately and the lack of tread was a clear indication that his trainee needed a brush up with the basics.

"Take a double," Malik instructed, turning his hand, index finger extended, in a rotating motion. He nodded towards the doorframe whose black shadowed secrets could carry millions of untold dangers to the Revival, "I'll swing back for the boys".

On his way back around, Malik scoured the benches as closely as he could without drawing Issa's attention. There was no evidence of wildlife or rodents which made Malik smirk internally, the poor kid was just as sucky at lying as he'd been at that age. But lying in these circumstances, to

7

your superior nonetheless, was simply unacceptable, and he would need to confront Issa about that soon.

Issa grabbed his light and moved toward the second room without caution. '*Take a double*', sure, it would have been a double if Issa had bothered to check the space the first time. Having shrugged off his responsibilities, his entire team would be at risk as soon as Malik brought them in, so Issa needed to make haste and search for any signs of tampering.

The room was dark and dusty, much like the rest of the building, and held nothing of interest. Some books, dusty and rotted. A few cloaks, also dusty and molded. And a few folded tables, you guessed it, dusty. But no obvious machinery or hidden cameras, and certainly no signs of life. Issa took a deep breath as the sounds of the Revival came bounding through and interrupting the quiet sanctuary. Issa stood still, frustration seizing him. This was his duty, his responsibility, and he'd done a piss poor job of it. He was given a chance that no one else had, and he hadn't taken it seriously. If the Revival fell tonight, it would be all his fault. He made a mental note that he would not bail on his responsibilities again, he would not risk his team.

Before leaving the blackened space, Issa stopped for one final moment. Grabbing his necklace, he thought of Bethany. Had they led a different life, been born before the war, she would have enjoyed a chapel like this one. Issa kissed his necklace as he had seen his sister do many times before, wiped away the anxiety from his skin as if it were an overcoat he could slip off, and walked back into the main room to join his team.

The Revival was full of life, their laughter filling the empty space as if they had no fear in the world. Issa was in awe of how careless they all seemed, how easy they clamored in. Could they not see the potential dangers that the space held? Did they not second-guess the capabilities of their scout, of Issa, that could have led them into their own coffin? In the front row, one boy was climbing over the bench while two others engaged in a wrestling match beside him. Behind them, four more sat in idle positions, leaning on one another and kicking their feet up over the top of the benches. Six more lingered into the room in a pack, weapons draped across their chests, having just come off night duty surveying the borders. While four of them engaged in easy banter, Issa's attention was drawn to the two who appeared to be having a disagreement.

Outside, there was undoubtably ten more boys whom just took over their morning post. On the far side of the room, you had five boys throwing a weighted sack amongst them as they spread further and further apart, their weapons parked in the pews and perched against the broken windowsills. Taller than the rest, Malik joined this group, jumping in the middle and seizing the toy as he stalked off. The boys let out grunts and gawks as Malik pocketed their plaything and ordered them to their seats.

The boys were in various stages of cloth. Those coming off the night shift were in full gear, their black Velcro bullet-proof vests secured tightly across their chests and dark, cut-up jeans adorning their waists. A few of the more fortunate souls wore elastic waisted shorts and t-shirts, but the majority of the team were bare-chested, their legs covered by the short brown-leather pelt that the commoners boasted.

"Alright, alright" Malik bellowed, bringing the bantering to a halt as he waived his hand in the thick air, "sit so we can get on". He was fully suited, Issa had yet to see his leading commander out of gear, ready to pounce on his prey at any moment.

The flies in Issa's stomach fluttered as he allowed himself a moment of exaltation, perching several rows behind his colleagues, distancing himself from the wrestlers and the sleepers. *'He did it,'* he thought to himself. *'He did it; he joined the Revival. He may not be 'one of them' just yet, but they'll come around as he proves his worth, he'd make certain of it'.*

"Second, enter!" Malik hollered, commanding his Second-In-Command to leave his post at the entry and join the team for the meet. "What's our total head?" He asked as Xavier sauntered in.

A hooligan turned commander; Xavier led with a chip on his shoulder. Issa hadn't been fond of the guy before joining the Revival, and his opinions only further soured once he joined. The guy had a foul attitude, potential ulterior motives, and his squinty eyes told of unspoken secrets. He pushed them hard at drills, bullied the younger recruits, and excused the behavior as 'skilled training tactics'. As if there weren't enough reasons to dislike the guy, he stood several inches above Malik, always looking down on his commander, both physically and mentally.

"Twenty-one end count, sir," Xavier flashed. I did the numbers myself and he was right. There were twenty-one warm bodies in the room. With ten men stationed at the morning border, that meant two heads were missing from the count. Malik clearly did the math himself as he did a quick survey of the room.

"Why are we short?" Malik asked, masking fear in his tone. Having earned his spot at a young age, Malik gained a reputation for being one of the strictest leaders the Revival has ever had. But with strict leadership, came great rewards, seeing as how both the Revival and the neighborhood had surpassed headcount records that dated more than 20 years in the past.

"Nunez is out sick, I checked on him myself. He has the best hands ensuring he gets back on ASAP," Xavier explained and Issa's mind wandered. His father was most likely tending to Nunez; the elders would want the most skilled medic to ensure a member of the Revival is back to work promptly. It's the third day of the week too, which meant that, had Issa not given up his studies to join the Revival, he would be at his father's side, learning the healing practices so he could take over for his father one day. "Reyes welcomed his baby girl this morning, five pounds, nine ounces," he smirked, leaning back and propping his feet up smugly, his pelt sliding back and revealing veiny muscled legs. "Our Third-In-Command will be back at his station this evening". Both missing members were fine, well for the most part anyway. Xavier could have started with that, but he liked to get a rise out of Malik when he could. But as always, Malik pushed his ego back down and refused to give Xavier any response besides a slight tightening of his eyes, imperceptible to most. But Issa was paying attention, he'd watched Malik for months and was fairly well attuned to his queues.

"And the neighborhood check, what's the status this morning?" Malik questioned, his eyes lingering on Xavier as he waited for one of the record-keepers to chime in. One of the boys feigning sleep dropped his legs from where they perched and dragged the disheveled stack of loose-leaf pages onto his lap. How the teenager earned his role was beyond

Issa's comprehension, clearly the kid wasn't organized well enough for his duties as he muddled through the pages.

"The ughh-" the boy stammered, searching for his answer, "the. Neighbor. Hood. Check. Is," he accentuated each word, drawing out time. Malik was growing irritable. This was not the team he cultivated. This was not the team that would save their neighborhood. This team wouldn't survive a raid, nonetheless a true camp of soldiers. No, this was a team that would walk themselves right into the hands of the Troops and smile as a soldier sticks a knife in his back. A new pit settled in his stomach, adding to the wall of rocks that could come down in an avalanche with the slightest breeze. "Got it!" The boy announced proudly, raising the page up for all to see before realizing he still needed to answer the question. "Got it, the neighborhood headcount is heavy by one this morning, courtesy of Mr. and Mrs. Reyes," he chuckled, "total up to a new record high of one-hundred and fifty-seven."

'One fifty-seven,' Malik thought, a surge of pride filling his chest as his outside features remained stoic. The moment of pride didn't last, he couldn't let this success overshadow his shortcomings.

"Get up!" Malik shouted, surprising the sleepers as everyone jolted upright. Pulling the sack out of his pocket, he launched it at the huddle of boys. "Up, now! Get up!" The boys huddled together as Malik stepped in their direction. "What is this? A fucking daycare?! Am I your nanny?!" Malik yelled, turning his back on them. "You're too comfortable, all of you! That's how we make mistakes! One fifty-seven is a victory, but this war is far from over and we have to stay on top of our game if we want our numbers to grow. And that means staying awake when you're called to a meeting!" He turned back around; his typical pale complexion reddened with fury as he looked around the room cautiously. He had boys sleeping, some playing games, and he even caught the Chosen One bailing on scout duties this morning. They were too comfortable, forgetting the true harm that awaited them if they didn't remain sharp. He had a new class of graduates amongst him, this was the time to tighten up, to show them what they've signed up for. "You will all do double drills today", he announced and was immediately met with the low grumble he anticipated. "No? You're too good for drills now, is that what I hear?" No one responded and they averted his gaze as he glanced around the room; all but one. "Issa" he called, hoping the boy wouldn't disappoint him. While he liked Issa, he felt a kinship with the kid and knew that the young talent needed to be properly groomed. "What do you think? Do you think this clan deserves double drills for their behavior here today?"

Issa felt heat surging up his face. He knew his team hated drills and the sun was quickly melting the few remaining clouds in the sky. But Issa? He loved drills. The feeling of the hot sun on his tanned skin, his body sweating away his weakness, his young muscles developing with each new set. "I think-"

"Louder," Malik commanded, his head bowing towards Issa as he sent a telepathic message. '*say yes*'.

"Triple", the words fell out of Issa's mouth like a flood and immediately earned him sharp gleams from his onlookers. Malik was surprised, but he tried not to show it. Triple drills in today's heat would surely separate the weak from the strong. While he enjoyed the challenge, he also didn't want his team too tired that they become ineffectual.

Issa reveled in the idea of rubbing his sore muscles this evening, the gift from a good day of hard work. This is what he wanted; it's why he joined the Revival. "I think we could do triple drills".

Malik paused, uncertain how to respond. Maybe he wasn't doing so bad training the kid after all. Maybe, just maybe, the kid stood a chance at the redemption the elders gossiped about. Maybe Issa would be the one to see them through the dark times. "Triple, huh?" He pretended to ponder the assertion. "You know, I think you're right. Does anyone object?" Malik found Xavier in the crowd and silently urged him not to respond. He knew Xavier and Issa did not get on, but pushing against Issa now would only serve to undermine him. "No takers?" Malik questioned, silently counting to three as stillness surrounded the room. "Hmmm, good, then triple it is. Now, I want a boundary report".

One of the night crew members that appeared to have been in an argument upon entering the hall cleared his throat. Issa recognized him as a teenager named Geoff who boasted translucent skin and was one of the few neighborhood members with blonde straight hair. "We found a huddle of buildings to the West that look promising. About 5 miles. The roads are fair. If we can push a small team there to scout, it should only take a couple days to clear." Geoff shared, a haunted look in his emerald eyes as he glanced at his neighbor.

"What aren't you saying?" Malik asked, a darkness settling over the room as the room waited for a response.

The boys hesitated before the one known as Cable gave in. "There were some tracks spotted along the Northeast border. Maybe two or three miles out." The words were an omen and the entire group shifted in their seats. Malik knew they had been here too long, but the comfort of a solid shelter and nearby water source was too attractive for him to force them back to the road. "It could have been some stragglers, maybe even a small neighborhood," the boy carried on, making excuses to avoid the inevitable, "they disappeared in the grass, so we don't know how close they came".

"Were they bare?" Xavier spoke as he leaned forward in his seat, dark eyes revealing the same fear that Malik felt. Malik leaned his head down, holding the bridge of his nose as he shook his head. His team shouldn't be making excuses, they shouldn't have held back this information. Valuable time had already been wasted, who cared if the feet were bare at this point, they all knew what this meant.

Cable, a stumpy boy with unruly sandy brown hair and freckles, looked uncomfortable as he looked down at his naked, burned, and scratched-up feet. Issa couldn't help but wonder how Cable could have joined the Revival, his stomach hung over his shorts and he clearly hadn't missed a meal in a while. "They disappeared in the grass, so we don't know how close-"

"Were. They. Bare?" Xavier repeated, accentuating each word.

The boy shook his head before mumbling, "no".

The intensity in the room lit up like a summer storm. Issa watched as Xavier turned to Malik. "They could be here tomorrow. If they're scouts, there could be a whole raid upon us in less than twenty-four", Xavier stated, his eyes wide. But Malik already knew, had already come to the same conclusion that every boy in the room was thinking. Unlike the terror on Xavier's face, Malik's fear displayed itself with vengeance.

"Sound the alarm," he commanded of Xavier. "Geoff, Zeke, Taylor, Ben, Hareem", he paused as he looked around the room and came to a stop at the Chosen One, "and Issa, suit up. I want you to go to the new heading in the West." Malik looked back, pointing at Geoff, "5 miles?"

"Yes sir," Geoff confirmed.

"I want you on the road in 30 minutes, set your watches", Malik commanded. Immediately the six boys did as they were told and began their timers on their watches. "Search in twos, if you spot anything, see if you can dismantle. If not, send three back and the remainder of you continue to push on West. If all is clear, five of you sleep and one keep watch. When we arrive, I'm sending the first five back out on a new hunt to keep pushing West and then one will stay to debrief." The boys acknowledged Malik's instructions and all jumped from their seats to leave.

"Issa-" Malik called and Issa ran to him. Malik knew the boys well enough to know they wouldn't intentionally harm him, but he also knew that Issa would be the first choice to stay on guard when the time came. Malik bent over Issa and lowered his voice so that only he could hear. "You're ready, otherwise I wouldn't send you." Issa nodded. "When the time comes, get sleep, tell the others you're not to be the lookout, understood?" Malik could see Issa's disappointment, but Issa still confirmed the demand without hesitation. Malik tightened his grip around Issa's forearm for a slight second and then dropped his hold, "Go".

And Issa did. He ran out of the building, the heat of the sun already weighing down on him as he pushed himself towards his home. He knew his family would be scared and that he wouldn't have the time to give them a proper goodbye. He had just made it to his front steps when the sirens rang through the air, the alarm notifying everyone in the neighborhood to return home and pack their belongings.

Issa sprang into his house where he crashed into his mother. It only took a moment for her to register what was happening. "You're going," she asked timidly.

"I only have a few minutes" he confirmed. Her face registered the impact like a physical hit, but she didn't protest. He felt her pain as she covered her mouth in an attempt to hide the wail that her lungs pushed out. But Issa didn't have time to console her. He pushed on, skimming up the steps to the room he shared with his sister.

Besides the weapons he already held, the remaining guns, knives, and grenades were already packed and ready, just as he intended they be in the event he needed a quick exit. Nevaeh was in the closet grabbing the few stuffed toys their parents allowed her to keep and shoving them into her luggage. She paused as he pushed above her to grab his military vest and the only pair of cargo pants he owned.

He moved out of the closet and pulled the pants on, their heavy material foreign to him after years of not wearing leggings. He'd only just become used to wearing the loose elastic shorts the Revival found at a gym during a scout. Half the boys protested the shorts, electing to keep to the neighborhood's traditional beliefs, but Issa acquiesced to his mother's pleas to look more formidable around Nevaeh.

As soon as the buckles of his vest were shut, he leaned down to kiss Nevaeh's forehead. Had they not been separated by years, many would have sworn Nevaeh to be Issa's twin. They shared the same olive complexion, thinly sloped cheeks, and bone-y stature. Issa's heart clung to her as he wrapped his arms around her tiny frame, but when it came to her, he didn't care that he was wasting precious time.

Her hair, half braided and half flat, swallowed him as he took a deep breath of her earthy scent. Her big eyes sought answers, but he didn't give them. He turned to leave just as Nevaeh pushed her favorite toy towards him, the crusted wool brushing against his hand as he picked up his bag. Issa hated to disappoint her, but he knew he couldn't bring the toy with him.

"Keep it for me, save it for when you see me again." He patted her head as she sulked, pushing the rogue hairs behind her shoulder. "Pack your things first. If you have time, try to grab some of mine. I've got to go," he clicked his watch, illuminating the thirteen minutes he had remaining.

Issa bounded down the stairs two at a time. "Where's dad?" He asked as he pushed into his parent's bedroom. His mother was dutifully packing, tears filling her eyes as she willed herself not to cry.

"He hasn't returned from Medic," she stammered. Issa sighed, looking back at his watch. He had twelve minutes and he still needed to meet the boys at the far end of town, a six-minute jaunt on a good day.

"Tell him we're headed due West five miles. I'll find a safe place to settle in," he informed, and then added with a laugh, "get a good leg up on a mansion" he smiled, trying to ease the tension of his first real mission with the Revival, "with king beds."

"Don't you worry about us, just keep your head down and stay alert", she demanded, pulling Issa in for a teary-eyed hug. When she pulled away, Issa swore he saw Bethany, his mother's oval face and high bun a signature Bethany look, but the image faded as soon as it arose. He decided that it was a good omen and he turned to leave.

Just as Issa read ten minutes counting down on his watch, he heard the front door slam, and he ran to the door with his mother in tow. His dad was nearly bowing over in exhaustion, his brown curls draping over his face as his lungs screamed for air. No matter what disengaged front his dad put on, Issa knew that he really cared about his children, his heart was just too haunted to reveal it. The two men exchanged a quick nod. "Do your mom and I proud", he asserted, putting his hand on Issa's shoulder.

Issa stood dormant; his feet tied to the ground as the seconds ticked by. Looking behind his parents to the stairwell, Nevaeh sat perched between the iron rods and Bethany sat behind her. She smiled timidly and the weight holding Issa lifted. He quickly turned and pushed through the thin opening of the front door and began his jog towards the West end checkpoint. At the end of the street, he stopped to look back. His family hadn't come outside to watch him leave; they'd be too busy packing up their house once again. The ninth home Issa had known, and that's just counting the ones he could remember. But eleven months in one home was unheard of in the North, which made it that much harder to pack up and leave. He'd come to enjoy this home, his routine, and it would once again be erased by the presence of the Troops.

He glanced back down at his watch, eight minutes to spare. He set out at a fast sprint, barely recognizing the buildings as he swerved his way through the broken streets, dodging fellow neighbors as they rushed home to pack.

When Issa arrived, his body was slick with sweat and his joints were on a slow burn; he loved it.

"Hey kid," a boy he had come to know as Taylor, said as he walked toward Issa, his hand out with a bottle of water extended, "I figured you wouldn't think to pack one. This is on loaner until we can find you a good one". Issa took the bottle thankfully and opened the lid, taking a massive gulp from the top. "Slow down," Taylor quipped as Issa wiped stray beads of water from his chin. "We've got a long trip; you need to pace that or you'll get sick. Take small sips when we stop running, but don't make extra stops and don't hold us back."

"I'm the fastest runner here," Issa reminded, cocky from the multiple drills and relays he'd won.

"You're fastest because you're untrained. Out there" he motioned towards the streets that disappeared into the sunset, "it's not a contest; it's about endurance. Keep pace with us, don't overdo it or you'll regret it. We've all been the fastest runner at some point, but there are more important things than speed."

Issa's mind drifted back to his Revival lessons and the test he had to pass. There could be buried mines, hidden dugouts, they could even run right into a band of Troops. Sure, Geoff had already scouted the pathway, but new dangers could appear without notice. Issa attached the lid back to his bottle just as their sixth member, Ben, approached.

"You ready?" Geoff asked, turning to them each individually, eyes landing on Issa last; he nodded. "Holler when you need to stop, don't get more than 20 feet behind, and don't slow us down. Out there, we are a team, but you better believe it is every man for himself if you don't keep up". With a slight tilt of his head, Geoff took off and set the pace, the boys quickly joining in a 'V' formation as they headed into the unknown.

CHAPTER 2

ELEVEN YEARS OLD

I ssa combed his hands through her hair, little strands knitting together and straining against his tiny fingers. *"Ouch, be gentle,"* Bethany winced, holding her head back as Issa continued to play.

"Are you listening?" Rafael chided playfully, *"I have an important decision to make here,"* he reminded her.

"I think you'll be great at any of them," she smiled. She was laying on her stomach, her head resting in her hands. Rafi was laying beside her, his chin propped up against his fists until he folded them and ducked his head into the mattress.

"You're no help," he scolded, closing his eyes in an attempt to ease the pain behind his eyes. *"I can't wait 'til next year when you have to choose, you better remember this and how you bailed on me".*

"I'm not bailing," she laughed, pushing Issa off of her and turning onto her back.

"Yeah, she's not bailing," Issa mimicked. *"Besides, she's going to be a nurturer like mama,"* he hopped over Bethany and jumped onto Rafael's back, Rafi letting out a large roar

21

as he turned and grabbed Issa by the hands, picking him up and launching the kid over his shoulders as he reached to tickle him.

"Oh yeah, and what about you, then? What will you do next year when your sister graduates and begins her assignment?" He asked as he tormented Issa, finding the sensitive spot around his hips. Issa wailed as he scratched and thrashed at Rafi, using all his strength to escape his captor's strong hold. When Rafael caved, he settled Issa back down on the ground.

Issa pushed his wild hair out of his eyes and righted himself. "That's easy, I'm going to be a medic like dad."

"Is that right? You've got to be smart to help your dad, that's a tough skill," he goaded, knowing the seven-year-old would have many years to deliberate and change his mind. But for Rafael, time was a luxury he didn't have. Month twelve was coming to a close and the neighborhood would soon be celebrating their next year and, being his thirteenth year, Rafi would be one of the few celebrating his graduation and asked to decide his assignment. While he always imagined himself a gatherer or hunter, the current unrest in the neighborhood had him wondering if it was selfish to ignore his innate talents, his speed and agility making him an excellent candidate for joining the Revival.

The neighborhood had been forced to pick up and move a lot lately, a band of Troops hot on their heels. In the last raid, the Troops paralyzed the Revival by seizing two of their best sharp shooters and their fastest scout. In the raid before that, they nearly suffocated them as they stole and destroyed the little food supply the gatherers had managed to collect. The latest Revival updates indicated that the soldiers were still hot on their tails, having only given them half a day's *rest before following in their footsteps. The elders were growing weary, spreading rumors of splitting the neighborhood into two in an effort to minimize the destruction. But with the Revival numbers dwindling to an all-time low, the notion to split the artillery was inconceivable.*

"Yup, I'm going to be the best," Issa claimed, pulling Rafi back to reality. The little boy knocked on his chest with his arm like a gorilla ready to charge his enemy, "All the sick people will come to me to make them feel better and I'll heal them instantly!"

"There's more to it than that," Bethany chimed in.

"Yeah-" Rafi interjected, "so if I get hurt in the Revival, you gonna come stitch me up?"

The air sucked out of the room, Issa's brown eyes widening as he stepped back and looked up at Rafi. Rafael and Bethany had been friends since before Issa was born; the two were practically inseparable. Since Bethany practically raised him, Rafi was like a brother to Issa, which made the announcement painful.

"You're joining the Revival?" Issa questioned, glancing between them as they moved to the edge of the bed. Rafi looked at Bethany and pondered how to respond, but Bethany avoided his gaze. She couldn't lie, but she also didn't want to be responsible for singing him to sleep after tormented nightmares of gaping bullet wounds and bloody severed limbs.

Bethany instinctively reached for her necklace and both boys watched her silently, the lighthearted banter gone. Issa reached out for it and Bethany let him hold the thin gold cross as he moved closer and pushed into her lap.

If We Don't

"You know, Issa, not everyone in the Revival gets hurt. There are some jobs that don't even need weapons," Bethany informed, trying to ease the tension.

"Like what?" Issa pondered, poking the sharp edge of the cross behind his nails, pulling up black dirt.

Bethany pushed down on the chain, forcing the idol out of his grasp, and then pulling his hands up to investigate. "You sir, need a bath," she scolded. But Issa just looked at her, refusing to be deterred.

Before either Rafi or Bethany could muster up an intelligent response, the world around them rang out. A loud alarm blared and startled them, pushing them all to their feet. The clamber of the bells sent a surge of adrenaline through their veins. They moved together, each with a different mission. Bethany ran to the crib, grabbing their baby sister who's screams she tried to muffle by placing her hand over the toddler's mouth. Rafi was at her side, grabbing the baby's bag and stuffing her blanket, diapers, and other essentials into the bag in a frenzy. Issa did the same with his and Bethany's belongings, grabbing only the necessities before leading the team downstairs.

Issa was the first one into the hiding space, a small cannonball circle carved into the wall under the stairwell. As he jumped in, he threw his belongings on the floor and turned back, grabbing Nevaeh as Bethany shoved her into his arms.

"I have to go," Rafi announced breathlessly, handing Nevaeh's bag to Bethany.

"No!" Both Cruz siblings shouted in unison.

"You can't leave, not now-" Bethany pleaded, but Rafi pulled her into his chest, wrapping his arms around her.

Bethany held him, a weight in the pit of her stomach holding her in place.

"I have time, I'll make it back," he soothed, "I have to try".

He turned to leave, but Bethany grabbed his hand and pulled him back, the siren blaring like a ticking bomb. She looked hesitantly from Issa to Rafael. She knew her duty was to her family, but the thought of Rafi getting caught on the streets alone, defenseless, was unbearable. His family, if still alive, would be waiting for him. But he wouldn't stand a chance alone against the Troops.

"Issa," she exclaimed, "you know what to do. You put the mask over her nose and mouth, it needs to be tight-"

Issa's brows drew together. "What do you- No, I-"

"I have to go, Issa. You're safe here." Bethany reached for the heavy wooden console, but Rafael was already pushing it, closing up the hole until only a small space remained. "Mom and dad will be here soon, and I'll be back as soon as I can-"

"No-" Issa begged, his small hand barely escaping the hole as he reached for her, his fingers grazing the tips of her shirt as she pulled away. He felt the cold metal against his hands as the necklace snapped and landed on the floor. Bethany turned back, seeing the cross fall to the ground. She halted, a brief moment of hesitation as she considered turning back for her sacred jewel, but the ringing of the bells forced her forward. Grabbing Rafi's hand, they ran out of the house, the screen door slapping against its frame as Issa grabbed ahold of his handle and pushed the barrier closed, blackness enveloping the crawl space.

* * * * *

Issa jolted up in his bed, the image of Bethany running away from him fading into the recesses of his mind. Her long, dark hair dangling down to her thighs in the oversized light blue sack their mother made her wear, her eyes sparkling as the descending sun cast her shadow on him. She was there, she was safe, she was alive; but the dream was a trick. Perhaps a sign of over-exertion or dehydration, a clear reminder to Issa of what he was working so hard to achieve. The awful torment it played on his mind, him still a seven-year-old child with his older sister protecting him, caring for him, dreaming of the future with him; a future that would never come true.

Using the shredded blanket, he wiped at his face, removing any signs of weakness. The room was crisp as the blanket fell away and he surfaced from his makeshift pallet, his breath visible in the air. He looked over at his sister who turned uncomfortably. He picked up the pieces of his blanket and placed them over her as best he could and then he walked out of the room.

"Issa," his mom said as she saw him lurking in the doorway. "Best get ready," she chided.

Issa looked down as if to make a point to his mother. His feet were bare which wasn't uncommon for children in the neighborhood. Finding suitable shoes was a luxury and typically reserved for the Revival members. Issa, against his wishes, was still too young to join, and therefore would have to suffer his way to school without shoes. Similarly, Issa had outgrown the pants he had been given when he was a boy and was now reduced to covering himself with a short brown loincloth like most of the other traditionally-clothed kids.

"I am ready" Issa snarked, gesturing towards his attire. His mom looked up from her cleaning and observed her son. Dissatisfaction written all over her face. Of her three children, Bethany was the only one that favored Mariam. Although still considered young amongst her tribe, Mariam's wrinkles and peppered grey hair aged her beyond her years, looking more like her children's grandmother. And while food was always scarce, her body remained thick in her curves, the pudgy softness alluring to the newborn babies she cared for.

She never wanted kids of her own, not living in this world, but she never let her pessimism corrupt her as she nursed and nurtured the orphans. Mariam knew any children born in the North would face the same day to day challenges she had growing up, always on the move, living in fear of being caught by the Troops. It wasn't Issa she had to worry about getting caught. She had confidence in him. The elders teach the Revival about what they would face if they get caught. True, some young boys like Issa are given leniency, allowed to join the soldiers if they renounce their lineage. But young girls and older boys are of little use to the Troops. It's hard to know which is luckier, allowing your body to be used for target practice or to be tortured as a slave; while one meant a painful death, the other surely meant a painful life. That's why the Revival is taught to save a bullet. When Mariam's brother told her the story, she was mortified. '*If you're faced with no other choice, you do what you can to alleviate the pain, but always save one bullet for yourself,*' she remembered him saying, '*it's better for your family to die at your hands than at the hands of your enemy. No true Patriot would dream of being used against his kin*'. The day he told her that was the day she promised she would never have children. Even when she met her Joey, she swore to him she would never have children. But they were young and foolish back then, and getting pregnant with Bethany was a surprise. She willed God to take her baby from her so she would never have to understand the pain of the life they had been given, but God gave her a strong child. So strong that, at only three years old, she survived the plague that took the lives of nineteen of the twenty-eight children in the neighborhood. She was weak and feeble and Mariam was convinced God had finally come for the child she pleaded he take. Only, Mariam *did* want her, how could she not have loved the tiny life she created? And her heart grieved as she watched her daughter cling to life. But God made true to his promise eventually, and he took Bethany in the worst manner conceivable.

"Just go-" Mariam sighed, brushing off her son, "and I want to hear good reports from your teachers," she called out to him as he swung the door open.

It wasn't that Issa had misbehaved in class; teachers actually commended Issa on his behavior and grades. But he often skipped school and no one knew where the boy would go. And when he would resurface? Issa was often dirty, his pelt bearing new holes and dried mud. And when he'd show up to class late, he was often distracted, gazing off in the distance or drawing stick figurines on the desks.

As predicted, Issa didn't turn left to go to the makeshift school, but instead hung a fast right and sped off in the opposing direction. He had no intention of attending school, not when the education he needed was somewhere outside the walls of the educational center.

Issa had taken off too early for the drills to begin, so he ducked into the shadows of an unsecured building and waited. He hid in the cold shadows, cupping his bare hands around his mouth and he blew warm air to soothe them as he waited for the evening crews to leave their posts.

The Revival was broken down into 5 parts: grunts, maps, scouts, security, and leadership. When the evening scouts passed the corridor, Issa knew they had signed out and the morning crews would be starting their drills. Waiting several moments after their departure to ensure he wouldn't be spotted, Issa headed to the Northeast corner of the neighborhood where the grunts and muscle would be lining up. He found himself a dugout on a hill behind some old dumpsters. Looking around to confirm his hideout's seclusion, Issa watched as one of the muscles gave the instructions and he followed their motions as the men began their sets with lunges.

Malik looked on as the grunts heaved through their beginning drills on the cold blacktop. He knew the youngest boy was thirteen, as per their rules, but he couldn't help but think the boys were getting younger each year. Their limp bodies and avid complaints gave him little hope in his current lineup of grunts. That is, all except for the Cruz boy.

"He up there?" Xavier asked as he fell into step beside Malik. Malik didn't like Xavier, couldn't stand the boy's attitude and skepticism, but he couldn't deny his skillset either. Xavier was Second-In-Command and should have been next to move up to First when a buried mine took out their leader. But the elders had a different plan in mind, bringing Malik up from Third. Malik couldn't blame Xavier for his bitterness; he'd stolen what was rightfully his. But Malik needed trust in his Second, and there was a small part of him that feared Xavier's loyalty, feared that, behind the chocolate eyes and school-boy haircut, was a ninja ready to pounce. "Earth to Malik," Xavier cooed, waiving his hand in Malik's face. Malik brushed his hand away and lifted his eyed to the hilltop where he knew the boy was hiding.

The Cruz boy was too young to join the Revival, but Malik could see the determination in the kid that was lacking in most of the other grunts; the boy had a fire in him.

"You kidding?" Malik coughed, "Can't you hear him?" The first time Malik caught the boy, he thought it was a soldier spying on them for a raid. He was relieved to see that it was just a neighborhood boy, one of the healer's kids, the one who'd lost his sister. Malik didn't have to question what sparked the fire in the kid's eyes, but he did wonder if he was doing the right thing to ignore the boy's attendance at private Revival drills.

"How long you gonna let this go on?" Xavier asked, taking the words straight from Malik's train of thought. Malik understood law and order. He knew he should have turned the kid in, at least let his parents know for the kid's own safety, but he couldn't do it. He'd heard the prophesies from the elders. Maybe he was naïve to apply them to the boy, but he could feel that there was something special about the kid.

"I've been thinking of bringing him to a round table," Malik implored. Xavier turned to him immediately, his face drawn tight in an emotion that resembled... anger? "I want to see what the elders think of him," he defended.

"The elders?! Seriously, MK?" His eyebrows knit together and Malik wondered if he was being rash. "Nah, man, you're asking for trouble. You know they won't approve, it's a clear violation, the kid's too young."

Malik knew Xavier wasn't wrong, but he had a gut feeling about that he didn't want to ignore. He'd watched the kid a few times, even saw him occasionally behind abandoned buildings practicing drill sets. He was impressed with how far the kid had come and would bet his rations that the kid could beat a few of the current grunts, especially the thick one. If he couldn't get that kid, Cable, to take some pounds off in the first few months of training, Malik knew he'd have to find something more suitable to his abilities. The Revival's numbers were strong, but not strong enough to cut the hefty kid without at least trying. But the Cruz kid, he could be a real diamond in the rough, and Malik wanted to be the one to clean him up.

"Are you saying that because you're jealous, or because you really think he couldn't handle it?" Malik questioned, knowing that while his intentions may be muddied, Xavier's opinion was far from honest.

Xavier didn't answer the question. Instead, he jumped into the line, screaming at Cable. Malik was beginning to doubt that Cable could pass the cut on his first try. But he also knew the flak he'd get if he failed the kid since his grandad was one of the elders. But Cable would get two more tries if he didn't get in right away, that's how the exam worked; you get three chances to pass your entrance test, each time the bar lowers slightly. That's why he wanted to give the spy a chance. If the kid could keep up with the others, regardless of his age, why shouldn't he be permitted to join? It would give him a greater chance of truly making an impact on the Revival.

His mind made up, Malik watched the drills and waited until the last set before allowing his Third-in-command, Saylor, to take over. He followed a footpath up the hill and found the boy intently watching Saylor's instructions.

"You gonna stay up here forever?" Malik asked, surprising the boy as he jumped back and pulled a rusted knife from his pelt. "Your parents know you have that?"

The boy looked stunned as he looked from Malik down to his knife. "I-" He didn't bother finishing his sentence; Issa knew he had been caught and it wasn't worth denying. Months of planning and watching, and he could see it unravelling before him.

"What's your name, kid?" Malik asked, swiping the dull blade from Issa without hesitation. Issa bounced back, pulling his arms up defensively, scolding himself for being an easy mark. Malik brought the knife up for examination. It wouldn't kill easily, probably wouldn't cut much either, but if a wound was inflicted, it could probably cause a good infection. "When your First-In-Command asks a question, you don't make him repeat himself", he was on a power kick, asserting his dominance.

"Issa", the boy announced as he straightened his back and dropped his arms. It was a good show of confidence and Malik was impressed.

There were so many things Malik wanted to ask Issa, but he needed to play this right. Sure, he probably should be consulting an elder before making rash decisions, especially knowing his Second isn't on board, but Malik pushed the thought away. "Does your family know you're up here, Issa?"

The boy, Issa, never flinched. He was thin, too thin, but he had strong muscle development, probably from practicing the drills. His dark brown hair was long and tangled, probably hadn't had a decent cut since he'd been born, and he was in desperate need of a bath. Malik could make out the markings of several tattoos around the back of his neck, but none on his forearms or legs which Malik found interesting. He tried to glimpse down at the boy's wrist to gather his age, but the boy turned evasively.

"How old are you?" Malik asked. He'd guessed twelve, not quite old enough to join, but just close enough that the boy would want to know more about the Revival. When it was clear the boy did not intend to respond, Malik held out his own wrist and showed Issa his markings. He remembered the first time he learned the truth behind their markings at one of the round tables. When born, the nurses label the birth year on each baby's wrist with permanent marker. Individual birth months and days are ignored, but as a community, a birth year is celebrated collectively on the first day of the new year. On the fifth birth year, the number is permanently etched on each child's wrist with black ink; it's their first real marking, but hardly the last. For the select few lucky enough to join the Revival, they go one step further, and brand the sacred 'R' with the lightning-bolt tail onto your shoulder.

After the war, the plain-skinned lackies claimed the Southern territory, forming the wall and permanently separating the cultures. The free-spirited Northerners may have won the war, but the destruction and lack of structure ultimately caved and gave way for new leadership to stake its claim; that's when the Troops arrived. And since then, small tribes of neighborhoods have scoured the land, hiding from the soldiers and forming small bands; forming the Revival. And when they're ready, they will retake the land that is rightfully theirs.

Issa glanced down at Malik's scratches, '89', and then looked back up at his leader. He hesitated, but knew hiding wouldn't make a difference at this point. He'd been caught and the only saving grace would be to earn Malik's trust. Slowly, he lifted his hand up and Malik grabbed his arm. '100', the kid was eleven years old, born exactly one century after the collapse.

Malik's eyes met Issa's as his mind began to unfold; he couldn't think of any other kid he'd met with that birth year. Slowly releasing Issa's hand, Malik gazed intently at him. "Have you ever heard of a round table," he asked.

Issa's brows furrowed. His first thought was that his First-In-Command was an idiot. Of course he'd heard of a round table, he wasn't living under a rock, his family had many different tables in the homes they'd settled.

"Not a dinner table," Malik announced, laughter in his tone.

Issa thought harder. Not a dinner table, then what? The tables found in the living space? Or the ones he'd seen inside school buildings?

"It's not a table at all, it's a figure of speech," Malik clarified. "There is some historical significance to it, but it's really just a meeting that only Revival members are permitted to join. The elders meet with us and teach us the stories of our past; there's the times that predated the war, the events that led to the period of trials, the peace settling after the wall was built, the arrival of the Troops, and," Malik hesitated, "everything that's happened since." Issa listened intently, and then shook his head and Malik nodded in understanding. "If you're interested, I want you to join me, we're meeting tonight."

Issa's eyes widened as his gaze lifted. He couldn't believe what he was hearing. Not only was he not in trouble for snooping in on Revival trainings, but now he's being asked to join in on a secret meeting? To heck with *interested*, Issa was thrilled.

"I can't promise the elders will agree to you joining," Malik continued, "but I will talk with them. If you meet me here when the sun sets beyond the horizon," he pointed to the skyline, "I'll have an answer by then and perhaps you can sit in on a meeting."

Issa was elated. Sure, it wasn't a guarantee, but now that he knew about the meetings, he had another tool in his belt. If the elders didn't approve, he could simply follow the Revival to the round table and listen in on their meeting.

"Okay, but for now, I need you to pack up. I can't have you spying out here, you need to go to school. The elders certainly won't bend the rules if they know what you've been up to." Issa nodded and turned to leave, practically skipping as he ran off. He'd been caught, by the First-In-Command no less, but he wasn't turned in. He thought he was hiding so well, but clearly his leader was more attuned than Issa had thought. He had to hope that the elders would agree; otherwise, his gig was up.

Issa returned to class as instructed, but didn't hear a word that was said during the lesson. A 'round table', a secret meeting that only the Revival knew about, a chance to learn about the past and the great war from a viewpoint beyond his father's rantings. All the other boys in Issa's class, did any of them know about the round table, had they kept it a secret from him? Did his dad know? Should he ask him? Had Bethany and Rafael known?

The thought of Bethany sent a surge through him. He was one step closer. Maybe there was still a chance; a chance she'd be alive, a chance he'd find her, a chance he'd rescue her and bring her home. But no, he knew there was no hope.

When the light gave way to darkness, Issa was back at the hill, pacing back and forth as he waited for Malik.

"Hey kid," Malik chimed as he came around the corner of one of the far buildings. Issa glided over to him, eyeing the clothing Malik held. "Put this on," Malik indicated, shoving the clothes towards Issa. "I think they should fit". Issa held out the garments. The black silk shorts had a draw string waistband and, although they looked a bit large, he knew he could knot the strings to fit his small frame. The white shirt, on the other hand, looked several sizes too small. "We may have to cut off the sleeves, might fit better."

"Did they agree?" Issa asked, not caring about the clothes.

"Yeah, yeah, but there are some rules you'll have to follow. Change first and we'll talk on our way," Malik informed. Issa changed from his pelt as Malik ripped off the sleeves, the ripping sound of the cloth foreign to Issa. Once fully clothed, Issa followed Malik as they set off at a fast walk. "So, normally you'd learn the rules as part of your training for the Revival, but I'm going to give you a quick rundown," Malik began. "First, you're not to talk. You're simply an observer there, so unless directly asked a question, don't speak. There may be some members not happy to see you there, so I want you to blend into the background, got it?" Issa nodded. Malik continued to inform Issa of the stipulations around his presence as they continued towards the outer barriers of the neighborhood, outside of the permitted safe zones.

Issa knew when they had arrived at the round table, but to his surprise, there was no table in sight. They had travelled just far enough outside the town that their small fire wouldn't be visible to the neighborhood, and all the Revival boys and the elders were gathered around it in the shape of a circle.

What was even more of a surprise to Issa was the smell surrounding them as the boys took turns roasting food over the fire; Issa had never seen such a large display of food outside of the neighborhood. He wondered how they managed to find the food, where it came from, why they hadn't shared with the others, but he knew better than to ask.

"What's he doing here?" Xavier called out as he caught sight of Issa, trailing cautiously behind Malik. Xavier knew Malik's intentions, he just hoped that Malik would wise up and change his mind. Since that clearly didn't happen, his next motive was to poison the Revival against the kid, convince the elders he was too young to join, and prove that he, not Malik, was best fit to lead the Revival.

Malik, on the other hand, was prepared for Xavier's retaliation. He even mentioned it to the Elders when he sought them out for counsel that afternoon, how bringing in new meat unexpectedly had the potential to cause a rift in the leadership and also within the Revival. Always one step ahead of Xavier, Malik was confident the kid could withstand the spotlight, and he'd forewarned Issa in anticipation of exactly this.

"All will be revealed in time, mind your own," Malik chided, his calm tone easing the unsettled boys as their cautious glances returned to their food roasting on the fire. Malik found one of the grunts and took a stick, passing it along to Issa who quietly grabbed it. Moving down the line, Malik took some meat and hooked it onto Issa's branch and then his own before directing Issa towards the open flame.

Issa eyed the meat, his stomach turning and boiling as the smell wafted down to his gut. He rarely ate meat as it was a commodity his family could rarely afford, but he knew the benefits the protein would provide and his mouth watered as he mimicked Malik and held his stick over the fire. He didn't want to assume the food was for him, knowing he had not done anything to earn the reward, so he pushed down the hunger that raked through his body. When the meat was toasted and brown, both Malik and Issa pulled their items away, and Issa watched as Malik blew on the torch before taking a large bite from the side.

Malik knew he was taunting the kid, but he wanted to see how well he could obey his commands. But as he bit into his dinner and savored the delicate meat, he was transported back to the first time he had encountered a round circle and decided to put the boy out of his misery. He whispered toward Issa as they both took a seat on the ground, "If we are to protect the neighborhood, we need protein to replenish our bodies and stay strong. We don't over-indulge, and we keep all information here private. You may not be one of us yet, but you're held to the same standards. If you eat that," he gestured to the meat dangling off of Issa's pole and almost laughed at the boy's visible desire, "you're agreeing to these terms, you can never tell of what you see, hear, or do here."

Issa's gaze fell on Malik as he registered, and he nodded, slowly leaning forward to take a bite. The gritty texture was foreign to Issa as he sawed off a portion of the fatty meat. He savored each bite he took and finally swallowed when the bite had been ground down to a paste in his mouth. All at once, he felt the heat from the fire warming his face and a resurgence of energy climbing in his body like a firework.

"It's good, huh," Malik chimed as he took another bite into his food.

"What is he doing here?" Xavier goaded as he approached Malik, his footsteps hard against the dirt path, intentionally making a scene. "That belongs to us," he exclaimed, eyeing the meat that Issa was devouring, "he doesn't belong here!"

"Wrong," Malik shouts, standing up and looking down on Xavier, "that belongs to anyone I say. I make the decisions here, not you." Xavier huffed and Issa watched intently, certain the two would end up in a brawl, but just as Xavier went to speak, a new voice intercepted, and the crowd fell silent.

"Sit down boys," the voice commanded. Issa wasn't certain if the directions were aimed at Malik and Xavier, but all at once the Revival gathered into the circle and everyone sat, facing the four elders whom each sat perched on a wood stool. "We have a unique topic to discuss with you all tonight," the same elder exclaimed. The elder sat second from the left, toying absentmindedly with the cane draped over his lap. They all looked alike, boasting shiny heads that danced with the colors of the fire, layers of wrinkles like hills mounting under their sunken eyes and soft skin. "I guess first we need to address our newest guest," he began, all eyes following his toward Issa who quickly swallowed his last piece of meat. His face was red, but it wasn't clear if that was from the light casting off from the fire, having just gorged himself on a luxurious meal, or from embarrassment as all eyes fell on him. The group was silent, sharing a collective thought surrounding the intruder; who was he and why was he there?

"Tell us your name boy," a new elder, the one that sat on the far-right side, demanded. Issa looked at the elder, his long nose pointing at Issa like a big 'he doesn't belong here' sign, and then turned his gaze towards Malik who gave a slight nod.

Issa raised his head confidently as he spoke in an unwavering tone, "my name is Issa, son of Joey and Mariam Cruz."

"Issa-" the name rolled off his tongue, the last vowel hanging in the air. "Tonight boys, we have come to an impasse," the third elder, sandwiched between the former two speakers, indicated. "You see, when the great war settled and the peace time ended-" he paused, closing his eyes as he searched for the words he had once heard from his predecessors, "with the arrival of the Troops, the neighborhoods were formed." Malik instinctively looked back on the town where his people slept. No alarms were sounding and the only light he could see was half covered by errant clouds.

"At first, the Revival thought they could take on the Troops and reclaim the land they had just won," the elder smiled as he shook his head at the foolishness of his ancestors. "But the Troops didn't come from the ravaged Southern borders, they came fully shielded from across the waters, and they came with a vengeance". The elder opened his eyes, but looked out beyond the circle, at the dark land that surrounded them. Land that held new mysteries each day.

"When it became clear that the victory that claimed the Northern hemisphere had now given way to a new authority, neighborhoods, like ours, fled." He said the word with disgust, emphasizing the weakness of his predecessors. "It's unclear as to their motive; whether the intent was to regroup and refocus their forces against the invaders, or perhaps to encroach upon the South since the borders were still so new, but it didn't matter."

Malik's mind wandered. He often thought about the South and how, after they lost the war and the wall was resurrected, their former neighbors abandoned the North. When the boats arrived, it would have been so easy for them to flee to the South, re-build the ruins and forge a new partnership, creating an alliance that could have pushed the Troops back to the water. But the doors were locked and guarded. Rumors had it that there were thousands of bodies stacked up less than a mile from the wall, serving as a warning to any Northerners who might try to cross the border; a reminder that they're unwelcome. Hell hath no fury like a Republic scorned.

"The large bands of neighborhoods split up, quickly learning the dangers that the Troops presented if they fought against them. Winter hit hard, as you all can imagine," the boys shivered in unison, the mild fire barely easing the cold bite of the pre-winter chill. "Plagues killed off children and adults alike, and families were destroyed as they bargained their own flesh just for a chance at evading the Troops". Malik glanced at Issa who visibly shook, his face tightening. "And somewhere along the years, we lost our focus. Days were spent trying to stay alive, not planning, not strategizing our comeback. Occasionally the neighborhoods would cross paths, join ranks, share stories of our battles with one another. And at some point, no one really recalls when, or how, but a new myth formed." The elder hesitated, looking once again at Issa who was sitting forward, listening intently.

Malik knew the battle the elders faced. There were very few things the elders disagreed on, and this happened to be one of the biggest controversies of their time. Perhaps it was wrong of him to suggest it in the first place. Malik did not think himself a religious man. Like most Northerners, he lacked the understanding and education to understand or praise a higher power, so who was he to flaunt this kid in front of them and suggest that he could be the 'Chosen One'?

CHAPTER 3

FIFTEEN YEARS OLD

The voices faded, moving further into the recesses of the old building. Their words were a soft mumble and Issa knew he would have to get closer if he wanted to hear them. Swiftly peeking around the corner, he ensured no one could spot him, and he rounded the wooden barricade as he inched closer to the secret meeting. More footsteps descended upon them, and Issa hesitated as he eyed the green light from his watch, knowing he needed to return to his post. But instead of leaving, Issa took deep breaths, slowed his heartrate as he leaned in closer, trying to make out the third voice. Surprise caught him when Malik's deep voice filled the vacant space. It didn't surprise Issa that Xavier and Zenhara would be caught in a secret meeting, but now Malik?

Both the neighborhood and Revival were stunned when Malik announced Issa as the Third-In-Command. Sure, he deserved it, he was stronger, faster, and had better instincts than any member that had preceded him, but there was an order to these things. Zenhara had been training for the third position, his mentor Xavier pushing him to the brink during their private drills. And while he lacked the natural confidence and intuition that Issa possessed, there were several among them that faulted Issa's promotion as Malik's unwarranted bias towards the 'Chosen One'.

Issa hated the insinuation; he hadn't wanted to be a prophecy, he simply wanted revenge. Pushing himself harder than the others, Issa's intentions were strategic and built upon a mountain of vengeance. Being promoted to Third-In-Command, while an honor amongst his tribe, was simply a building block to the ultimate reprisal. But from the moment Malik brought Issa to the first round table, saw the boy's passion for the history of their little clan, he knew he would guide Issa towards leadership, ensuring the boy have every opportunity available to avenge not just his sister, but their entire neighborhood. He knew there were skeptics living among them, Xavier and Zenhara among them, but he refused to allow the critics to gossip. So, Issa wondered, why would Malik justify the posse by hosting an unsanctioned meeting without inviting him?

Seeing a mirror along the far side of the wall, Issa positioned himself so that the reflection focused on his comrades.

"Just hear me out," Xavier plead. "We haven't had indication of soldiers for over a month; the city is clear. That building is a fucking stronghold. We could house the entire neighborhood within the upper layer and leave the entire ground route for training and drills." Xavier spoke with his hands, pointing to the sky as he continued, "with eyes camped on the roof, the elevation would allow great visibility and protection, it's a game changer."

"We don't occupy a space that large," Malik protested, "it's not-"

"I know, I know," Xavier interceded, turning his back to them in frustration as he pulled his hand over his forehead, exasperated, before turning back around with a fury. "Look man, we are the fucking Revival!" He pushed into Malik's face, his hand now gesturing towards himself and then outwards. "We are the only force these people have against the Troops. At what point do we stop from running and finally put up a strong front against our enemies?"

The room fell quiet as the question lingered. Zenhara spoke next. "We need to start thinking about laying down roots. If there are other neighborhoods out there, we can send scouts out and bring them to our stronghold, there's plenty of room. Our numbers have never been this strong."

"The last time we-" Malik protested, but Xavier cut him off.

"Bullshit! There have never been conditions like this and you know it! You are our leader, MK, but you are not the only one here with ideas. We deserve a chance here; we should at least talk to the elders. We-"

"Okay," Malik succumbed, his eyes forcing closed with the weight of his decision. "Well ask them. I can't promise…"

"I want to be there," Xavier demanded. "You're against this plan, so you should serve as the opposition. Zen and I can prepare the rebuttal, that way there is a fair argument."

Malik considered the proposal and nodded, "okay, we can present at the table tonight".

Xavier's mouth twitched up into a half smile. "Thank you," he clapped his arm on Malik's shoulder. "Either way this comes out, we can put it to rest." Malik nodded again and Xavier looked at Zenhara, both turning to exit. Issa pushed against the wall and slid around an open doorframe, alluding them as they rounded the corner to leave. When their footfalls were quiet, Issa tiptoed back to the corner and saw Malik crouched down in a huddle, his head buried into a cavern enclosed by his arms and legs. Issa watched in awe, his heart aching as he watched the weight consume his leader as a hushed cry escaped his lips. The twenty-six-year-old was clearly exhausted; tired of fighting, tired of pushing, tired of all of the decisions and struggles he had to battle daily.

Issa stepped back, he knew his leader wouldn't have wanted him to see this vulnerability, but an errant misstep onto a rotted plank heaved an ambient creak, and alerted Malik to his visitor.

"Who's there?" Malik questioned, his head popping up. Issa hesitated, wondering if he remained silent whether Malik would pry further. "Issa?" Malik's eyes met his, their gazes refracted off the mirror. Issa let out a small sigh, hung his head, and rounded the corner into the empty space. The meeting was clearly intended to remain private, but Malik did not show signs of concern when his Third shuffled into the space. After a moment of silence, Malik let out a chuckle and looked up at Issa, "You never were good at spying", he could recall the frail boy up on the hill many years ago, his grunts and moans as he practiced the drill sets.

"I'm great at spying; I hide in plain sight." Issa chuckled as he moved inward and sat beside his leader. Issa wanted to ask about the meeting, he wanted to know what Xavier was stirring up, and more than anything, he wanted to know why Zenhara was involved and not him. But he didn't ask, the silence enveloping the two men until Malik spoke.

"There's a structure on the North side of town. An old mall or something," he heaved. "Three stories tall with a good view of the city." He stopped as Issa failed to connect the dots. "Xavier wants us to scout it as a potential headquarters of sorts. If the integrity inside is as promising as the outside, the whole neighborhood could move in."

"To what end?" Issa pondered aloud.

"To *the* end," Malik chortled absently. "If successful, we'd never have to run again. There's a stream that shoots alongside, there's fish; it could be a perfect solution."

Issa was skeptical, nothing in the North could be that perfect and not already have claim. "What's the downside?"

Malik blinked and shook his head. "Our options are risky either way, it's just a matter of making a choice at this point. Assuming the building is clear."

"So, what's with all the smoke and daggers? Why haven't we scouted it?" Issa prompted, his blood sizzling with anticipation, but Malik sat quiet. He was tired of the strategic planning, tired of everyone looking to him for guidance. He recalled the last time a vote was called, the last time a First tempted fate and upset their order, and they lost far more than they bargained for.

The Troops had been following them, a game of cat and mouse. With every forward stride they would make, the Troops sat back and watched, choosing when to interrupt. They'd destroyed countless lives and, while the recent raids consisted mainly of stealing food and supplies, the soldiers reached a new low when they seized their neighborhood last night. They had captured fourteen souls and killed half for sport. And just when he thought they would allow the others to return home, their lieutenant held onto the girl.

If We Don't

*　　　*　　　*　　　*　　　*

"This one's mine," he concluded as the others scurried behind the Revival. It was clear he surprised his own team with the announcement as they turned to him in question. She was a kid, probably hadn't even started bleeding yet. But the lieutenant didn't care as he brushed his hand through her dark hair.

"No!" a boy protested, pushing past one of the muscles who instinctively held the kid back. The soldiers laughed and a bullet rang through the air, landing an inch from his feet. The First-in-Command eyed the muscle who wrapped an arm around the kid's mouth. A cry escaped from the girl as she reached for her neck, pulling at the hem of her faded blue dress.

"She earns you" he paused, debating as he pulled her closer, leaning closer and breathing her in, "four days," he announced, trolling his finger down her cheek. The gift melted the pain in his chest as the First agreed; four days was a godsend that he would be a fool to deny. The Troops had terrorized them for weeks on end, every other night like clockwork, and this allowance would permit them their first real chance of escaping.

Malik couldn't bear the thought. What could the girl do for them that would hold their attention for that long? What pains would she endure in her remaining days?

The Troops backed away and they held still, cautious of any bullets that may fly back toward them if they moved too soon. When the last soldier disappeared behind the walls, the muscle released his hold on the boy, who immediately fell to the ground, his knees scraping on impact.

"What are you doing?" he screamed, tears staining his face. "We have to go after them, we have to save her!" he demanded. Malik searched the eyes of his leader, knowing they would never see the girl again.

"Send an alarm for a round table," the First commanded, his gaze landing on the same muscle that captured the boy who took off at a sprint. "Second," he fired, "get a count of injured and deceased. Have a record join you and inform their families." He turned to Malik, "take the boy to his family and then find a map and meet at the table." Malik turned and grabbed the boy. He protested, but Malik ignored him, pulling him to his feet and pushing him toward the city. The alarms rang out in a loud roar, the three quick bells and single deep chime signaling both that the Troops were dismissed and that the remaining Revival and elders needed to meet.

Malik found the boy's home, his grandfather stepping outside as they arrived. Malik recognized the elder immediately, and grief seized him. The Second-In-Command would not have arrived yet to inform the family of the girl's departure, so the responsibility fell on him.

"We have to go, papa, they took Bethany!" the boy proclaimed, grabbing the elder's arm as he tried to lead him away. But the elder held firm, leaning down and holding the boy at his shoulders to keep him in place.

"I'm sorry, Rafi-" he mourned, hooking an arm around the boy. Although the boy had to have been nearing his teens, he looked small in his grandfather's arms. His soft black hair pulled back in a tight bun, falling loose as his grandfather lifted him into his arms. The transaction was inaudible once the door closed behind him, but crying rang out when the elder reappeared in the doorframe. Malik

didn't hesitate as he jogged off in the direction of the meeting place, the elder following suit behind him.

"We've lost ground," the Second-In-Command seethed as he joined the circle, his chest rising and falling with his labored breaths. "We lost nineteen." All eyes fell on the First-In-Command, the revelation shocking him into silence. "We need to make a move," the Second continued, as he made his way to the center and pointing towards the faded lines that were erased following the last meeting. "We have four days! We need to split the neighborhood in two and separate. When the Troops resume, there will be two footpaths to follow and at least half of us could stand for a clean break."

Malik listened intently, having newly been appointed as Third, he didn't want to assert himself yet.

"Are there any other options" one of the elders asked, pushing past Malik to get a better visual of the map.

The First-In-Command remained silent as he turned and faced the elders and his subordinates. He moved toward the map and the plan that he had previously turned down. "If we were to ever try, now is our best chance. Both sides would have a four-day lead, it just might work."

Malik didn't like the plan, knowing their numbers were stronger as one unit. But when they called for a vote, Malik watched the hands fly up in agreement, his own arm hesitantly rising as he saw the overwhelming favor.

They had split the odds down the middle. The First and Second-In-Command split, Malik joining the latter, and the elders were divided equally among the two tribes. The next morning, the neighborhood was divided and Malik's neighborhood watched on in despair as the other tribe set off in the opposing direction. The boy, Rafi, held up the tail end of the disappearing clan, remaining in a tight embrace with another family until his grandfather called for his return and he skulked away.

*   *   *   *   *

Malik remembered the events, the pain fresh in his heart as he recalled later hearing that the Troops lied. They hadn't waited four days to follow, and the neighborhood that was last seen heading in the southeasterly direction was absconded within two sunsets. A few survived to tell of the tales, Rafael's grandfather being the sole surviving elder who, after twelve days alone in the wild, stumbled upon the footfalls of his former allies and rejoined his former ranks.

In total, only four survivors from their former neighborhood had re-emerged. The stories of each survival and near-death experience just as astonishing as the first. Malik never asked the elder about his grandson's fate. He'd heard rumors throughout the years, the elders were targeted first, their families slaughtered for their defiance against the monarchy. It was a pain he could see in the elders' eyes even now, years later.

Malik stood in front of the neighborhood, the cold beating down on him as he distanced himself from the flame. The ground was harder now, cold; a harsh winter knocking on their door. He braced himself as eyes drifted toward him and he fought back the urge to vomit.

"We've been provided an… opportunity," he claimed, his teeth chattering. "I've called this meeting tonight so you can hear both sides equally. None of this should be shared to ears outside of this table, but you will be given the night to consider. We will meet again tomorrow to cast a vote, majority rules, and that will be it. Whichever way the votes fall, I expect everyone to get onboard and support the choice of the majority, understood?" The boys looked around, silent headshakes confirming their agreement. "Your First and Second will explain your options, both the positives and the negatives to both, but we will not assert our opinions. We are here simply to give the details, not to sway your decisions. Your Second will start with the pros," he informed, moving aside for Xavier to address the team, "the floor is yours".

"There's a building on the far end of town," Xavier began. He explained his ideas in great detail, information that Malik had already shared with Issa. The building would be a safeguard, they would remain dormant, the intention to stay in one place, build their forces, and prepare for a battle with the Troops that would undoubtably come. The benefits were irrefutable; a safe, warm place to take shelter. No more injuries or deaths at the hands of mother nature. A safe place to welcome weary travelers such as themselves.

But it also meant deviating from their traditions; a major risk for a small tribe that had withstood more than a century on the run from the soldiers. They could survive a week, a month, perhaps even a year or more, but to what end? The Troops would certainly find them eventually. And when that would happen, they would have nowhere to go, nowhere to run or hide, and they would be forced to confront their aggressors with whatever strength they could summon.

Once both sides were revealed, Malik opened the floor for questions. After a long silence, Malik dismissed the Revival, reminding them of their responsibility toward silence.

Issa, much like the others, was torn on how to vote. He was worn down and tired, his feet scarred from years of travelling on relentless terrain in the shivering cold and squelching heat. But he also didn't want to sit around and wait to be a target of the Troops. He wanted a certainty that neither option could provide. When day turned to night and Malik called for the vote, Issa's hand remained at his side, falling victim to whatever fate his team demanded.

CHAPTER 4

15 YEARS OLD

Issa waited until the final boy disappeared into the abyss before motioning for his team to move in. Three leaders, three floors, three separate teams; that was the plan for scouting the building they had coined as a 'mall'. Issa being the youngest and newest leader, his team was the last to enter and, while his partners would begin their venture upwards to the higher floors, his team was responsible for clearing the bottom layer of the vast building.

They started at the first sign of morning light, having prepped for two full days to ensure each member knew their responsibilities. While they were strategic enough to coordinate leaving half of the members behind to guard the neighborhood, they were still uneasy about the final decision to allow all three members of leadership into the compound. If there were trip wires, hidden mines, or even soldiers lying in wait, they could lose all three of their most skilled commanders in one fail swoop. There was also an argument for leaving Issa behind, seeing as there remained some who considered him the prophesied 'Chosen One', but the final decision came to Malik, and there were few that Malik trusted to do the job properly.

Having waited the required time for the two preceding units to enter, it was Issa's turn to finally have a peek inside the mysterious structure. Day one of the invasion was simply to scout; to look for weapons, survey for traps, and to generally secure the building. Once clear, two men would stay behind on each floor, a total of six members holding down the fort until new morning light. Day two would be to gather any items within the structure that were left behind that could be of use for the neighborhood or the Revival, the maps would begin charting the layout of the grounds, and the leaders would begin strategic planning. Day three would begin the transition. The elders would stake claim first; following the guidance of the leaders, the elders would find their designated locations, apart from one another, and the muscles would assist in relocating mattresses and any additional home-like commodities that would make the elders comfortable in their newest bunks. From there, the Revival would slowly aide the entire neighborhood until everyone was locked in and signs of their presence outside removed.

Issa wordlessly flagged his team to follow as they moved toward the building entrance. The large building casting a shadow over them and eliminating the warm comfort of the sun. Issa could see that doors to the building would be hard to secure and that, in time, they would have to restructure the long corridor of broken glass doorframes. Worse than that realization was the fact that this was only one of four entrances that all resembled each other. He glanced down at his feet as the broken glass shards cracked under his weight. Confirming the wind-blown pieces were soft and imposed no threat to his covered feet, he continued, making a mental note that they would have to clean the grounds before inviting in the families.

There were two sets of doorframes with roughly eight doors in each set. Issa couldn't fathom what sort of structure would need double entrance doors. It would provide protection, sure, but the quantity of doors and the length of the entryway would circumvent any protection the measly glass doors could have provided. When he cleared the entryway, the room opened up into a vast space that was completely ravaged.

Metal structures with hanging arms littered the walkway and had no understandable coordination. Issa paused, fearful that the structures were a weapon of a new variety. Issa looked back at the three sets of eyes that followed him, motioning to his team that they were to avoid touching the obstacles. He trusted his men, but wished he had more time to prepare with them. When they divided the ranks, Malik made the final determination, strongly positioning Issa's team since he would need the most support. Each team consisted of a leader, a muscle, a scout, and a grunt.

Issa knew his grunt well; Benji. He'd always liked the kid, but was wary of any thirteen-year-old who's best friend was three years his junior. When Issa joined the Revival, his one fear was leaving his baby sister Nevaeh unprotected. Sure, she wasn't a baby anymore. Five years younger than him, his younger sister had a confidence well beyond her years. And when Issa left, it wasn't long before Nay's circle grew. She was outgoing and vibrant, the complete opposite of Bethany and Issa, and cultivated friendships easily. Even though the age gap was concerning, Benji had become a good friend for Nevaeh. And now that Benji was training to join the Revival, Issa made a vow to take care of the pudgy-faced kid.

Hareem and Zeke were more of a mystery to Issa, having been in the Revival for years alongside him, yet never really intersecting with his patrols.

He watched them all closely as they followed in his footsteps. The layout of the room far beyond Issa's imagination. There were beams lifting out of the ground and connecting to the layers above and open walkways leading in each direction. A sign hung partially from a single hinge and dangled in the breeze. Issa tilted his head to get a better viewpoint. The sign pointed in all three directions before him, but he couldn't make out the words.

He knew now was as good of a time as any for his team to fulfill their purpose. Pointing at Hareem first, he signaled for the boy to take the pathway to the right. He looked around cautiously and decided he wanted to take the left wing as he could make out a broad opening in the corner that he wanted to explore, so he signaled to Zeke and instructed him to continue along the forward aisle. He nodded to Benji who followed his steps carefully as they turned to the left. The space was large and winding, but rather un-miraculous. The thick coat of dust a clear indication that nothing had disturbed the space in quite a while.

When Issa entered the next room, glass continued to litter the ground and Issa noted the vandalized glass desk structures. A crash alerted Issa and he jumped, seeing one of the metal forms somersaulting to the ground as Benji shrieked. At the same time, Zeke appeared in an opening behind the kid and his image flashed across several mirrors, creating the appearance of a raid.

Issa lifted his gun, his finger on the trigger, but he didn't pull. His heart and breathing harsh as he registered the foul smell of their surroundings. When he realized what occurred, he pushed his gun aside and heaved out a sigh, retracing his steps to where Benji sat tangled with the metal form and lifted the boy up.

The metal structure screamed with the movement, but no alarms of apparent harm came for them. When Issa looked at Zeke, the boy shook his head, indicating he found nothing of significance. Hareem joined the clan swiftly, his eyes averting to Benji and the jungle-gym, but he didn't speak. Together, the boys turned, facing the opening that Issa was originally drawn to. Beyond another wide doorframe, the building opened into a large abyss, with hundreds of additional doorframes leading to their own untold universe. On the rafter above them, Issa could make out the form of two of the other Revival members from Xavier's team. They hung low and clung to the walls as they moved into the abyss and aimed their weapons into a new doorway. The building was larger than Issa had thought.

Issa turned to his men, contemplating his strategy for tackling the large expanse. He had a feeling in his gut that unnerved him and he couldn't shake it off. He looked up at the ceiling, there were several security globes attached to the ceilings; an indication of a security presence that could be useful for the Revival to monitor their camp. The few globes within sight were shattered, but he hoped the mechanics were salvageable.

The boys followed Issa outward as he unveiled his plan, speaking in hushed tones. "We're going to split into twos, but you're to stay together at all times. We continue to move as a unit. Benji and I will take the East side and you two the

West. Take your time to survey everything, and you're not to move on to the next" he hesitated, not sure how to label the open spaces, "room until both the East and West teams have finished the current space. If your team finished before the other, come out to the center and check behind the desks in the middle." The boys nodded in understanding. Try not to talk unless there's an emergency, and do not touch anything," he resisted glancing at Benji. "If you need to stop or retreat, follow your same footsteps back."

The two teams separated, and Benji followed Issa to the right as they entered the next store along the East side of the building. This one was considerably smaller than the first, but it contained several of the same metal figurines. Issa looked behind the desk and found nothing of significance. He allowed Benji to take point as they burst through a doorframe that extended to an even smaller room. Boxes lined the room, a thick skin of dust, but nothing that warranted further observation.

Each set went on the same for the teams until they came to a fork in the road. The Westward wall continued forward, but there was a bend in Issa's route that led to a new wing of rooms. Issa hesitated as the West group looked to him for guidance.

Above them, Issa could see that he was making good pace. The teams on the second floor were just emerging from above the same openings along the Westward wall. They, too, were unclear as to how to continue and Issa moved outward to see the crew emerging above him and Benji. The third-floor team was more covert, hanging too close to the walls to be seen from Issa's viewpoint.

Issa flagged his team down, deciding to tackle the side wing before continuing forward. The boys set forth in his direction just as something caught his gaze. Turning back around, Issa caught the glaze of a tile in the center of the aisle. The tile, while seemingly identical to the ones surrounding it, a light sheen was evident and the tile sat a hair taller than the others in the line, an evident streak of dust trapped around the edges.

"Stop!" Issa shouted, his scream ringing throughout the cavernous walls. But it was too late.

Zeke crouched down instinctively, his right foot landing on none other than the illicit tile. The tile sunk down with his weight, but nothing changed.

On the top level, Malik peered over the edge. "What the fuck?" he whisper-screamed at Issa, disapproval evident in his tone, but Issa didn't pay attention. Onlookers from each level watched him as he slowly approached Zeke.

Issa was right, there was no doubt. The previously raised tile was now indented a centimeter below ground level. Issa looked at his teammate and peered around at the others. It could be a bomb, it could be a silent alarm, for all he knew, this tile could sentence them all to death or shoot confetti and singing clowns from the ceiling.

"Retreat!" Issa shouted at his audience, but no one moved. "Are you fucking deaf idiots?" He yelled, the dizzying circle surrounding him closing in on his peripheral as panic set in.

Zeke could see the panic, he felt it himself, and the sudden shock hit him like an avalanche that hoisted him upwards as he bolted from his spot. Issa tried to stop him, but the boy moved in a frenzy and Issa tumbled over himself.

On the floor, the tile righted itself and the silent world around came to life like a crying newborn baby hearings its voice for the first time. From the forward wing, mechanic whirls sounded as bullets sounded off and showered around them at every level. Pieces of the tile jumped up from the ground as the boys ran in the opposite direction. The bullets were sprayed in a vertical fashion, Issa just above the ascending line as he inched forward. But as Issa looked towards his exit, a black wall with clear slits descended from the ceiling, slowly cutting off their escape. Two boys, having safely passed the blockade, turned around to raise the barrier, but it wouldn't move and turned around hopelessly.

Running directly through the line of fire, Issa was determined to find a new exit, or die trying. Descending from the third floor, he caught sight of Malik just as a bullet pierced his gut and sent his mentor's limp body falling over the cascade.

"No!" Issa shouted as he contemplated turning back as Xavier crashed into him and yelled, "go!"

"But Malik-" Issa protested, turning back toward his First-In-Command, a pool of blood surrounding his tangled, lifeless body.

Xavier pushed him on, not looking back, "he's dead, so unless you want to join him, keep moving!" A new sound clamored ahead of them as a new barrier descended along the wall where the bullets continued to ring out. "Turn," Xavier commanded as the growing group of boys passed the corner to the East wing. They were nearly one-third clear of the mayhem when Issa looked back. Of the twelve men that entered, five followed in Issa's footsteps.

An errant step pushed another tile into the ground and Issa wailed, noticing the glossy tile too late, a new string of bullets unleashing from directly ahead of them. A step ahead of the others, Issa had already cleared the range and could only watch as his men fled backwards, red holes rippling through their bodies as they fell to the ground.

Above him, Issa could hear gauges switch and he knew another barrier would soon lock his crew inside the horror house. Moving quickly, Issa found a heavy desk and pushed it toward the invisible barrier, hoping the desk would keep the barrier from descending and buy his team some time.

Once in place, Issa doubled back, hoisting several of the metal contraptions and shoving them at the doorway and on top of the desk just as the wall came down around him.

In the opening, he watched as another Revival member fell limp to the ground. To his right, he could see Benji hiding along the edge of the wall, paralyzed in fear, but remaining seemingly unharmed. That's when he noticed the border of destruction, the edges and side rooms were untouched from the havoc the bullets created. The slow-moving wall was lowering, but Issa had time. He was, after all, the fastest sprinter they had. Re-emerging from his coffin, Issa kept to the side walls as he headed for Benji. Upon examination, Issa confirmed that Benji was unharmed and pulled the boy into an upright position.

"Help!" A voice rang out from the middle of the fractured zone, and Issa surveyed the land for movement. Issa spotted Xavier as he tried to crawl out of the line of fire. The bullets swept in a forward and backward motion; the return trip back having not yet started.

He pushed to his feet as the deafening sound started yet again. Pulling Xavier up in one swift motion, he hoisted his arm around Xavier's side and draped the boy's arm around his neck. He headed for the edges, orphan tile slices flying around him. A scream emerged from him as he thrust

Xavier's body toward the safe space of an open room, a bullet grazing the side of his arm as he dove for safety.

Disregarding his own injuries, he turned Xavier's body over to examine the injury. A bullet had pierced his left side and leg, causing a torrent of blood to pool from the open wounds. A large bang sounded out in the distance and Issa watched as the wall met the resistance he built. He watched as the metal figurines folded, the force of the barrier slowly failing.

"Benji!" Issa called, and the boy shuffled over to Issa. "I need your help to lift him," Issa instructed, having seen the kid move forces three times his weight during drills.

Benji looked at Issa apprehensively, but conceded, grabbing a lifeless Xavier by the arms as Issa pulled at his feet. Clinging to the sides, the boys moved quickly, the sound of the closing barrier pushing them forward.

As they arrived to the opening, the wall had pushed the barrier down and only a three-foot gap remained for the boys to sink under. They threw Xavier under and Benji climbed down, pulling Xavier free as he cleared the small opening.

Issa turned, searching for any remaining signs of life, but all he saw were lifeless bodies, sharp tile fragments, and littered bullets. Sliding under the gap seconds before the wall cut through the barrier and sealed shut, Issa hesitated, his breathing harsh and the ringing in his ears overshadowing Benji's pleas.

He climbed over Xavier and tilted his head over the boy's mouth, he could feel his breathing and see the rise and fall of his chest; he was alive. Gesturing towards his arms, Issa moved back to Xavier's feet as the two boys carried their leader out of the building.

The cold bite of the wind was a welcome feeling as sweat pooled off of them. They had barely escaped the building when a swarm of bodies assaulted them. The alarms were ringing and Issa listened cautiously. A long, continuous shrill indicated all he needed to know; as far as they could tell, no Troops were visible, but the neighborhood would be encouraged to hide in their homes, only medical personnel permitted on the streets.

He saw his dad first, but Xavier's obvious critical condition took his father's attention as a different medic began prodding Issa for signs of injury. He knew he had a gash on his arm and a possibly a head injury as thick blood stuck to his hair like honey; cementing the long curls to his bare neck.

CHAPTER 5

15 YEARS OLD

The trap was surely the doing of the Troops, no Revival could afford to waste the artillery that was spared. Which meant that the Troops could have left behind the death cage simply to inhumanely slay those that deny the monarchy. Or, the more likely conclusion, that the ruse would trigger a silent alarm notifying the Troops and that the blockade walls were put into place to capture any surviving rebels until the Troops could ride in. Believing the latter to be their goal, it would only be a question of how far the closest ranks were, and how long it would take them to arrive.

"Has a meeting been called?" Issa asked of Zenhara as a nurse finished taping up the gash on his arm. Issa had a cut along his temple, most likely from an estranged tile, and a bullet grazed the side of his arm directly under his Revival branding, but none of his injuries appeared life threatening.

"Malik is dead," Zenhara reminded him, "and Xavier is unconscious," Issa looked at him, but Zenhara stared back blankly, waiting for him to draw the conclusion.

65

"Meaning?" Issa exhaled, wondering if perhaps the gash in his head was worse than he thought. "Meaning I'm in command," he registered, the words weak as he spoke them into reality. Until, or if, Xavier stirred, Issa would be the acting First commander, he was responsible for calling a meeting. "Call a meeting, Zenhara. Now. Any Revival we have left," he stopped, clarifying, "except the night scouts, tell them to keep their eye on the horizon. And sound an alarm to start packing, we probably have Troops heading for our doorsteps."

Zenhara left and Issa hopped off the bed. He needed an update on what remained of the Revival; he needed to talk to Malik. Issa had never felt so discouraged and he bowed over with tears threatening to overwhelm him. The nurse ran to his side, but he held out his hand to encourage her to keep distant as he hurled into the bucket by his feet. He wasn't supposed to lead the team, not now, not yet. He was only fifteen and still had so much to learn from his superiors, but in a matter of hours, his entire reality changed and he could be responsible for leading an entire neighborhood to safety.

Issa approached the Church that served as the Revival's latest meeting spot and was overwhelmed with anxiety. They had always chosen Churches, though he wasn't sure why, it was one of the questions he never got around to asking Malik about. Was it symbolic? Was there a purpose? Or had the twenty-six-year-old simply liked the idea of gathering in a sacred place?

"Inside," he barked, as he approached, ignoring their rituals to survey the space before entering. Surely after the catastrophic losses they suffered in the morning hours, God wouldn't play any further tricks on them.

Issa instinctively reached for his necklace, allowing the piece of cheap gold metal ground him. The doors sprang open as he kicked them in and stormed to the front pulpit. Like most other buildings after the war, the Church was decrepit, gaping holes in the roof and windows shattered. As they approached new Churches, Issa always searched for any stained-glass windows, they were his favorite. But this location was hit particularly hard throughout the years, and the only remnants of colors he could find on these windows was the gold tinge of rust and black littered bodies of dead flies.

The boys filed in quickly, this time crowding along the front stairs instead of spacing out within the pews. "Do we have a record?" He asked solemnly, not having memorized the roles and faces yet.

"Yes," one of the older boys called out. Issa recognized the boy and was disappointed when he looked at his lap to see the disarray of pages shoved together. Issa would change that if he had time, they needed a better system. "We're at, ughh, one- one hundred and seventy-three. Down eight."

Eight boys, eight men. The entire third level team was taken out inside the mall, Xavier the sole survivor from the second level team, and Zeke from Issa's unit. Zeke had survived the onslaught and escaped through the first level exit before the first wall closed. But when they turned around and watched their comrades fall without any way to aide them, Zeke's mind soured and he put a bullet through his skull. At least that's what Hareem said, and there wasn't any evidence to the contrary. Hareem implied that he tried to pull the gun away, but he was too late and instead turned toward the city to warn the others, gathering medics, elders, and any remaining Revival the neighborhood could spare.

"How many in the Revival?" Issa asked, his voice nearly a whisper.

"Nineteen," the boy responded, his voice low. They each sat in silence in various phases of shock. Issa waited; certain a new confidence would emerge. He needed hope, he needed a second wind, he needed… anything.

"Okay," he drawled, "Zenhara, you're promoted to Third-In-Command, we'll celebrate later," Issa dismissed. "Until Xavier returns, you're acting Second-"

"Xavier's returned," a loud boom echoed throughout the room as Xavier pushed through the double-door entryway. His leg was in a boot as he hopped on crutches, his little brother running up beside him as he scrambled inside. His face was pale and Issa wondered if he was even permitted to leave medical, standing dumbfounded as Xavier moved forward. Scratches covered every inch of the boy's face and arms, his head hung low with a haunted expression in his red-rimmed eyes. "Move," he commanded of Issa. He obeyed, but didn't sit down among the others. Xavier's brother took a seat among the boys and Issa wondered why the boy hadn't left, he was too young to join the Revival. Xavier followed Issa's eyeline which landed on his brother and Xavier let out a blood-curdling laugh. "You jealous of the boy, Chosen One? You not want anyone breaking your record for being the youngest Revival member?"

"No-" Issa protested as Xavier turned to face him, balancing on his good leg.

"Well fuck you. I think we could use any extra members we can find right about now, don't you?" Issa didn't respond, he knew he needed to pick his battles carefully. He also didn't mention how they were in this predicament because of Xavier, seeing as it was he who fought to survey the mall and create a safehouse. "Fuck all of you bastards," Xavier laughed, his words echoing in the small room as several eyes glanced to Issa for assurance. "Do you boys even understand what we're facing?" He asked rhetorically. "Is this a game to you all? Don't you understand what it means when those sirens call?" He listened intently, the alarm still blaring behind the doors. "I know Issa does, you know what it's like to lose to the Troops."

The hair on his back stood up at the mention of insinuation. Issa didn't like to talk about it, but gossip is inevitable in their small tribe, and he knew word would get around about Bethany.

"Stupid bitch didn't follow the rules, and she paid for it with her life," Issa saw red. He moved toward Xavier, wrapped his hands around his neck and gripped tight. But as Xavier's strength depleted and he couldn't hold himself up, Issa dropped his grasp and sent his new leader to the ground, coughing up blood.

"Fucking Bastard," Xavier yelled as Zenhara came to his aide, "no fuck you," he groaned, shoving Zenhara away. "That your master plan, Issa? Kill your commander? You really think that will earn you the respect you need to run this place?"

Issa searched the faces around him, scared boys watching as their leaders struggled in a pissing match.

"I bet the Chosen One can't even kill," he chided. "If the time really came and the Troops got ahold of that pretty little thing in your house," he goaded Issa, "Ne-vay-ugh." Issa's first curled into a tight ball, he was seconds away from losing his grip. But Xavier was ready this time, dropping his crutch and aiming a pistol at Issa's temple. "Not so brave now, huh?"

The group gasped simultaneously and a quick glance at Zenhara confirmed to Issa that Xavier had fallen off the deep end; he posed a risk to them all. Issa's spine straightened, his confidence building as he began to calculate their options.

"I could blow you away right now," Xavier whispered, "but what about you, Issa?" He challenged. "If a Troop member had your sister in his arms now, knowing the fate that beholds her if he gets his hands on her, that young, sweet pussy," Issa drowned him out, he knew it was his only choice. Xavier was taunting him, and Issa was easy prey. "Could you do it, Issa? Point the gun between her trusting, big, beautiful eyes, and pull the trigger?" Xavier pulled the gun back, but still had it positioned toward Issa. "Could any of you do it? Could you kill your family so they don't become target practice for the soldiers? Or are you all too fucking weak?!" Issa could feel Xavier unraveling. He knew he had to stop him, but the gun was unlocked and loaded. Rushing him could kill Issa, and Issa wasn't ready to die. If nothing else, today taught him that, taught him that he wanted to live, wanted to protect his family, his sister.

Issa watched as Xavier's arm turned toward the audience, toward his brother, and all caution flew to the wind. He charged Xavier at the same moment as Zenhara, both men tackling him down as the sound of a bullet rang through the air.

The smell of the gunfire sent Issa into a panic. He was suddenly there, back in the mall, the bullets gliding past him. Issa crawled off of Xavier, lifting a hand toward Bethany's necklace as he kneeled over, panicked and fighting for breath.

"What the fuck!" Zenhara cried out, standing up and distancing himself from his best friend.

Issa turned, surveying the scene. The boys were scooting away from Remi's lifeless body, blood pouring from the young kid's chest. Issa was dumfounded, stunned, perhaps finally in shock from the stress of the day. But when Issa saw Xavier lift the gun again, he reached for his own pistol and not one, but two more bangs pierced the air. Issa waited, the moment drawing into infinity. Smoke billowing from his pistol as Xavier dropped his weapon.

Zenhara, the victim of the second round, fell to his knees; his stare full of surprise as the life exited his body and he toppled over, his body and blood intertwined with Xavier's.

Issa couldn't move, he couldn't breathe. He'd just killed someone. He'd just killed his commander. Eight bodies, now eleven. What the hell had happened? Why hadn't he voted in the meeting? When the tally count came out to a fifty-fifty even split, forcing them to flip a coin, why hadn't he voted?! He could have stopped this, prevented it. Malik would still be alive; they would all be alive.

Like a beat on a drum, a new alarm sounded in the air; the Troops were within sight. They needed to run, they needed to hide, they needed to pack their things and wipe away evidence of their presence. But Issa couldn't move.

The boys rose, one after the other, still looking to Issa for reassurance.

The sudden ringing of his watch is what caught his attention. Xavier's watch followed suit. They had set an alarm earlier that day, it was part of their plan. In the event they lost track of time, each leader had an alarm set to guide them out of the mall and back to the city.

Snapped from his daze, Issa looked toward the remains of the Revival. They were terrified and he needed to reassure them, he couldn't allow more bloodshed.

"Go home," he instructed, a practiced confidence in his voice, "go home and hide. Make sure your gear is ready, you know what to listen for. We will regroup in the morning and pack to leave." He hesitated, understanding the responsibilities that would fall on his shoulders in the morning. He would need to appoint new leaders and orchestrate a pile-up. Then he, and he alone, would be responsible for leading the neighborhood out. "Meet at the West at dawn, we'll reorganize there."

The boys turned to leave, but Issa spoke up again, halting their movements. "Xavier was scared," he blamed, "he was angry". I know you're all afraid now, but don't be. This changes nothing, we honor the fallen by doing what we have always done, and we're going to make it." He lifted his gaze and straightened his posture. He was in control now. "Make me proud of this team."

With his final words carrying them, the boys dispersed. Issa knew he needed to follow them out, he needed to find his way home and help his family hide, help Nevaeh hide, but his legs were glued to the ground, weighing him down like a thousand-pound anchor. Issa wasn't strong enough for this, he couldn't lead the Revival, stand up in front of the neighborhood and guide them, pretend like he has some ultimate plan that he conjured up overnight while his superiors' bodies decayed. Surely there had to be a better leader, someone older and wiser that could take the helm.

Panic set in as movement outside caught his attention, the alarms continuing to blaze. The Troops had come. Gone was the time for Issa to run, he'd have to make a stand or die trying. Issa raised his hand to his shoulder, feeling the rough edges of the 'R' that marked him a traitor, granting him an immediate execution. They would give no leniency to him and he accepted that fate when he agreed to join, but it wasn't just his fate he sealed in. If he died, who would be left to care for Nevaeh? His mother couldn't lose another child, she wouldn't survive it. And his father, the poor lad was already a waste on society. If it wasn't for his strong medical capabilities that could out stitch his three closest colleagues while riding horseback, the neighborhood would have dropped his drunk ass along the road years ago. But Issa was their final peg, the glue holding the pieces together once all the stitches were cut. If they lost him, Nevaeh wouldn't stand a chance. She'd become an orphan, left alone to gather and hunt and provide for a life that was pre-destined for failure.

And the neighborhood, what would happen to them? They were all looking to him. If they woke up in the morning to find Issa dead along with the others, they'd surely fall apart. No leadership, no direction, no one even partly trained in understanding their methodology.

Issa couldn't give up. With all the odds stacked against him, he still had to try. Removing the taping around his wounds, Issa moved with haste. He looked down at the massacre he'd witnessed only moments ago and concocted the plan he hoped would be his saving grace. Tentatively he lifted Zenhara's limp body and crawled beneath him, lying face down. The boy's warm blood a blanket on Issa's torso as he grabbed Xavier's free hand and draped it over his back. His head wound properly revealed, Issa closed his eyes, feigning death only moments before a crashing sound indicated a foreign presence.

He held his breath, the fear surging through his blood as he lay still, commanding his body not to move. A sick thought entered his mind as he imagined the soldiers' disappointment, finding that they had missed out on the show. Slow footfalls growing louder alerted Issa to their proximity and he nearly winced when a misplaced foot crushed his outcast hand.

"Looks like we missed one hell of a party," a voice exclaimed, and the absurdity of it made Issa grimace as he held back a growl. A slow ache formed in Issa's chest as his brain plead for oxygen and he distracted himself by counting to the monotone sound of Xavier's alarm. Beep-one, beep-two.

"They all dead?" another voice queried and Issa could feel the light shake as one of the soldiers jostled Zenhara's body with their rifle. Beep- five.

A loud boom echoed in the room as a gun went off, but Issa didn't move, didn't dare to inspect himself for any new injuries, allowing his body to warn him of any critical wounds. Beep- eight. Luckily, no new pain surfaced, but he was losing time as his lungs fought for air. Beep- nine.

"Yup," the man groaned dismissively as another called out 'building's clear'. *Leave*, Issa begged them, the burning in his chest spreading throughout his body. Beep- twelve.

A silence consumed the room and Issa knew his time was up, his body pleading as his mind turned to muck and his fingers tingled. Beep- fifteen.

"Start the fire', a voice commanded and footsteps carried away. Beep- seventeen. By his estimate, there was only one solder on guard now and Issa fingered his belt for his gun, but it wasn't there. Beep- nineteen. His options were limited. He was strong in a fight, but his body was tired, his muscles weak. Beep- twenty-one. And as soon as the other could hear the altercation, he would surely return and, even on his best day, Issa's odds were slim. Beep- twenty-five.

Loud and rapid fire sounded outside and the soldier turned. Beep- twenty-seven.

"Let's move," he heard as loud footsteps covered his exhale, his chest heaving as his threat disappeared to investigate the new slaughter.

Rising from the carnage, his body slick with blood, he saw his gun and maniacally stumbled his way until his fingertips crossed the cold metal. Falling over, he turned and held the gun towards the door, but the men were gone. Issa fell back, his chest heaving as he sucked in a large breath of air. A gritty taste filled his lungs as his mind registered the scent. Fire.

Could he not just catch a break? Issa wondered as he pushed himself up. The continuous bang, clang, pop of bullets out front warned Issa of imminent dangers and he turned to survey his other options.

Several broken windows framed the room, but he would surely be seen if he attempted to exit them. The front doors were not an option, so Issa's best chance would be to find a back exit.

Charging through the doorframe that lit up with hot flames, Issa covered his face with his arm, blocking smoke from invading his recovering lungs. Another doorway looked promising, but a quick tug on the searing handle stopped him, the door was locked. Stepping to the far wall, Issa readied himself and he launched his body toward the frame, the door billowing as he forced it open.

Smoke pultruded around him as the flames clung to his foul shirt, but Issa wasn't done. He was a target in an open field and his time was running thin as footfalls descended upon him.

He pictured Nevaeh. His scared little sister, alone in a dark space, her only protection in the form of a thin bookshelf concealing her hideout. She needed him to return, needed the security that only he could provide. But his body was tired, his adrenaline fading. Blackness marred his vision and his limbs were putty.

With the last strength he could muster, Issa ambled his way to a neighboring building. He mustered enough strength to descend the stairs to the basement, but lost his footing and fell the remaining feet to the bottom. There was no guarantee he was safe and he didn't have the strength to camouflage himself. Peering long enough to see that the room was untouched, Issa gave in, allowing the exhaustion to take over his body and the world around him fell to darkness.

CHAPTER 6

FIFTEEN YEARS OLD

Bum. *Buh dump. Bum dump. Buh dump. Issa's head pounded, a heavy throb beating in the back of his head. Bum. Buh dump. A loud shrill deafening him as he leans up, lifting his hand to the sensitive gash on his head. Buh dump. The room is dark and he fumbles to his feet, following the single stream of light invading the space. Buh dump. He knocks his feet on something and glances down. Stairs, he's at a stairway. Can he climb it? Buh dump. Yes, his legs lift, his brain sending silent commands as his feet carry him forward, hauling the heavy mass of dead weight towards the light. Buh dump.*

The door creaks open without hesitation and the bright sun attacks him. Buh dump. The world is empty, a large open field silent with the exception of a small boy who runs hastily across it. Bum. Buh dump. Issa remains invisible, cast in the shadows of the dark room as his vision clears and the world comes to view. Buh dump, clang! Buh dump, clang!

An alarm rings, intercepting the placid silence as his hearing slowly returns, his head throbbing violently in tempo. Buh dump, clang! Issa rubs at his head again, dried crusty blood shedding onto his hand.

He steps into the light and acclimates himself, the warm sunlight a welcome friend. Looking to the left and right, he makes out the torched remains of the Church. The Church! It came to him in a flash, the dead bodies, the Troops, the fire, Nevaeh.

Issa rushes home as fast as his feet will carry, surveying the empty streets as they slowly fill with signs of life as the chime sounds. The neighborhood doesn't know yet, but soon they will all be looking to him for guidance, for reassurance.

He turns down the lane and spots his house, no movement visible from the street. He is cautious as he approaches and he braces himself for the worst. Signs of the raid outside were apparent, yet minimal on his street; they still had a chance.

He propped open the door and slid in, eyes roaming the open floorplan as he searched for his parents. On high alert, Issa reached for his pistol. Surely his parents could hear the sirens, so why weren't they responding? Mom should be packing their things while dad left to aid the medic teams in their search and rescue attempts. Clearly empty, Issa moved away from the living space and headed to the basement. When the landing came into view, his heart dropped and his body tinged with remorse. Laying in a bed of thick congealed blood, his parents' bodies were limp. He rushed in, feeling his mother's pulse for any sign of life. But her body was cold and stiff, and Issa deflated. Tears pricked at his eyes, but wouldn't surface as he looked to his father, his body wrapped around the rocking chair, a black hole marring the back of his head and blackened blood stained the wall behind him. The gun lay on the floor, discarded. 'At least they fought back', *Issa thought.*

A shuffle behind him caught his attention and he turned, removing the pistol from his waistband. The Troops knew their tricks, surely they hadn't left Neveah unharmed. That is, unless they were still there, hiding. Bracing himself, he pushed back the bookshelf in one swift movement and readied his weapon.

She was there, but she wasn't alone. Holding her from behind and silencing her screams, a soldier was waiting for him.

"Issa!" she screamed as the hand fell from her lips, pulling a gun toward him. "Run, Issa!"

"Issa! Issa-" he jolted awake, sweat pouring from his temple as he pushed his sister back and caught his breath. He looked at Nevaeh, meeting her gaze and letting her know he was okay. In the dark night, he could barely make out her form so he pulled her closer, gently tucking a stray hair behind her ear.

It was a dream. A nightmare. Well, some of it anyways. He did wake up disoriented and confused, but when he came home to find his parents dead, Nevaeh was asleep; alone and unharmed in the small crook carved into the wall. His vibrant, energetic sister had sunk ten inches overnight, her body curling in on itself as she fluttered awake. She was afraid, but her big brown eyes softened when she recognized her brother. She jumped out of the hole like a monkey, hurdling herself toward him and latching herself onto his torso as she cried. He held her, throwing his gun over to the bed as he turned her away from the carnage. She was petrified, her tiny bones shaking as she wept in his arms. But she was safe, she was alive.

If We Don't

He surveyed the quiet land around him and laid his head back down. It was still too dark for them to cross over without suspicion. Issa was the first to admit that his plan had flaws, but as soon as Nevaeh came ambling for his chest that morning, he knew he had to do everything in his power to save her.

"It's okay," he cooed, petting her long hair. "You're safe". He rocked her in his arms like he was burping an infant. How the Troops found his parents and not Nevaeh was a mystery to him, but he was thankful. In less than a day, he had lost his commanding officers, been promoted to First-In-Command, lost both of his parents, and became the sole custodian of his sister. It was enough to send anyone over the edge, but Issa clung to Nevaeh. She was the only good thing he had left in the world. Holding her head to keep her from turning, he escalated the stairs and outside the house.

"Issa!" a record-keeper and scout shouted, approaching him. "We've started the tally, sir, and we're telling families to pack their things and meet at the Western checkpoint. I think we should be able to set out by noon." The news was good. Just as he had hoped, the Revival was still alive.

"What's the current mortality at?" Issa asked, nodding to the record-keeper's notepad.

The boy eyed Issa cautiously. "We've counted eighty-one so far this morning. Crews are still scavenging".

Eighty-one. Eighty-one dead. What was the headcount at just yesterday? One seventy-three? That's nearly half of the neighborhood!

"Does that include the eight from yesterday?" He asked, afraid of the answer.

The boy's response was timid. "It doesn't include the eight from the mall".

Eight more. Eighty-nine dead in total and the crews hadn't even finished searching. Add his parents and the numbers were already in the nineties.

"There's two more," Issa stammered, "In the house behind me, have the crews collect them for burial."

Issa walked on, carrying Nevaeh. Part of him wanted to run. Run fast and hard and never stop, never look back, not even more a second. But he couldn't. He had a responsibility here, a responsibility to his team and the elders and Nevaeh. Nevaeh, God, how could he raise Nevaeh? He's still just a boy himself, he doesn't know how to care for a child! And when he has so many others looking to him, he can't watch her, too!

He set Nevaeh down and grasped his head with both hands, walking in a broad circle. 'Focus Issa, Focus,' *He chided. He could ask the nurturers to care for the girl, her parents did die. Surely they could make an exception for him. But then what? She's what, ten years old now? She's got a steady head on her shoulders, she could figure it out. He was only a year older than her when he joined the Revival, she can take care of herself.*

But as he looked at his sister, Bethany's tortured eyes stared back at him. She had trusted him to take care of their youngest sibling. He had already lost one sister, he couldn't abandon the other. But could he give up his post? Had anyone ever stepped down from the Revival before? Who would lead the neighborhood to safety? Could he truly face his peers knowing that he abandoned them when they needed him most? He hadn't reviewed the maps, he didn't have a plan, he had no idea where they had been, nonetheless where they should go.

If We Don't

Issa faced the small crowd as he sought higher ground. He had return home long enough to pack his things and develop a plan, and then he joined his neighbors at the checkpoint. The crowd silenced, a hush falling among them as they turned to him; the Chosen One.

No one knew when the rumors started, but the prophesy spoke of a boy, raised among two identities, who would face an unspeakable loss and, with a stomach full of fire, would tear down the foundation that betrayed him, and lead the forsaken to destiny, freeing them from the pains of their century. Once Issa was brought to the elders, the prophesy was dissected further. He was born a full century following the Great War. And losing Bethany? It was all part of the greater plan; the loss filling him with a rage that consumed him. Joining the Revival was the final step; giving him a new purpose, a new identity. And so, the elders took a step of faith and trusted in the bigger plan.

But after all Issa had been through, he couldn't help but think they were wrong. Either the prophesy was a lie, or perhaps the interpretation was incorrect.

"I don't-" Issa's voice cracked. He didn't know how to begin, how to apologize, how to form the words. The faces surrounded him were tormented, agonized. He clutched tighter to Nevaeh's hand. "I'm leaving," he finally managed to say. "You're welcome to join me," he paused, unsettled, "but I don't think that you will." His heart thundered, his limbs ached, numb clouds forming in his eyes as invisible streaks slid down his cheeks and dampened the ground at his feet. His feet bare for the first time since he joined the Revival, his torso unclothed as he handed in his vest. "I'm going to the South," he announced, and as predicted, screams of disapproval and hate were tossed at him.

Variations of 'you can't', 'that's a death sentence', 'but you're the chosen one', 'that's suicide', 'you can't betray us', and 'you're leading us to slaughter' hit him as his neighbors protested.

"Please, please-" he called out, begging for mercy, "you have to understand-"

'Coward', 'dirty bastard', 'fool'!

"My family is dead!" he spit angrily, silencing the abuse. "I have nothing, we all have nothing! We're not living, we're barely even surviving! I'm tired of running and I'm tired of pretending that this life is worth my pain!" He paused, catching his breath as his chest heaved from his outburst. "Now whether you like it or not, my compass is heading South. I may not stand a chance, but I will die trying!" He lifted Nevaeh's hand for the crowd to see. "She's innocent! She's a fucking child! They're inhumane if they can't look at her innocent face and bare skin and at least offer her a chance at retribution!" He glanced down at his sister, hoping he was right. She only had one tattoo, her birth marking. They may find him worthless, his body to marred and his mind too old to salvage, but he had to at least try, for Nevaeh's sake.

*   *   *   *   *

And so, some twenty-six days later, he was ready to reap the consequences of his actions. They travelled mostly at night, aiming to allude any wandering Troops that might enjoy the side action of a ten-year-old girl while perfecting their aim on her brother's broken skin. Recalling his lessons on gathering and hunting, he kept food in her stomach and provided a solid four hours of rest when the sun was at its highest peak. And while the venture nearly stole all nine of his spare lives, as the sun set on the twenty-fifth day, he could just make out the grey barricade on the horizon. While his body ached for salvation, he wouldn't dare cross the border in the night. He needed any favor the Lord could give him if he stood a chance at the South accepting his surrender, and showing up in the darkness of night would surely land a bullet to his chest. Even he knew the mantra, *'shoot first, ask questions later'*.

To his knowledge, it had been years since a Northerner attempted to cross the border. In the early years following the Great War, peace existed among the nations and some Northerners even assisted in the creation of the wall. So it was a surprise to them, when the monarchy descended and the ships arrived, that the walls wouldn't open; their days of peace and friendship come to close a modest two years later. The North had won the War against the South, but when the chance to rebuild presented itself, the South had a vengeance to settle, and they watched as the monarchy did the dirty work for them.

His food source was low, so he knew he couldn't hold off much longer. And as he watched the stars that night, a southbound shooting star provided the sign he was waiting for. But it didn't stop his heart from pounding as he watched the sun rise that next morning.

Nevaeh eyed Issa cautiously. Besides a few mumbles here or there, and of course shouting his name to wake him from the dreams that plagued his sleep, she hadn't said a word since they left the village. His sister, previously an untamed hurricane with cataclysmic winds, now a sad little duckling that didn't trust her wings.

Issa dropped down to his knees, making direct eye contact with her. He wanted to talk to her, wanted to encourage her or provide some sort of reassurance, but the words failed to come. Instead, he simply tugged her hands, and then turned, ready to face their destiny.

Issa didn't know when they passed the barrier, or even if they had passed it, but standing with his feet inches from the metal barricade doors, he assumed the invisible marker had been surpassed. When they were withing a quarter mile, Issa could hear the alarms sound and now he could hear the clamoring behind the walls, the heightened sense of urgency in the tone as he leaned his head closer to hear. Even the smell was different as they closed in on their neighbors, but he couldn't say that he preferred it much. When a loud metal clang sounded, Issa took a step back and pulled Nevaeh with him. As the doors folded open and parted, an onslaught met them, silent words passing between them.

He hadn't given this much thought, he suddenly realized. He hadn't quite thought he would make it this far. He didn't know much about the South, he almost imagined them as green-eyed aliens, but to his surprise, they looked quite a bit like Issa and the neighborhood he left behind. Though a bit more well-nourished, donning heavy coats and boots, faces and limbs clean and unmarred, and hoisting machinery far more complex than the pistol Issa buried that morning, the monsters facing Issa didn't look as foreign as he'd imagined.

Nevaeh looked up at Issa and broke the silence, "are you going to say something?" she asked, her blunt innocence slowly returning.

Issa looked back up, holding her by the shoulders. "My name is Issa, son of Joey and Mariam Cruz. This," he tapped Nevaeh's shoulder, "is my sister Nevaeh." No one flinched, the guns still trained on them, "she's only ten-" he trailed off, glancing down at his sister once again. "We won't be any trouble and we could really use your help."

When the barricade remained silent, Issa wondered if they didn't understand him, if, after all these years, they adopted a new form of communication. But just as Issa's hope faltered, he heard a voice ring out over a com. "Can anyone give an update? Over."

He heard it; he recognized the words. If he could understand them, then- "Drop you weapons," a female voice commanded as a woman stepped forward, the row behind her pushing back and raising their guns to the sky. "Issa, do you have any weapons on you?" She addressed him, her soft tone forced.

"No, I buried them in the field," he answered honestly and earned a close-lipped smile.

"We're going to search you, do you understand?" She was tall, her face was lean, but not concave like those he was familiar with. Her bright red hair sleek and tied behind her head and plastic rims dangled on her nose and ears. Issa consented to the search and two men approached cautiously, patting down Issa's pelt and Nevaeh's thin shirt that dangled below her knees. When the men nodded back, the lady's smile re-emerged, this time showing brilliantly white teeth. "My name is Caroline," she informed, "It's very nice to meet you Issa and Nevaeh."

"All clear" a man spoke, pulling the radio to his lips. "Two outsiders entering."

"Are you ready to come inside?" Caroline asked, the human barricade cracking and allowing space for the three to walk together. Issa grabbed Nevaeh's hand and led her, strategically placing himself in the middle as they moved inside; the doors banging shut behind them. Long beams of artificial light pierced through clear boxes in the ceiling and left blinding white blobs in his eyes when he looked away, blinking furiously.

"My eyes-" he gasped frantically, throwing his arms outwards, creating a gap between himself and those surrounding him. Immediately guns were raised and trained on him as he pulled Nevaeh into his circle, his back hitting a wall. "My eyes!"

"Calm down, boy," someone demanded, but Issa was hysterical.

He yelled louder, "my eyes! What have you done to my eyes?!"

Through the commotion, Caroline stepped forward, a calm resonation in her tone. "Issa, please, listen to me. You're not used to the lightbulbs," she spared a glance upward. "If you look straight at them, it temporarily impairs your vision."

"Temporarily?" Issa question, his gaze moving to the white tile flooring beneath him.

"Yes, temporarily. Just keep blinking, it will slowly disappear." Issa did as she said, the white blob shrinking in size, changing color as his vision slowly re-emerged. "See, it's fading," she narrated as the blob slowly morphed into the recesses of his eyesight and blended in with the scenery. "It's okay," she whispered as she held out a hand, easing the tension and directing the weapons downward. "Just tell me when you're ready and we'll keep going". Issa waited, measuring up the squad that surrounded him; several wearing white coats mirroring Caroline's appearance while others wore variations of green camouflage military vests, matching canvas pants, and high tan combat boots. They looked very similar to the dark green and black uniforms adorned by the Troops, but instead of the gritty scorn on the opposition's faces, he saw hesitance and reluctance.

Issa nodded, straightening his posture as he followed Caroline down the hallway through the sterile sleek, silver door that led to an intensely lit room with white walls and a smell that seared Issa's throat. Images of his father sewing up arms and teaching Issa how to draw blood flashed before him, but his father wasn't among the faces that stared back.

"This is a hospital," Caroline informed. "If you allow, we would like to clean you up, get you something to eat, and run a few simple tests." Issa blinked back at her. He wanted to trust the woman, her honest green eyes settling the fear that riddled his body, so he agreed; it was his choice to come to the South and he needed someone he could trust.

"Can Nevaeh come with me?" Issa asked, his grip tightening on his sister's small hand.

"We'd need to separate you," she informed, but quickly added, "just for a moment. We will bring you both back to this room as soon as you've cleaned up." The answer didn't sit well with Issa, and he tried to think of an argument. "We separate the male and female bathrooms and showers, for privacy and safety reasons," Caroline added. "If it makes you feel better, I will promise to stay by her side." His heart thumping faster, he slowly agreed, letting go of her hand as Caroline turned toward another man. "Issa, this is Byron. He's going to help you until Nevaeh and I return." Issa watched as the man as he eyed Caroline, something sensual in his gaze, a comfort or familiarity that he felt with Caroline as he watched her step aside. Issa greeted Brody with a nod, both men watching Caroline as she led Nevaeh to the other side of the room and through a wooden door.

Byron was tall and slender, Issa presumed in his mid-thirties, wearing the same white overcoat and light blue shirt as Caroline. He resembled what Issa imagined he could look like in fifteen years, given a nice haircut and bath.

"Are you ready?" Byron asked once he managed to pull his eyes from Caroline. Issa followed Byron through the door beside where Nevaeh disappeared, steam billowing toward him as the door closed; thin square tiles slid under his feet. "The shower is here," he stated, pulling back a white sheet. "Turn this if the water is too cold," he pushed the left silver knob protruding from the green tiled wall, "and this if the water is too hot." He moved away and the white curtain fell back into place. "This," he exclaimed, "is a bar of soap to clean yourself with," he indicated to a white brick the size of Issa's hand as he placed it on top of a towel. "You'll dry off with this," he handed both items to Issa and walked away. "This basket is for your-" he hesitated, looking down at Issa's loincloth, "clothes". He opened a drawer and pulled out a white bag, "here are some clean ones to put on when you're done." He led Issa back to the shower and placed the bag of clothes onto a stool beside some lockers. "Oh, almost forgot," he half jogged as he returned to the shower and pulled the curtain back, "this is a shampoo and conditioner combo. You'll put this in your hair." He pointed towards a doorway, "I'll be out there when you're ready. If you need any help or have questions, just knock. No one else will be allowed in while you change." The information overwhelmed him. Soap, conditioner combo? Leave clothes in the basket, and what else? "Issa, do you want me to go over it again?"

Issa shook his head fast, not wanting to look stupid. But Byron must have sensed Issa's lie, because he pulled in closer and leaned against the protruding wall. "We haven't had many of you, but I've met a couple in my time," he informed. "There's a lot to take in, and you won't remember half of it tomorrow. Sensory overload we call it," he sighed, making direct eye contact with Issa for the first time. "You are safe here, that much I can promise you. So just take a deep breath. If you need me, I'm happy to come back in and help, but we find it best to give you some space, let you acclimate. And I'll be on the other side of that door," he pointed to the door they entered through, "if you need me for anything." Byron walked away, pausing and looking back at Issa before letting the door closed behind him, a loud click once the door was shut.

The room was fairly large, two rows of showers connecting in an 'L' shape around the corner. Issa backed away and returned to the shower Byron had indicated. He turned the cold knob first and the water sprayed down from the ceiling in a fast stream, startling him as he turned it back off. Slowly this time, he pulled the level again and watched as the spray ran down the curtain and disappeared through a metal grate. Stepping in, the cold water stung against his skin, and he slipped to the ground as he tried to escape. '*What the hell*'? He thought, afraid to go back in. But this time he was prepared and he turned the left lever to adjust the water to his preference. He rubbed his body with the soap, white foam popping on his skin as yellowish-brown water flushed off his skin.

When he looked at the, what was it called? A combo? Well, when he looked at the combo-thing, he could see a blue liquid inside a metal tube, but the tube was stuck on the wall and he couldn't figure out how to apply it. Opening his curtain, he looked to make sure no one was watching, and he stepped out into the cool air, running to the shower beside him and finding the same contraction stuck to the wall. He scurried back to his shower, allowing the warm water to run down his body, the tiny pellets massaging his sore joints. Ducking below the combo, he pushed a small lever, releasing the blue jelly onto his face and into his mouth; a terrible, God-awful taste as he spit the thick paste out and rinsed his mouth with water. He decided he didn't need the combo goo and waisted long minutes under the heavy stream of water, enjoying the pressured sensation, until he heard a knock on the door.

"Everything okay, Issa?" Byron's voice boomed through the doorway.

"Fine, everything's fine!" He yelled, cutting off the water and grabbing the towel to dry off. The towel was fluffy and soft, smooth as it whisked away the beads of water his skin. And his skin! He'd never seen it so perfectly clean, having washed away fifteen years of mud and dirt and all sorts of foreign substances from his dark, now borderline olive, skin. Using his teeth to tear open the bag, Issa fumbled into the clothes, the waist band of the blue shorts a perfect fit around his thin frame. The white shirt smelled of a heavy perfume and Issa fanned the shirt before pulling it over his head, the long sleeves and high neck disguising Issa's tattoos and branding.

Leaving the room, Issa searched for Nevaeh immediately, finding her sitting on top of a flat table on the far edge of the room. A man hovered over her, peering down her throat. "Hey, hey," Issa, shouted, stumbling over to her and looking for Caroline, "what are you doing to her?" He questioned, pushing himself between the doctor and the table.

"Issa, it's okay," Caroline hummed, appearing out of nowhere. "We're just starting some tests to make sure you're both healthy."

He looked quizzically at her and countered. "You need-I'd like it if you would test me first, please."

She smiled and agreed, "we can arrange that, go ahead and hop up," she a white cloth that draped over a cushy bench. "I will be the one to examine you if that is okay?" She looked at him for an answer, but he turned back over to Nevaeh, watching the man intently. "So, tell me Issa, how old are you?" she asked, lifting her rolling chair to better meet his gaze as she fitted her hands into blue gloves.

They explained each test in detail as they continued, taking their blood pressure, samples of blood, and asking questions about their family and neighborhood. When the tests were done and they were cleared, they were provided a new pair of shoes and escorted to a lobby to await their ride.

"Your driver will take you to your apartment," Caroline informed him, sitting beside them as they waited, "that's where you will live until you're old enough to find new quarters. As a minor, you're not allowed-"

"What's a minor?" Issa interrupted, trying his best to ask the 'right' questions even though all he wanted was to find a dark place to lay his head and sleep.

Caroline dimples curved into a light smile, "it just means that you're not an adult. You have to be at least seventeen here to make you own legal decisions as an adult." Issa nodded in comprehension and she continued. "We want you to have privacy, but we also can't allow you to be without adult supervision, so we'll assign you a caretaker. I've already spoken with the city and they're assigning you to a lady named Annette Gabriel. Ms. Gabriel will help you enroll in school, make sure you're completing your studies, and she will also make sure you've got a homecooked meal every night. Her apartment is beside yours, but she will have a key and a side entry directly to your suite."

Apartment, key, suite... the words overwhelmed Issa as he tried to keep up. His brain was a fog, the sun just beginning to set on what had been the world's longest day.

"Now, the apartment isn't free, you're going to have to work to pay and you will also be expected to chip in for the food that Ms. Gabriel provides, but you'll have some monetary assistance provided by the government as long as you continue to work and prove you are a contributing member of society."

'*Is she still speaking English*'? Issa wondered, nodding along as he pretended to understand her.

"Looks like your ride is here," Caroline indicated, standing. She shuffled them along to a Jeep where another woman was just exiting from the driver's side. Issa had seen many vehicles in his time, but had never actually ridden in one, and the prospect thrilled him. "Issa and Nevaeh, this is Ms. Gabriel, she will be the caretaker looking after you both," Caroline introduced, and Issa shook the woman's hand.

Annette Gabriel was a middle-aged brunette woman with soft eyes and an affinity for floor-length skirts. Her long hair was tied up into a bun that reminded him of Bethany, and her warm smile eased the tension that had been building in his spine.

The car ride nauseated Issa, and when they finally arrived at their destination, he felt like muck. The day was exhausting and emotional, and as he glanced at the mountain of stairs leading to their apartment, Issa thought he'd rather park himself on the solid ground below and sleep outside. But his manners won out, not wanting to set a bad impression for Nevaeh.

The apartment was built on stilts, the lower lever forming a shelter for the vehicles which contained a descending door that sent a shiver down Issa's spine, reminding him of the black walls that foreclosed on him in the mall. Issa forced his body up the rickety wooden stairs and into their apartment on the second level. The furnished suite boasted two-bedrooms, two bathrooms, a designated living space, and kitchen with an extended countertop to eat at.

"My home is next door and I have a key to your loft and will conduct random searches to ensure you're obeying the rules," she informed them as she opened the door and flicked on the lights in the open room. "I'll cook dinners for you and help monitor your stipend until you can get honorable work," she continued as she opened and closed various cabinets in the kitchen. "The apartment on your left belongs to the school custodian and he also serves as my part time handy-man. If anything breaks or you need assistance, he should be able to help," she stated. "He actually should be coming home any time now, I'm sure he'll be eager to meet you."

"Why?" Issa questioned; the notion incredulous, but he apologized immediately, recognizing the crudeness of his question. Luckily, his question didn't seem to bother her.

"Hasn't anyone told you about him?" Ms. Gabriel, Annette as she requested to be called, asked. A shake of his head pushed her to continue. "He's like you, from the North."

The world around Issa froze. There were more of them? Yes, yes there were… Brody- Brock- Brice, whatever his name was, he said something of the sort earlier, hadn't he?

The memory was faint as he tried to bring it to the forefront of his mind. They were in the locker room preparing for his shower, he leaned against the wall and- yes. He did. He'd said that there were others like him.

"There's more of us?" He questioned, feigning ignorance as he tried to pry out information from her.

"Not many, but there are a few within the districts, though he is the only one who has remained in the district." Districts? Annette could read his puzzled expression. "We'll have plenty of time to brush you up on the history, but it's been a long day and tomorrow will be just as brutal. I suggest you both get some rest." She turned to leave, "I'll have dinner ready in an hour and I'll bring some over." And with that, she closed the door behind her.

Issa sat on the striped couch in the living space, finally able to piece together the events from the day. He was puzzled; he did it. He made it. He travelled countless miles on numerous terrains, managed to outwit the Troops, found the border wall and wasn't killed, and now he had a roof over his head in a sturdy building that had actual working bathrooms and lights. And he wasn't alone! There were others! He laid down, the stiff fabric itchy against his arms and neck as he stared up at the ceiling. Nevaeh joined him, cradling in the crook of the sofa, and the world around them darkened as their adrenaline faded and they fell asleep.

Thump, thump, thump! A rapping on the wall startled Issa as he pawed at his eyes, reacclimating himself with his surroundings. "Issa!" A male voice called out from behind the front door. Thump, thump. "Issa!" He jumped up, fear seizing him as his back hit the wall, Nevaeh curled into him. He had yet to encounter a threat in the South, but he wasn't sure what to expect from the unknown interloper. Thump, thump! "Issa, it's Rafi, please open the-"

Rafi? Did he say Rafi? Issa's heart raced, knocking past Nevaeh as he ran to the door and fidgeted with the lock. The door flew open, the incessant knocking halting as the door fell back. Issa's eyes adjusted the to the darkness and he stepped back to get a better look. The man was tall, his long arms and bulging muscles much larger than the thirteen-year-old that Issa had once known. But as he scanned the man's face, the crooked nose, eyes so dark they were almost black, and five-head, Issa was certain it was him.

"Rafi?" He whispered breathlessly, but Rafael didn't answer as both men stepped forward, their bodies intersected into a hug. Rafi was here! He was safe! Issa cried, losing his battle with the emotional roller coaster he had fought for nearly a month. "You're here!" He cried out, "How are you here?!"

Rafael took a step back, his gaze moving onward to Nevaeh who had picked herself off the ground and hovered in the corner. "Don't-" he exclaimed, "don't tell me that's little Nevaeh?" He shouted, entering the apartment, but stopping several feet away from her. Issa reveled at the sound of Rafi's voice. The tone so familiar, yet huskier than he remembered. And the dialect swift and more robust than he'd recalled. "My God, you've grown so big," he smiled, "You probably don't remember me, I'm your uncle Rafi." He extended his hand to Nevaeh and she grasped it cautiously, looking to Issa for reassurance. Uncle Rafi? *Uncle* Rafi. That's right. He was dating Bethany before she was taken. They had planned a future together. She would be a nurturer like their mom, and he, well, he hadn't decided what he wanted to be. Rafi said he wanted two and a half kids and Bethany teased him about the possibility of a half kid. 'We *'ll adopt an orphan*', he said, '*while I won't want to, you won't be able to resist and you'll show up on our doorstep with a baby in tow and, because I love you, I'll cloth and feed the kid*'.

But then the alarms went off and Bethany was taken. And Rafi's family was separated into the other neighborhood unit during the split and… And what? Issa thought he'd died. When his grandfather showed up in the middle of their journey and announced the raid, everyone has assumed Rafi was dead. "You were only two the last time I saw you," he recalled, "so you must be, ten now?" He turned to Issa, gabbing around Issa's shoulders and fisting his knuckles into his hair, "and you! When did you grow up to be so big?!"

Issa pulled on Rafi's arm, forcing his lost comrade to face him as Issa surveyed the man he'd once known so well. His eyes drew together in confusion. "How did you- how are you- how is this possible?"

Rafi's eyes turned down and he sighed. A smell drafted in as Annette kicked the half-open doorway. "Issa, I hope you don't pick up on Rafi's bad habit of leaving the door open. You'll let in bugs," she exclaimed, and the two boys stood dormant, eyeing each other cautiously.

"I'll tell you everything," Rafi promised, "now let us sit for dinner first."

"Tell him what?" Annette questioned, sitting the food down on the counter.

When Issa hesitated, Rafi continued, "I've had full day of work and came home to find a ghost," he explained, drawing a confused expression from Annette, but she didn't push any further. She searched the drawers and pulled out a long spoon-thing, sticking it into the dish and heaving it onto a plate.

"I tried to make a simple meal," Annette informed, "I remember how picky Rafael was about his spices when he first came."

Issa looked to Rafi again, a knowing gleam in his friend's eyes as he took a seat at the counter. Annette stood opposite from him and Issa watched their exchange. She was too old to be his wife or girlfriend, so perhaps a mother figure? Issa's heart warmed. His friend was alive, healthy, and happy. And if Rafi could come to find a home in the South, why shouldn't he?

Issa sat beside his comrade, his stomach growling as he registered the smell of the potato casserole; feeling at home for the first time since he'd lost Bethany.

CHAPTER 7

15 YEARS OLD

Issa walked to the front, all eyes on him as he searched Malik's face for a sign, but his face was expressionless. Surely he couldn't have been in trouble. He'd performed admirably and he'd been on his best behavior since he'd joined the Revival.

"Come on boy, hurry up," the elder chimed. "Tonight is a special night," he indicated as Issa hesitantly approached and the man wrapped an arm around him. "We know several of you have been putting in extra hours and drills, and the hard work has been noticed. Your leaders are very proud to see the team coming together and forming the strong bond of a true tribe. And while we wish we could honor each of you, there are only so many roles we can offer." Issa's eyebrows curled together in confusion, turning his head slightly toward the row of elders that watched him. "Malik, would you do the honors?" The elder asked, stepping back and allowing Issa a clear path to Malik.

"Today, we honor you, my friend, for all your hard work and dedication to success." Malik turned back to the team. "Issa, I'm the first to admit that I enjoy playing jokes on you, *calling you the 'Chosen One', and sending you on wild goose chases that you take so very seriously,"* that caused a giggle to arise from the tribe, *"but I have also been witness to what an incredible asset you've become for our team. Your stealth, stamina, and intuition are just few of the reasons you are someone we have come to rely on. So, on behalf of the Revival, I would like to ask you, Issa Cruz, to be our Third in Command."* Issa whipped his head, his eyes wide as he questioned his leader. The team surrounding him roared to life, several members popping into a standing ovation as they shouted his name. To his left, he could barely make out Xavier's movements as the boy stalked off behind the tribe. Third-In-Command? But he was only fifteen! And Zenhara was next in line, wasn't he? Or was that not how the process worked? *"So, what do you say,"* Malik questioned as the cheering died down, *"do you accept the nomination?"*

Issa looked at his team, several of them ready to jump up and attack him. How had they kept this a secret? The elders to his left nodded approvingly as he glanced their direction. Although in shock, Issa managed a response. *"I do,"* he declared confidently, a surge of joy overtaking him as Malik slapped his back. He could barely hold his feet still, wanting desperately to run home and tell his family of his promotion.

"Okay, okay," the first elder interrupted. *"The elders want to extend our sincere congratulations to you, Issa. You have certainly exceeded our expectations and we are confident your hard work will help to guide, strengthen, and fortify our neighborhood and Revival."*

"Thank you for this opportunity," Issa smiled as the team erupted with cheer.

"Okay boys, let's not draw too much attention," the elder goaded. *"Let's go ahead and take our seats. We have an important lesson for you today."*

Issa and Malik returned to their spots as Rafael's grandfather cleared his throat. The fire danced in the elder's eyes, eyes that had lost their spark since he returned to the neighborhood.

"For our newer grunts, this will be the first time you've heard this story in full, so it is vital you pay attention. One day, you will each be charged with remembering this and telling these stories to your future descendants." The group silenced in anticipation, the crackling of the fire the only interrupting sound. *"There's an old saying... that 'history repeats itself'."* He glanced up, making eye contact with several members before landing upon Issa *"We tell you this, not to make you fearful or to inspire hate in your hearts, but to teach you a lesson. So that one day, when you each have the chance to make a change in this world or in this neighborhood, perhaps you'll be wise enough to make the choices to save our nation, and keep our history from reoccurring. So that maybe you can stop another Civil War."*

Issa was apprehensive. This was the first time he'd heard the story of the Great War. While he'd asked Malik to tell him several times, his only response was an inaudible shrug as he paled, a haunted shiver climbing up his spine.

"It all started in the twenty-first century. The country formerly known as the United States of America was divided. Politically, socially, racially, you name it, there was some sort of argument to be had." Issa conjured up an image in his mind. He'd seen books, pictures of busy city streets,

101

individuals with their faces buried in their phones or computers.

"It was after the dawning of the technological revolution; a thing called social media became the forefront of news almost overnight. False news, radical media, was omnipresent. The old blamed the young for corrupting their society with their music and violent videogames and movies, while the young blamed the old for their lack of vision and their reckless destruction of the planet. And politically," he shook his head, *"all sides were corrupt. It wasn't a matter of who was or wasn't lying, it was just a matter of who would get caught or who could pay the most to hide the evidence."*

"What made it all worse," another elder interrupted, *"was that very few people had access to honest news sources. Some kids wouldn't even study politics, taking the word of their friends, their colleagues,"* he laughed hauntingly, *"you know, I heard once that a guy voted for his President simply because his favorite singer told the audience to vote for the guy, so the boy did. He didn't do any research, didn't ask questions, he simply accepted the artist's viewpoint as his own because,"* the elder held up his finger into air quotes, *"'well, if we like the same kind of music, why wouldn't we also like the same President?'"*

The other elders hung their heads in dismay. "We will have future lessons to explain the racial tension and the differences in the political parties, but for today, we just want to give you a high overview," Malik announced, *speaking up from his spot amongst the Revival. He nodded for the elders to continue and Rafael's grandfather's gravelly voice broke the silence.*

'Right," he hesitated, collecting his thoughts. *"so the tension boiled and clear lines were drawn. In the first Civil*

War in the United States, the division was primarily focused on race. It was still a topic of note in the Great War, but it was merely one of many undertones. In all reality, the idea of racial injustice was far worse than the actual race crisis. I'm not saying it didn't exist, but the media had a talent for illuminating racial inequalities in adverse measures."

"What does that mean?" Cable called out from the group.

Rafi's grandfather coughed, looking toward the row of elders, offering up the chance to further explain. Finally, the third elder on the bench took over. "It means that, every race faced discrimination. It didn't matter what solutions were put into place to counter-act racial injustices; people hung on to the past, and they wanted retribution for prejudices that some had never even encountered. A vengeance that ended up causing a new racial imbalance. There were some who believed that schools needed to stop teaching about the Civil War altogether, since it served to be the sole catalyst for teaching future generations that the color of their skin separated them from their friends."

"But once again, that was only a splinter in the foundation, not the whole crack," Malik interjected, maneuvering the conversation back on topic.

"That's correct," Rafi's grandfather agreed, years of dust and dirt wheezing in his lungs as he tried to regain his momentum. "The biggest fragment came from Religion, or lack thereof, since so many of the 'hot topics' and disagreements could be traced back to religion. The wall that now closes off the Southeastern corner of the land, that is a portion of land that used to be known as the Bible belt. Down South, there was pretty much a new church on every

street corner. *Different denominations, slightly different interpretations, but a strong intolerance to outside values."*

"Meaning what?" Zenhara asked, leaning forward.

Rafael's grandad sighed and looked towards the others. The second elder, sitting directly to his left, spoke up again.

"There were strong beliefs surrounding the Bible. For example, a major topic at the time was focused on gender. The Bible teaches that God first created man, and then woman. At this particular time in the twenty-first century, it was becoming more common for individuals born of one gender, to reclassify themselves as the other gender. Or in some cases, they claimed they had no gender at all, claiming they were born non-binary." Confusion marred the faces in the crowd.

"But how is that possible?" An unknown voice rang out from the back.

"Well, that's a great question, but unfortunately, I don't have the answer to that," he heaved. *"The point we're trying to make here is that the there was a large divide that was growing. And while there were religious individuals across all parts of the country, it couldn't be denied that the division crossed almost evenly across the horizontal center of the country. Then, to make matters worse, one of the more conservative states, formerly known as Texas, was in the height of scrutiny. First it was the creation of a wall along their Southern border, reducing free travel among the neighboring country, but it continued with highly prejudicial governmental rulings; control on female reproduction, and then the final string, religion in schools."*

"At this time in history, there were riots, shootings in school, so much hate" the last elder interjected vividly, standing and pacing in front of the others, *"and many*

believed this to be due to the lack of religion in the classroom. Texas was the only state in the Union allowed to fly its flag at the same height of the American flag, they had their own state pledge, and rumors of secession were heightened because of the dominant political and religious affiliations in the state."

Rafael's grandfather continued, "many in Texas agreed that taking religion out of school was the root cause of the country's dismay. So, they passed a new law, adding a formal course on Religion to high school mandatory curriculum. And that was just the beginning. There was an uproar, Christian families not wanting their children exposed to Muslim practices, Atheists not wanting to be forced to study any religion; the arguments were endless. But to many, it actually made sense. The class wasn't designed to recruit students to a religion, but simply help educate them on the many different ideologies. Lawmakers said that there was no guarantee a student would go on to need physics, algebra, or economics following graduation, yet students were still required to attend courses on these subjects; so why not also study religion? Soon after, school districts changed their holiday policies, making them more diverse in nature. Before the change, Christians celebrating the birth of Christ would get two weeks off for the holiday, whereas those who recognized similar religious holidays didn't get any recognition. So, policies were adapted, giving equal consideration to holidays and religious events of all students. It wasn't an easy transition, but the attempt was in good-faith; it just didn't last long.

"Several surrounding states attempted similar legislative action, but with so many different principles and practices, it wasn't manageable," Malik explained. "That's when the

states in the North, Massachusetts and Minnesota among the first, took the opposite approach, fully removing religion and religious practices from their districts. School calendars changed, keeping students in-school for the winter holidays and striking an imbalance that didn't stabilize until the conclusion of the Great War."

"When war broke out, the more liberal believers navigated North, and the more conservative people moved South," the last elder explained, reclaiming his seat on the bench. "And the tension only grew. First it was religion, then race, sexual orientation, then gender, and so on."

"So, because we live in the North, we don't believe in God?" Taylor asked, stealing the words from Issa's mouth.

"No, not at all. It just meant that people chose to interpret religion in different ways in the North. And not to make it applicable in public schools." Malik responded, receiving a nod from the elders.

"However, you are onto something there," Rafi's grandad announced, "as several of the topics of dispute greatly impact how we operate today. For example, most, but not all, Southerners believed that marking your skin was a sin. Because of that, it was… recommended for people to hide their tattoos in public or in workplaces, or just not get them at all. But the farther North you'd travelled, the viewpoint altered so drastically that, over time, it became acceptable to walk nude in public in an effort to showcase one's art. That's why so many of our ancestors refused cloth and why many of our people today still only wear a pelt." Realization dawned on the tribe as members slowly eyed their companion's choice of covering, the dark markings and raised brandings clear on their open flesh. "It didn't mean that the North or the South were correct, but the facture

expanded along the border, and it didn't stop until war broke out."

"But the North won," Xavier reminded, *his loud voice breaking up the silence.*

The last elder exhaled, "that is true, but winning isn't all it's made out to be. You see, these people had once formed a country; a Union. By taking a side in the battle, it potentially meant separating yourself from your friends, your family. When the first bomb went off in the Texas panhandle, the bomber took the lives of eighty-one civilians, among them was his own cousin. And the stories grew worse from there."

"How long did the war last?" Issa asked, his heart pounding as he allowed the information to sink in.

The elder shuffled in his spot. "With the aid of various countries, allies supporting their cause, the war lasted for more than three years. The peacetime that followed only lasted about two years."

"Why so short?" Issa demanded, but the elder remained silent.

*　　　*　　　*　　　*　　　*

Issa leaned over the kitchen table, pushing his empty plate aside. "Why didn't it last?" Issa asked, sitting across from Rafael at the kitchen table.

"The dictatorship," he said evenly.

"Dictator? I thought it was a monarchy?" Issa questioned, puzzled.

But Rafi shook his head. "Nah, the monarchy didn't take sides in the battle; they washed their hands of the dirty Americans. But that didn't stop other forces from recognizing the potential. The North claimed a lot more land than the South after the war. So, with the wall firmly in place, the Troops sailed in and forced their reign, and the newly established Democratic States of Northern America fell almost overnight."

"But if the North won the war, why couldn't they just fight off the Troops?" Issa asked, dumbfounded.

"The war lasted too long. Food was scarce, buildings capsized, artillery used. The United States used foreign imports to support so much of their business, without new shipments of goods, the country was paralyzed. Plus, besides the few who helped resurrect the wall between the new nations, the North was too busy celebrating their newfound victory, they never even saw the soldiers arrive. There was no time to formulate a new government, having abandoned past political structures, it was almost too easy for the Troops."

Issa pushed up from his seat, rubbing his head as he marched. "And these assholes wouldn't help?" He cried.

"It's not like that Issa-" Rafael defended.

"They let us die! They left us for dead! They lost the war and sauntered off and built a wall and forgot about us!"

"They didn't Issa! The war decimated them! They had only two years to rebuild and restructure their new government. They couldn't risk the North coming back in and causing turmoil. And they didn't know how bad it would get. By the time they were strong enough to lend aid, it was too late."

"It was never too late! I watched my neighborhood decimate in size only one week ago while you've been here for eight years! Eight years Rafi! Do you know how many people have died in eight years?!"

"Of course I do, Issa! And we have tried! You don't think I've tried?" The tension in the room was thick. Both boys now standing, Rafi took a step closer to Issa, his face red with anger. "I can't do it alone, man."

"I can't forgive them," he replied honestly.

"I'm not asking you to. I'm just- you have to learn their ways, understand what caused their fear and anxiety. It's the only way we can empathize with them and get them to trust and understand." Issa sauntered; his heart not ready to cave in. "I don't think they want forgiveness. They just- they have a lot to be mad about too. Issa, you should see the land. There is so much that hasn't recovered, so much destruction-"

"And I should care about that when they left us to die?"

"Issa, they've tried. The North left them for dead well before we were born. These people weren't even alive when the wall was built and when the Troops arrived. They're a lot like us; just trying to understand a terrible past that has haunted the walls they rebuilt."

Issa looked up, finally making eye contact with Rafael. "I have to go back. I have to try and save them," he confessed.

"I know," Rafi whispered, leaning on his friend. "But we have be smart about it."

Forcing back tears that pried at his eyelids, anger surged through Issa. Or perhaps it was passion. A new force grew inside his heart and his mission became clear. He knew why he was brought to the South, why the elders called him the 'Chosen One'. The legend said it would be a child born of both worlds. They had thought it meant he was to be raised by the neighborhood and the Revival. But Issa knew better now, knew the truth. He may have been born in the North, but he felt the new life breathed into his soul in the South as he considered the mission ahead. '*I'll do what Rafael said*', he thought, '*I'll learn the ways of the South. Then, when they time comes, I'll return to the North; stronger and ready to fight*'. He looked at his friend, his hope revitalized. "When do we start?"

PART 2

CHAPTER 8

SEVENTEEN YEARS OLD

He knew the answer, he was certain of it, it was just at the tip of his tongue. There were seven districts with three leaders each: religious, military, and… and what? It wasn't social or public or governmental… what was the word?!

"Do you know it or not?" Rafael asked Issa, the two of them perched on the tailgate of Rafi's pickup.

"I do, I know it, I just need a second," Issa snarled. *'Public? Social. No, public,'* he thought, his mind swirling in a haze of confusion and double. *'Could it be public'?*

The three pillars of each district were charged with upholding their duties and ensuring the safety of the entire Republic. With seven districts, that amounted to twenty-one active community leaders. Never allowed to serve more than twice, the officials also could not run back-to-back sessions. Plus, each leader could only serve for three consecutive years, spending the first half year learning the ropes from their predecessor before he/she steps down, and the final half year teaching the ropes to their replacement.

During their three years serving, it is the middle full year of their term that their specific pillar takes lead, and every year it switches.

'*Religions, military, and... something,*' Issa's mind was spent.

And because there is one representative of each pillar in every district, there is always an odd number serving for the pillars, so majority votes would win during votes. As far as the term limits, the pillars rotate terms, one year there is an election for the seven new religious leaders, the next year the election is for the seven military leaders to switch power and re-elect, and the following year it's the... "Okay, I give up, just tell me."

"What's your best guess?" Rafi challenged, watching the horizon cresting over the tall trees in the distance.

"Well, I know there's religious and military, my best guess on the third is... public?"

"Hmmm, so close," Rafi teased, jumping down from his perch and began hauling bags of soil into the bed of the dilapidated blue truck. "Political."

"Seriously?" Issa chided. '*Political! Duh'*! he chastised himself.

"Don't beat yourself up, you've been studying hard, you were bound to forget something." Rafi knew how hard he challenged Issa in the last year and a half. Since they devised their plan to petition the council, he's forced Issa to study every book he could to ensure he had a firm understanding of the culture and what opposition he would face.

"I should have known that," Issa admitted, scolding himself as he jumped down to aide Rafi. Everything he worked for depended on him passing the test. If he failed, he would have to wait another six months before he could retake it and that was time he couldn't waste.

When he came to the South, Issa knew he would have to work to adapt to the new way of life, but catching up on fifteen plus years of educational material in a year and a half was exhausting. That, working alongside Rafi as a custodian of the school and several government office buildings, and watching Nevaeh, he barely got three hours of sleep at night. But he knew he had a higher purpose, and he needed to do everything in his will to set foot back up North as soon as possible.

With the elections looming for the Military pillar, Issa knew he needed to pass his exam so he could petition the council. Unfortunately, even given his unique circumstances, they refused to break their traditions for him. In the South, the education and government were far different than the North. Here, students went through fifteen levels of education. Levels, not years. Because the society recognizes that individuals learn at different paces, you get to level up at your own pace. However, to reduce individuals from overwhelming the system and leveling too fast, the exams to level up are only held once a quarter. But you can only level up twice in a year. Then, if you fail to pass a level exam, instead of waiting the three months until the next exam, you're penalized and forced to wait two quarters until you can retest. This forces students to study and ensure confidence before registering for their level exam.

Then, to vote, you have to wait two years after your final level-fifteen graduation before you can vote. The thought is that it forces you outside of your comfortable youth and gives you time to acclimate to the structure of the outside world. And even then, you're not guaranteed voting eligibility. Because the voting process is so critical to the success of the Republic, you have to prove that you have a working knowledge of each candidate's platform. All debates are televised and, in order to vote, you must prove that you have watched a minimum of five of the seven live debates and be able to pass a pre-election exam.

Issa thought this was absurd and could hardly imagine this sort of leadership lasting in the North, but he was surprised to find out how well the system was working. Education was fairly equal across the Republic, so the ability to vote truly depended on whether each individual person actually desired the ability. The debates are recorded and therefore accessible to all individuals on the library monitors at their own convenience. Plus, forcing the people to watch the debates encouraged people to think and create their own conclusions, versus simply following the paths of their friends and like-minded individuals.

Issa and Nevaeh; however, were granted an exception to the educational structure, which was apparently incredibly rare. Because of their short time in the South, it was determined that they would not undergo the traditional fifteen levels of education. Nevaeh was permitted to begin at level nine, whereas Issa was allowed to start at level thirteen. Rafael studied with Issa intently, spending all of their free time in the library. And even when the men reported for their work duties, Rafael would quiz Issa as they mopped, swept, and cleaned.

And although he would be ineligible to vote, it was determined that Issa would be given full authority to challenge the council upon successful completion of his level-fifteen exit exam which was scheduled to begin at eight.

Issa rested uneasily against Rafi's truck. "What if I don't pass?" He questioned, timidly raising his glance to Rafael.

"Issa, you'll pass. You know the material better than some who've spent their entire lives here."

"But still, what IF?" Issa prodded.

Rafael stopped loading the top soil and exhaled, a bead of sweat prickling down his neck as the emerging sun's reach began to heat up the air around him. "What do you think will happen?" he asked, turning towards Issa.

"Well, I couldn't petition the council for starters," Issa cringed. "And I would have to wait six months to retest."

"Yup," his lips twitched to the side as he waited for a response.

"Which would mean I'd miss the window to petition the council this term and would have to wait until next year's election. And that would mean more people will die and there may not be anyone left to save and I would have done all of this for nothing," Issa rambled, catching his breath with the last word.

Rafael hesitated and leaned over for another bag of soil. "Was coming here a waste of your time?"

Issa paused, truly considering the question. He slept at night without fear of a raid and his nightmares were less frequent. He never had to worry about whether he'd be able to find food to eat. And most important of all, Nevaeh was safe. He may not have saved his neighborhood, but her safety was what mattered most to him. "No," he answered honestly.

"Why?" Rafi pushed.

"Because," Issa worded his response carefully. "There was no way we would have survived in the North. And I couldn't let that happen to Nevaeh."

"So even if you don't save a single person from the North, you believe you made the right choice to come here?"

"Yes, but-"

"No-" Rafi interrupted, throwing down a bag and then pushing Issa back, a sack falling from Issa's grip as he stepped away. "No, buts. You coming here wasn't a mistake. Even if you don't save a soul from the North, you're here and you're safe. Now, would it be amazing to go back there and help bring more to safety? Abso-freakin-lutely. But that's the dream, it isn't necessarily a reality, Issa. And I need you to recognize that."

"Recognize what?" Issa growled, his stature growing as he held his stance and allowed Rafael to crowd him.

"That even if you do it all right- study, pass the exam, petition the council, whatever- you still may never save anyone."

"That's not an option," Issa demanded, anger seething in his words. He hadn't come all this way, abandoned his neighborhood, faced the border wall, studied until the mid-morning hours each day, only to fail now. Even if it meant he would go alone, he knew he had a mission remaining in the North.

"That's a pipe-dream, kid. You need to accept that you may never see the outside of these walls again. That my tattoos may be the only ones you ever see again, that the life you left outside these walls may already be gone-"

"No!" Issa screamed, pushing Rafi's chest with his palms until he toppled over and Issa leaned above him. "I refuse to give up, there's no other choice for me! I'm not meant to stay here, to sit idle, while my friends die!" He turned away from Rafi and clutched the cold metal cross around his neck. He was too late to save Bethany or his parents. But out there, beyond the walls, there is another First-In-Command leading a neighborhood to safety, another boy who shouldn't have to watch his sister die in slavery, another orphan that shouldn't lose his parents.

"That's the boy I remember," Rafi chimed, dust flying around him as he clapped his hands against his pants as Issa turned back to him. The two exchanged a silent glance. "Now I don't want to hear the doubts anymore, because no matter how long it takes, we both know you're going back up there, even if it means we go alone." Issa's eyebrows drew together and Rafi smiled as he ducked his head. "You think I'm letting you go have all the fun?"

Issa's watch chimed, alerting him to the time. He only had a few minutes before he needed to be at the school. "I'll finish up here, you go kick some ass." Rafi smiled, and he watched as Issa turned and fled toward the schoolyard, imagining the little boy he had once abandoned.

*   *   *   *   *

"You're joining the Revival?" Issa's tenor voice questioned, his eyes clouding with fear.

Rafael hated upsetting the boy, but he'd thought a lot about this question in the past weeks. He didn't want to tell Bethany, but secretly, he thought joining the Revival was the best option for his future. He was stronger than many of the current boys, and he had great instincts. He could make his mom proud. But it also meant he couldn't choose a stable life with Bethany. She'd always wanted to be a nurturer, and everyone could see she was made for the role. But she'd want to settle down, raise a family, watch Issa and Nevaeh grow up. And if he chose to join the Revival, he'd couldn't be worried about her. Worried about whether she could protect herself, whether she could get to safety before the soldiers started attacking, quieting the baby from within the thin walls of an abandoned home. And he couldn't risk leaving her alone to raise their kids without a dad. No, she needed someone that could be there with her, help her provide for the kids.

Bethany reached for her cross necklace and wouldn't make eye contact with him. He'd told her about his desire to join a few weeks ago. And while she was polite, he knew she wondered the same things as he did. If he chose to join, he'd have to break things off with her, they'd have to go their separate ways. And while he only ever wanted a future with her, he knew joining the Revival was more important, and he could always watch out for her.

Issa reached for her necklace as she pulled him into her lap and cuddled him like a babe. Rafi's heart swelled for the beautiful woman he had grown to care so deeply for. There was no doubt what her future would hold, it was only a question as to whether Rafi would be beside her.

"You know, Issa," her smooth voice broke the silence, "not everyone in the Revival gets hurt. There are even some jobs that don't even need weapons." Rafi's heart ached. He had just said the same words to her not even a week ago.

Issa's head popped up and he looked at Bethany quizzically, "Like what?"

She tugged at his chin, revealing yellowed teeth as his lip jutted out. "You sir, need a bath," she sighed, changing the subject.

Bang, bang, bang! The alarm sounded and Bethany pushed Issa off as all three jumped to their feet. Rafael's heart jumped, a knot forming in his stomach. He needed to run home, make sure his mom and grandparents were safely hidden. Nevaeh's loud roar rang out in chorus with the alarm and Issa followed Bethany to the crib as they quickly packed the infant's belongings. Grabbing the essential items, Rafi shoved them into the bag he knew belonged to the toddler and then followed Bethany as they headed downstairs to the hideout.

He handed the belongings through the hole to Issa, the alarm like a ticking time bomb reminding him of the urgency; he needed to leave. "I have to go," Rafi said after he handed off the last item. He pushed Bethany towards the hole with one hand and the wooden entertainment center with the other, but Bethany didn't move.

"No," she and Issa exclaimed together, the look on her face tortured.

"You can't leave, not now-" Bethany exclaimed, her eyes pleading for him to stay.

"I have time," he reassured. "I'll make it back," he held her arm, tightly squeezing her hand. His dad had died when he was a boy and he was all that was left to take care of his mom. Sure, his grandma and grandpa were around, but his grandma had heart problems and needed constant care, and his grandpa was an elder who could be called to fight alongside the Revival if the circumstances were dire. He couldn't risk leaving his mom alone to care for his grandma, and he knew it was his job to take care of them until he aged up and his grandfather could retire. "I have to try," he exclaimed as he pushed away, but she held his hand firm as she turned away.

"Issa" she whimpered, fear and sorrow evident in her trembling words, "you know what to do." She folded a blanket over him and reached aside for the blockade. "You put the mask over her nose and mouth," she instructed as she grabbed the medical mask and put it against Nevaeh's face, "it needs to be tight".

Rafael could hear footsteps closing in outside, most likely neighbors retreating home as they fled from the approaching Troops. Issa protested, but Bethany didn't falter as she moved toward Rafi. He turned towards the front door, reaching back for her and he felt her hesitate, but he knew their time was limited so he pushed on, assuming she'd follow if she truly wanted to join him.

The streets outside were growing dark as the sun had already disappeared beyond the far buildings. They ran in the direction of his house, quietly rounding the corners to avoid detection. The bare streets an ominous sign that they had waited too long to leave.

Two streets away from his current brownstone, Rafi pushed Bethany backward as he caught sight of Troops. Turning back, he calculated they would need to run back a block and take the far side around to evade detection. He pushed Bethany in the direction, but quickly reeled her back when green blobs emerged from the opposing streets.

"In here," he whispered as he broke open a window to an abandoned basement and pushed her down into it. He could hear footsteps quickly approaching, knew they'd been spotted, but he pushed downward, ignoring the jagged glass that pierced his arms and hands as he sunk down. He had barely cleared the window, when a hand reached from behind him and grabbed his hair, pulling him back. The hand clasped his face and tore at his eyes as he tried to claw free.

"Rafi!" Bethany exclaimed, but the number of hands grew to four and Rafi was being lifted out of the space before she could protest. Laughter rang out as his feet hit the *pavement and he tried to jolt free, but he was hoisted up high and lost his footing.*

'Just keep fighting', *he thought.* 'Keep them busy and she'll get away'. *He clawed at his captor's arms and the soldier slapped him across the face, but he barely felt the blood as the cut darkened across his cheek. A misplaced arm crossed him and he leaned forward, opening wide and clamping his mouth down with force as he tried to free himself. A scream pierced the stale air and Rafi felt pride at the pain he knew he was inflicting, but a new hand emerged and a punch to his eye caused his grip to loosen as his victim pulled away. A black cloth fell over his face and the world around him went black.*

*   *   *   *   *

The memory faded and he reminded himself to breath. He had replayed that day over and over in his head, praying he could rewrite history. The last time he saw Bethany, fear etched her timeless features, as she was pulled away from him on horseback, and it was his fault. The Third-In-Command took him home that night and his entire family had survived. He had pulled her out to the streets for nothing.

Though he hadn't been able to face the truth yet, he knew he needed to talk to Issa about that day, about how Bethany was taken. In many ways, that day is the reason they were both in the South. It was that raid which caused the neighborhood to plan a new strategy and split into two units. It was his unit that was then later seized by the Troops and murdered. But Rafi escaped. He hid in nearby brush, pretending to be dead, and waited until the Soldier's left. He spent days searching for his former neighborhood, but hungry, alone, and scared, he fled South.

And for Issa? Rafael couldn't be quite sure how Bethany's disappearance had impacted the boy. But what he did know was the man that showed up in the South was far from the goofy, carefree kid he'd last seen in the North. And he could only imagine that losing Bethany was a big part of the chain reaction that led him there, trying to protect the one sister he had left.

Issa jogged to the upper school, replaying the facts in his head. Twenty-one leaders, seven districts, three pillars each: political, religious, and militant. The schoolyard was relatively empty, it was a Saturday and the only ones in the yard were there to take their level tests. Issa spotted Kathreen by a tree, sitting on the three-foot log border as she waited to be called in, her head shoved in a book.

"What are you reading today?" He asked as he skid over to her, she jolted as he approached.

"Jeez," she exclaimed, "warn a girl, why don't you." She teased, adjusting her sitting position to accommodate him.

They'd met when Issa first began classes. He quickly learned that she was the one to keep an eye on, and they'd spent countless hours together since. He didn't want to admit it, but she captivated him. Her chocolate skin several shades darker than his own, was so soft that it glowed. And her eyes? He'd never seen any so remarkably golden and energetic. Her smile was dazzling, effortless and heart-stopping.

She tilted her book inward, allowing him a glance of the cover.

"Ul- Uli- seez?" Issa sounded out timidly, falling to the ground beside her.

"Close, Ulysses," she corrected.

"What's it about?" He pondered, peering around to see the description on the back.

"Read it and you'll find out," she smiled, closing the book and laying it on the ground beside her. Awkwardness settled between them and she could feel the tension pouring out of him. "You're ready, Issa," she chimed.

He blinked back his fear and doubt, nodding his head. "I know, but there's a lot riding on this."

She smiled weakly, having sat in several meetings with Rafael, Hunter, Annette, and Issa as they planned the aftermath of the exit exam. Hunter was a strategic leader, having previously served one term in the military office serving the fourth district. He'd coached Issa on how to confront the council. Hunter was ten years older than Kathreen, and until Issa's arrival, they had grown quite close and many expected her to marry him. But her heart was conflicted with the arrival of the foreign boy. Her parents encouraged her to keep her distance from him, especially knowing that Hunter spent time with Issa, but she found herself emersed in his stories, bonding with his sister, and she was caught eyeing him fondly when he'd leave their group settings. And with her exit exam today, she knew it wouldn't be long until Hunter was expected to propose to her. While she had previously daydreamed of a life with Hunter, marrying him, carrying his babies, watching them turn into miniature versions of themselves, her dreams as of recent brought a different image to mind.

She looked at Issa, thankful he couldn't read her thoughts. She knew the world he was destined for, a life beyond the wall, riddled with danger, and knew she couldn't follow. But her heart tugged at her, her mind plaguing with thoughts of *'what if'*.

The front door to the schoolyard opened and Ms. Gabriel held the door, allowing for the few that gathered to enter. She was glad when she heard Annette would be one of the proctors during the exam today, knowing the confidence it would lend Issa.

Issa stood, dusting off his pants, dead slivers of grass clinging to his pants. It was hot outside and Issa was the only one not wearing shorts or a t-shirt. Kathreen thought back to the first time she has ever seen a Northerner. She'd seen the guy only once or twice before he was shipped to a new district to settle down. His arms were covered in dark stretches of black, delicate lines emerging from hidden caresses of his body. As new arrivals trickled in, the rules for the Northerners adapted. Being among the highest priorities, Northerners were to hide their skin from the Southerners, wearing long pants and sleeves as a band-aid to cover the scars from their former lives. Even in the near one-hundred-degree heat of summer, Issa and the others were expected to abide by the rules.

Kathreen recalled the first day she caught Issa at the lake, wearing a long swim top and wind breaker jogging pants. She doubted he would join them in the water, but was surprised when he was the first one to hop onto the swinging vine and plunge into the cold water. For a split second, his face softened and she saw a boy emerge, one who didn't carry the weight of a revolution on his shoulder and who only wanted to live carefree in the outskirts of the South.

She eyed him a lot that day, and his gaze always seemed to follow her path, so when she disappeared beyond an old decrepit pier, she wasn't surprised that he followed her.

Their hearts beating in unison, the soft water grazing their chin, his rough hands timidly seeking permission to hold her. The wet shirt clung to his skin like a waxy resin and she could barely make out the few black lines that encroached his neckline. She pulled at the neck, seeing the dark stripes fade down his chest as a warmth spread up her body. She'd never felt this heated with Hunter, and although it was discouraged, she wanted to peel the layer of fabric away from him and follow the lines as they crossed his toned warm olive skin.

But he stopped her, grabbing her hand and slowly pushing it back as their feet touched the murky ground below the water. She imagined him leading her up the small island and to the hidden shack. So many of her young friends had lost their virtue on the island, and while she had yet to defy her religious upbringing, she felt a new desire burning in the pit of her stomach, and she clenched her legs together. If he'd wanted her, she would give in to him. His face edged closer, his breath soft against her skin, but he didn't kiss her.

"You ready?" Issa asked, holding his hand out to her as she shook off the memory and heat that coiled between her legs. She smiled, allowing him to assist her carrying her books.

Although they were from the same year, Kathreen and Issa were nestled on opposite sides of the room. It was common for men and women to be separated to some degree, but Issa was pushed off to the far side corner behind rows of nearly bare bookshelves. While she hated to acknowledge it, he was an outsider and many still did not trust the innocent façade of the Northern boy that survived the trip to the South. She hated to think he would spend his life an outcast, pushed to the far edges of every social gathering, his skin carrying hard evidence that he didn't belong.

The same thoughts plagued Issa's as he took his seat away from the others, looking mournfully over to Kathreen. His last day in the school bringing back memories of the first day he stepped foot inside. A year and a half before, he'd been a very different person. Almost shy, he'd cower in the corners of rooms, allowing Nevaeh to hide behind him when given the chance. At lunch, he found it nearly impossible to withstand the surveying glances. Ms. Annette had expressed the importance that he try to blend in, that he behave, but when he overheard a group of boys conjuring up stories, he mustered the courage to confront them.

He approached the circle of boys rapidly, so fast they barely had a chance to react to his presence. He pulled at the hem of his shirt and peeled it back, the group silencing as they took in the black lines and raised edges of brandings and scars that marred his body. After a healthy dose of time, and before any adult onlooker could see, he slipped his shirt back on, covering himself. "I'm not poisonous," he seethed, "if you touch me, it won't burn, you won't get a fever, or a rash. It's just dark paint; it isn't dangerous." He looked at the boys in the group, their skin all different, ranging from pale white with pimples, to freckled olive skin, and dark skin that would blend into the dark recesses of the night. How could they all be so different and yet treat Issa like he is the only unique one among them? "I'm just like you," he claimed, lowering his sleeves and adjusting his shirt. When no one protested, shock still outlining their features, he turned and stalked off.

"Wrong," one of the voices rang out, stopping Issa's descent. It was a boy his age with dark black skin like

Benji's, so dark the black tint of the ink was barely visible. He gestured to the group around him, looking at Issa with distaste, "you will never be one of us." Issa turned and faced them, waiting for an additional onslaught, but no one spoke. They just stood there, challenging him. He felt bad for them, their vision so limited as to only see the worth in someone's skin instead of a man's character. Of the group of six, two couldn't meet his gaze, and he wondered if by chance they sympathized for him. But Issa didn't want their sympathy, he wanted them to stand up for him, to challenge the premise that he was ugly or dangerous or unworthy simply because of his external appearance. But they remained silent.

Issa ran out of school that day, not caring of the punishment. He found out later that the boy's dad was running for a political pillar and that an 'anonymous source' had turned Issa in for his crude behavior.

When Issa returned to the school later that week, he had a new mission in mind. He found the library and dug up any records he could find regarding the few Northerners surviving in the South. Including Issa, Nevaeh, and Rafael, there were only thirty-four that had ever crossed the border, all within the last twenty-five years. Issa printed off articles surrounding each of the Northerners' appearances in the South and articles related to the two attempts the government had made to cross into the North to rescue others.

Issa felt down to his pocket where the pages sat folded. He'd studied them carefully over the past year and a half, the pages wearing thin from refolding them each time he read them. He had devised a plan back then, and it all led to this. He needed to pass the exam, he'd petition the council, he'd join the military, and he'd head back to save the North.

"You have five hours," Annette announced as she pointed to a clock on the wall with bright red numbers. "Once you begin, you are not permitted to leave until you have finished. If you're unfinished after the clock chimes, you will submit your work incomplete." She looked over to Issa in his corner, silently encouraging him with a nod. "Raise your hand if you need to use the bathroom or if you're finished, and a proctor will come to you." He looked at the monitor in front of him, his name in the bottom right corner and the words 'exit exam' catching his attention. This was more than a level exit exam for him, it was also his ticket out of the South. "If there are no questions, sign into your computer to begin."

Issa sighed as the clock on the wall started to dance, the numbers trickling slowly down; this was it.

CHAPTER 9

SEVENTEEN YEARS OLD

S top pacing," Rafael demanded as he called out over his shoulder to Issa. "And come sit down for dinner." Issa looked over to Kathreen who sat on the couch with Nevaeh. She'd look up at him between pages as she listened to Nay read aloud.

The exams ended five hours ago and, although Annette indicated the results would be visible online after 7PM, it had not kept Issa from constantly checking the board for his results. Kathreen smiled at him, her plump lips curved around her brilliant white teeth, obviously confident in her results as evidence of fear was missing from her gaze. She lowered her feet, kicking the recliner leg shut underneath the them as she folded the book onto the side table. "It's time to get food in you," she smiled.

"I thought your parents wanted you home for dinner tonight," Rafi questioned, looking at Kathreen as she grabbed a plate, "finishing your exit exam deserves to be celebrated," he reminded.

"It's only worth celebrating if I passed," she exclaimed, "and I'm heading home soon, officer," she goaded. She enjoyed teasing him, but he was right. Her family, like most Southerners, celebrates the night of the final exit exam, and her family would be waiting at home for her return. Her mother would have made her favorite cheesy casserole and Hunter was probably already there waiting to join in on the festivities. Rafi had cooked Issa's favorite dishes while they took the exam and Kathreen loaded his plate with the baked goods. Green beans, macaroni, and chopped steak smothered in brown gravy with mushrooms and onions. It was fun watching Issa and Nevaeh explore new dishes in the South, their taste buds slowly acclimating to the foreign spices and textures of a homecooked meal. "I guess I should get going," she sighed, pushing the plate toward Issa as he sat at the countertop.

"You'll let me know?" He asked, gazing up at her. He hated to see her go, but knew he needed to keep his distance from her. Although always courteous, her father had made it clear that they were to remain only friends, and Issa couldn't blame the guy. As soon as he received positive results, he would begin his plight to challenge the council. He wasn't destined to stay in the South, not yet anyways. And Kathreen deserved a chance at the life she'd planned before he came through the front gates. While every instinct in his body told him to go to her, to touch her, feel her, love her, he knew she deserved more than he could offer. And he respected Hunter too much to cut in on their lives.

Issa knew Hunter planned on proposing tonight. Issa had helped her family put it all in motion, encouraging Kathreen to come to his apartment after the exam while her family could decorate after they finished work. But as the time clicked by and it was time for him to watch her go, he wanted

131

to hold onto her, to pull her back, to claim what he wanted as his own.

"Of course," she smiled, "meet later?" she questioned so only he could hear. His heart crippled. He knew she wouldn't be free to meet him, but she was completely oblivious.

He nodded, not finding the words to respond. Her smile tore at his heart, but he knew he was doing the right thing. If he passed, which he hoped to find out in the next fifteen minutes or so, he'd be one foot out the front gates, onto a risky adventure that she couldn't join.

Rafi eyed Issa as the door closed behind Kathreen, but he didn't say anything. He knew what that felt like, being torn between love and the obligation to do what is right. He'd been spared the decision, but he didn't know which was worse... watching her age beautifully, start a family, and grow old with another man, or knowing that she died loving him.

"There's an update!" Nevaeh shouted, and both men rose from their seats as they rushed over to where she sat at the home monitor.

"The results are posted," Rafi exclaimed, reading the screen. Issa wished Kathreen had stayed, that he could hold her as he saw his results.

He leaned over his sister who sat at the monitor and typed in his credentials. "Click it," he instructed once the page loaded and the giant 'find your results here' icon spread across the center of the screen.

Nevaeh hesitated, but grabbed the mouse and clicked the blue tab.

97th percentile. He'd done it! He'd passed the exam with flying colors.

"Congrats, man," Rafael chimed, pulling Issa in for a side-hug. He was shocked, his body raw with anxiety and terror and optimism and confusion. He'd passed. He'd learned fifteen levels and passed his exit exam after only a year and a half.

"I did it," he exclaimed, his body numb with surprise. "I should call-" he hesitated; Kathreen. He should call Kathreen. But she wouldn't answer. He knew she'd be otherwise occupied. Rafi seemed to sense his hesitation.

"We'll call Hunter in the morning," he indicated, "get the ball rolling for the petition." The petition. Right. Hunter was helping them prepare for the petition which, now that he passed, Issa could now file and get the date for his appearance.

"Right, tomorrow," he said, dread plaguing his senses as he imaged all the news that tomorrow would bring. Kathreen would be engaged to Hunter, Hunter would be helping him file to petition the council, a petition that would lead him back to the North and far away from her.

"Congratulations, Issa," Nay exalted, climbing up on the wood stool and wrapping her arm around his neck. He pulled her away from the chair, her feet dangling freely in the open air, as he wrapped his arms around her torso and held her against him. He had done it. He brought her to the South, saved her from the cruel fate in the North, and now he'd come one step closer to saving more. This was a celebration, he needed to remember that. Battling with his own subconscious, he pushed away thoughts of Kathreen and allowed himself to enjoy the moment with his baby sister.

"You helped me," he reminded her, "I couldn't have done it without you," he said as he set her back down, "and you, Rafi, thank you!" He hugged Rafael again, pulling him in close. The last year and a half had not been easy for them. While Rafi was always there to guide and protect the two siblings, Issa had not always been accepting of his old friend's assistance.

In the dark recesses of his heart, part of Issa blamed Rafi for their situation. If he hadn't left them that day, hadn't taken Bethany with him, perhaps they wouldn't be here now. Issa had never wanted to join the Revival, not until after Bethany's disappearance anyhow. Had they not left, had he convinced Rafi and Bethany to join them inside, they would have been safe. He would have woken up the next morning with Bethany's soft fingers brushing through his hair, her gentle words goading him awake. Issa would never have joined the Revival, continuing in his father's footsteps as a healer. He never would have been in the mall when the gunshots rang out and killed his friends, never have the memories of Malik's limp body falling to the floor, or nightmares of Remi's corpse coming back to life and blaming Issa for not protecting him from Xavier's wrath, and Bethany would have helped their parents hide so they'd never have seen the fury of the Troops. He wouldn't have been First-In-Command, never have been forced to choose his sister or his neighborhood; he'd never have travelled to the South.

But as soon as his heart attacked Rafi, his brain reminded him that Rafi was only doing what he had been taught, what he had been trained, to do. And he couldn't be faulted for that. Had the Troops never landed, had the monarchy never descended, had the Great War never flourished to begin with, the circumstances all would have been eradicated. Issa couldn't go back in time and prevent any of these circumstances from happening, but with the anger in his heart fueling his passion, he could certainly stop them from continuing. He could be an agent of change, saving other young boys from facing the ugly realities he did at such a young age.

Issa spent the evening working on his proposal, the plan he had put together forming in his mind as the pieces of the puzzle came together. He watched the clock strike 2 AM and knew that if Kathreen had made it to the hideout, she would have gone home long before now. He hadn't gone there as he had promised, and he unplugged the phone in his kitchen to avoid any incoming calls. He didn't want to talk to her, didn't want to face the hidden meaning behind her questions. He'd fallen for her in such a short time, and against his better judgement, he had allowed the impossible connection to deepen.

Needing fresh air and confident the streets would be empty, Issa slid on his shoes and walked outside. The air was muggy and the only sound was the silent hum of crickets and mosquitoes. He walked to the far edge of the district and followed the edge of the lake. If he had been born there, had the luxury of living relatively carefree, he would have lived in that lake.

Looking around to ensure nobody was around, he slid off his shirt and pants and dove into the water. The sudden cold chill sent a shiver down his spine and he dipped his head back under the water. He liked to come out at nights, enjoyed the peaceful still water as he gazed up at the starry night sky, free of the manmade chains that weighed him down in public. He imagined Bethany among the stars watching over them, hoping she was proud of him; proud that the was helping bring an end to the torture that she endured.

If We Don't

*   *   *   *   *

"Settle down now," Malik reprimanded as the boys put their stick-swords into the fire and sat down. "Today's lesson is a tough one, and it is very personal to several of our members, so I expect you all to give it the respect it deserves," he declared, eyeing Issa as he spoke. Issa always behaved at the circle tables, so he wasn't sure what he'd done to warrant the look from his leader.

"You've all heard the stories," an elder choked out, coughing into his hand as he caught his breath, "probably wondered which ones were true or what to believe. But I'm here to tell you, the very worst of it all, the things you can't bear to hear or discuss, those are the things that the Troops thrive on." The hair on his neck stood on edge as a sharp tinge nicked at his heart. 'Please don't', he thought, but the elder continued. "We've taught you how to use your weapons, how to fight back, how to hide your families, but tonight's lesson is something different; what to do if you get caught, and what you'll face if you're taken."

'No, no, no!' *Issa shouted inwardly, but he leaned forward, his face pale.*

The elder looked at his comrades apprehensively before diving in. "Young babies are too much of a hassle, so the Troops kill them off pretty quick. In our time, we've come across some abandoned Soldier training camps," he cleared his throat in discomfort, "there were babies strapped down to piles of hay, targets painted across their naked bodies, where they were used for target practice." A silent hush fell over the crowd, the whispers and faint movements ceasing.

"Sometimes they use ammo, other times we've found babies with full arrows protruding from their bodies. They

136

don't even bother to bury the deceased." A different elder added, sucking in a deep breath and exhaling loudly, the wrinkles on his forehead tightening as he rubbed his hand against his temple. "We've taught you that, if you're cornered, you should kill your families, especially the younger ones. Unfortunately, the bullets in your rifle are far more merciful than what the Troops would force your families to endure." The elder looked around at the boys cautiously.

"Boys, if old enough to walk and talk on their own, but not too old that they present a threat, they're typically safe, often times thrown into a cell to be deconditioned and trained up in the camps as a soldier." This caught several of the boys' attention. "That's why we wait until you're thirteen to allow you to join the Revival. We don't want one of you being chosen to join their ranks for fear you'd panic and tell them our methods. So, we wait until you're undesirable to them and we brand you with the 'R' so that they'll know you're an enemy to the Troops." Unease settled amongst the boys. "That's why we tell you to save a round for yourself. Dying with a bullet to the head is easy it's quick. But the Troops won't go that easy on you. You're their greatest enemy, the greatest force against them. They won't kill you, not right away. But they'll torture you, and make you wish you were dead." Issa's heart was throbbing, his breathing uneven. He knew the stakes when he joined, he knew the rules, but it was hard to hear the truth behind them.

"The older you get, the more set in your ways you are," a new elder spoke, "and therefore the less use you are to the Troops. Anyone above the age of thirty is typically shot dead on site. And it's rare that they've been known to take anyone older than their twenties. At that point they know you can't

be retrained to join them, so they'll kill you before they ever get back to camp." Issa looked around at the faces in the neighborhood, most were too young to qualify for this except for Malik who was in his early twenties. He found Malik in the crowd and his eyebrows furled together when he caught his commander staring at him.

"It does occasionally happen for young women," the elder explained, and Issa's attention was drawn back as an image of Bethany crossed his mind; she was twelve when she was taken. "These are some of the worst cases we've seen." Issa's breath caught in his throat and his heart felt like it was outside of his chest. "They don't typically suffer long, a few days usually, more or less. The girls are most often raped and tortured, sometimes gang raped. If they're lucky, their suffering ends there, but some are hand-selected to serve the Troops and they're led around by a choke collar and forced to cook, clean, and wait on the soldiers' every need. We've even heard of some giving birth to little soldier babies before they're killed." Issa felt the tears as they scarred his face. He couldn't stomach the thought of Bethany being tortured, raped, living life as a slave. "Sometimes they allow their half-breed spawn to live, I've heard of it once or twice, but the female infants are hung out for slaughter as soon as the cord is severed."

Issa jumped up and ran. His feet and body numb in the cold air as he pushed his lungs to fight for breath. 'No, no, no!' He wept as he sprinted back to town. He'd come within a half-mile of the borderline when his feet caved and his body surged forward, scuffing his hands and feet as he landed.

"No!" He cried as his body curled into the fetal position. It was too much for his heart to stand.

Slow footfalls descended upon him, but he didn't care to look. His body was numb and he didn't care if he was at risk. Bethany was gone. She had only lived twelve short years and the remainder of her days were presumably spent in an agony Issa couldn't bear to dream of.

"You knew?" Issa asked when he peered up and saw Malik hovering above him.

Malik dug his feet in the ground, playing with the cold dirt at his feet. "I presumed," he announced. "I was there the day she was taken."

Issa's head jolted up as he eyed his friend and commander. "You were-" he began, but the words caught in his throat. "You know what happened that day?" He lifted his body upwards and sat on his knees, searching his commander for an answer. "What happened to her?"

"You're better off not knowing," he exclaimed as Issa yelled, "tell me!"

Proceeding cautiously, he caved. "She was found during a raid. We had just caught the Troops on their way out and we had them surrounded. I was newly appointed as Third-in-command, and our leader held negotiations that saved the lives of half of the fourteen that were taken, but they only released six from the cage." Malik eyed Issa, but the boy was quiet and still. "But she wasn't in the cage, she was being held on horseback with one of the lieutenants. We thought they were releasing her, but they didn't."

"And you didn't fight for her?" Issa sobbed helplessly.

"It was a negotiation. If we forced our hands, they would have killed us all. Their lieutenant offered us-" he hesitated.

"What? What the fuck could they offer, tell me!"

"They'd been on our tails for weeks, causing commotion and raiding the neighborhood almost every day. Our

numbers were falling and there was no way out of it," he explained as level-headed as he could manage.

"What did they give that was worth her life?!"

Malik swallowed back his temper, his voice flatlining. "They offered us a four-day head start."

Issa pushed to his feet and stalked off, his arms holding his head up as anger fumed and his body cowered over. "Four fucking days?!" He wept, and Malik couldn't blame him. Issa had been a boy, he'd lost his sister in the most unimaginable way, and tonight he learned the fate that most likely befell her before her death. Worse was that the Troops hadn't upheld the deal, having come back for them within the following twenty-four hours and killing the entire pack that had sectioned off to mislead the Troops.

"Issa-" Malik tried to console him, but he pushed away.

"Don't you dare fucking touch me!" He screamed as he moved away. "We are supposed to protect this neighborhood!" Issa declared. "Not make bargains with their lives!"

Malik knew that bargaining was one of the only ways the Revival had to withstand the Troops, but he didn't bother explaining that to Issa. He knew the boy wouldn't be receptive to the information, not tonight anyways. So he allowed his subordinate to run back to town and he didn't follow.

CHAPTER 10

SEVENTEEN YEARS OLD

I ssa's heart beat in tine to the sounding alarm. *Bum, buh dump, buh dump.* The door creaks open in front of him, but the room is eerily silent as he pushes inward. His mom isn't packing in the kitchen and his dad's medical bag is open on the table, but they're not around. An uneasiness rocks Issa as he gathers himself, pushing through another doorway and descending the stairs to the basement.

He rounds the corner too quick and loses his footing, sliding down into the open space. When he lifts his gaze upwards, he recognizes why his feet failed on the cement flooring. A clumpy pool of blood covered his feet and he reaches for his gun instinctively. Laying in a bed of thick congealed blood, his parent's bodies were limp. He rushed to his mom, her body splayed flat across the mattress, and placed his fingertips at her neck; no pulse. Her body was cold and stiff, and he was clearly too late. He felt a surge of disappointment, the events of the past twenty-four hours crushing him as he knelt beside his mom. She's relied on him to protect her, to protect the neighborhood, and he'd let them all down.

If We Don't

Picking himself up off the floor, he travelled to his father whom was perched on the rocking chair in the corner. A black hole marred the back of his bald head and a splatter of his blood and brains painted the wall behind him. His hands were downcast and the gun sat idle on the floor below him, clearly discarded by the Troops. But as Issa stood up, he turned back towards his father's lifeless body. The hole wasn't at his temple like it should have been, he wasn't shot execution style. Issa pulled out his gun from his belt strap and lifted it to his father's lips, the line of fire matched perfectly.

'Since when did the Troops shoot through the mouth?' *Issa pondered. He turned and looked back at his mom. She lay flat on her stomach, her hands down and hind legs arched up as if she had been balancing on all fours before she fell forward. Issa returned to her side and lifted her upright, finding the entry wound on her chest.*

Had his dad come downstairs to find her dead and, out of sorrow, shot himself? Stowing away his pistol, he knelt down to the gun on the floor; three bullets missing.

Issa looked around the room carefully and found the stray bullet hole marking the ceiling. 'Evidence of what? A struggle? His mother fought back?' *He wondered. His skin tingled as his mind ventured to dangerous territory.* 'Fought back against whom?' *Issa heard a crackling and he turned around, his father's body now standing with a grim smile on the blood marked face, his eyes black and head tilted.* 'He couldn't be alive, could he?' *He stepped back as his father surged forward, reaching for the gun. He fell to the ground, a pool of sticky blood clinging to him as he tried to run. But the blood pulled him in like quick sand as he fought to escape. From ahead, he spotted Nevaeh in the hideout and he cried out to her for help, but his words were inaudible. She watched him, huddled in a ball and crying as he reached a hand out to her. The distance between them grew and the harder he tried to get to her, the further he would find himself. He turned back around and his father had his gun.*

The pool of blood finally faded as Issa reached for the gun to disarm him, and the two men struggled against one another, a single shot ringing out and plaster surrounded them as the bullet lodged into the ceiling.

Issa cried, but to no avail, and his father pushed him onto the mattress where his mother's body had disappeared. His dad sank back, falling against the far wall and into the rocking chair.

'No', Issa thought. He perched his body up on all fours and crawled forward, but his dad cocked the gun and pointed it at him. 'No, dad!' He yelled as the bang resounded in the compact room.

*   *   *   *   *

"No!" he yelled, "No, dad!" the sounds of his voice faded to the recesses of his mind as a new sound emerged, "Issa, wake up!"

Issa jumped to life, his lungs on fire as he filled them with air. He was wet and his hair clung to his skin like a fish net that he was trapped in. Nevaeh was in his room and she stepped backwards as his room came into focus. He wasn't in the North, wasn't in the house, hadn't been shot. But it all felt so real.

"Are you okay?" his baby sister asked as he breathing slowed.

He couldn't find the words to respond, so he nodded. He was alive, he was in the South, he was safe, but then why was his heart so heavy? He pulled back the images of the nightmare that was slowly receding in his head. Did he remember it correctly? The gun so close to his father's down stretched hand? His mother's body placement and the stray bullet hole?

For years now he consoled himself that his parents had fought back against the Troops, that they had died with honor, but was that true? And if so, why hadn't the Troops found Nay? She was barely concealed when he arrived, wouldn't they have taken her?

He looked up at his sister, her eyes still glued on him. Had he misread it all along? When he found her, she was shaking and she didn't speak for days. Was she traumatized by more than the idea of the Troops?

Issa and Nevaeh both jumped at the thundering sound of a knock on their front door. They exchanged glances, but neither moved until the knock sounded again. He pulled himself out of bed and followed Nevaeh out of the room until she perched herself at the counter. A bowl of cereal was waiting for her, and he guessed that she was having breakfast when she heard his screaming.

He moved to the front door and peered out, seeing Hunter. He slid the lock and opened the door, allowing the bright sun to filter into the dark apartment.

"What are you doing?" Hunter questioned, pushing past Issa into the room. "Man, why aren't you dressed, yet? Did you get my texts? They moved you up to this morning!"

"Shit," he exclaimed as he sprinted toward his room. His clothes were cleanly set out as he'd prepared every last detail for today's event.

"Come on man, we have to go!" Hunter chimed as Issa pushed into the suit.

After Issa passed the exit exam, he'd immediately prepared his petition letter to the council and, to Hunter's surprise, they were allowing Issa to speak at the next live debate. The military pillar would be having their final meeting today, so this was Issa's only chance to get consent to continue if he wanted to push forward during this session. He'd had only one week to prepare his arguments and he could feel his chance slipping away with tick of the clock.

"Let's go!" he shouted as he burst through his doorframe. He kissed Nevaeh's head as he jolted past and she shouted a hearty "good luck" as Hunter closed the door behind them.

Issa bounded down the stairwell, his dark memory following him as he cautiously took the final step to the ground.

"Do you have your cue cards?" Hunter asked, and Issa felt through his pockets, but came up empty. He halted, beginning to turn back.

"No, no time! I'll go back, you head to the courthouse!" Issa continued his jaunt forward as Hunter turned back to the apartment.

Rafael and Annette met Issa at the doors to the courthouse. "Where have you been?" Annette exclaimed as Rafael yelled, "Let's go, you have to get inside!" They pushed him in the doors and they followed him to the doors leading to the main courtroom.

"Do us proud," Annette exclaimed as she fixed his tie and Rafi pat his back encouragingly

"Hunter has my cue cards," Issa exclaimed, flustered. Annette's hands stopped and they all halted, the doors to the room pulling open for him to enter. "I need my cards!" he turned back, ignoring the guards at the doors.

"There's no time, man, you're late," Rafi exclaimed, "You know the material, you're just going to have to wing it." Issa looked at his friend, hoping to see a hint that he was joking, but his eyebrows were tight and his mouth flat. "You'll do fine," he nodded encouragingly, pushing Issa forward and beyond the doorway.

The doors clambered shut behind him and the swirl of fog in his head cleared as the magnificent room came into focus. There were three levels with master craftmanship decorations delicately lining each archway. He stepped forward cautiously as the rows of red stretched onward ahead of him toward the front pulpit where twelve men and women sat idly followed by a row of only three men.

"What is your name, sir?" One of the three top men asked. Issa was familiar with this, he'd studied it. The three men on top were the current reigning political, religious, and military leaders for his district; district 7. Below stood the individuals who wished to run for the current exiting pillar, in this case, the military pillar. The individuals would be able to hear and discuss his plight and they would form their stance and vote accordingly. Then viewers would be able to watch the event and decide their votes for the top seven who would eventually replace the current seven standing military leaders across the seven districts.

"Issa Cruz," Issa responded, looking around the room at the cameramen and news crews.

"Mr. Cruz, the floor is yours. Please address the court."

Issa watched the prompter carefully and hesitated as he took a step forward to the microphone. "I- ughh- am here to per-suade" he stuttered, a camera flash catching his attention. The leaders before him looked bored and the clock at the far corner was ticking down with his time, his tardiness counting against him with a resounding nine minutes and forty seconds left. "I am here to discuss a strategic opportunity for the South that would align the Southern Republic with the suffering Revivals in the North." He expressed, the words pouring from him like soft butter as he recalled the words he'd pieced together in his sessions with Hunter, Rafael, Kathreen, and Annette.

Eight minutes and fifty-seven seconds. "And what exactly would this allegiance look like?" The current military pillar for district seven asked into his microphone.

"That is a wonderful question," Issa announced, buying himself time to formulate a response. "I suggest that we create a campaign that would allow Southerners to sweep into the North much like the Troops have done, but instead of causing havoc, these individuals would spread the word of the safe haven here in the South." Eight minutes.

"And how would this differentiate from past attempts to enter the North?" the political leader asked. Issa watched as several of the electees nodded and others jotted down notes.

"I'm sorry, what?" Issa stammered, the long pause signaling Issa that he's missed a question. Seven minutes, thirty-nine seconds. He felt the urgency building in the room, a gentle sway distracting him as a blur formed around each of the chairs before him.

The political leader huffed and straightened in his chair. "And how would this be different from other attempts we have made to rescue Northerners?" The mechanical whirring of a swinging camera distracted him as he watched the black machine sway around the room.

Issa hesitated, scolding himself as he pushed down the nervous tick to reach for Bethany's necklace. "Well for starters, this would be different because we would send Southerners up to the North to-"

"We've done that before," the military pillar interrupted. "What would we do different this time?"

Issa cleared his throat, "we would send teams- I mean bands- ughh, just one band up as a test run," he paused, an awkward silence growing. "This would help Southerners get acclimated with the grounds and we could test in short runs until the band is more confident and can split into smaller teams."

Five minutes, forty seconds.

"How many would we send in this band?" The religious leader, the sole woman in the upper court, asked. Her glasses pushed down as she peered at Issa, her eyes narrowing at him as if he was a small ant she wanted to study under a microscope.

"Ughh, well, the size would be dependent on volunteers who-"

"So now we're accepting volunteers?" The military leader interjected. "What training will they have? We can't be sending untrained individuals out to the North. I think I can speak confidently when I say that none of my fellow military leaders would feel comfortable with this," he leaned forward, crossing his fingers as his hands created a pillar.

"Well yes, they'll have to go through several conditioning lessons and pass a certification exam."

"And what happens if these volunteers run into the Troops first? How do you expect them to fight?" The military leader posed, ready to attack. Four minutes thirty-three seconds.

"Each member would have combat and marksman training and we would prepare them by encouraging them to eat only common foods available in the North and by-"

"And what happens if they're captured?" the religious pillar enquired at the same time as the political pillar asked, "Have you thought about the repercussions that the South could face if the Troops found out we'd intervened in the war?"

"Absolutely. First, we would send the bands out without any of the advancements found in the South so as to ensure they blend in with other neighborhoods. Then, the plan would be-"

"So they would be without technology? How could families stay in touch? How would the government stay updated of any progress?" The political pillar cried out. Three minutes, twenty second.

"Unfortunately, we couldn't risk bringing technology with us. It would be a clear indication of the South's involvement and keeping this alliance a secret is of the upmost importance to ensure long-term viability and-"

"Mr. Cruz," the proctor exclaimed over the loud speaker, "we have passed the three-minute mark and we typically like to open the floor at this time for our electees to ask questions for their voters." She looked at Issa as if it was a question. Or was it a question? Two minutes, twenty-eight seconds.

"Okay?" Issa responded hesitantly, and the proctor turned to the nominees. A red light flashed over the candidate third from the left.

"Hello Mr. Cruz, I'm Hector Guzman running as a second-term military official with a background is special ops forces. My constituents have presented heightened concerns over this topic of the relations with our Northern residents. How do you plan to address their concerns regarding the potential loss of Southern ideals if we continue to flood the streets with refugees from the North?"

Flood the streets? Southern ideals? Was this guy a joke? "Well, Mr. Guzman, I don't think your constituents are really aware of the critical status of the North. In my neighborhood alone, we were nearly decimated by the Troops. My fear is that the longer we wait to travel North, the less hope we have of bringing anyone back through the gates and-"

One minute, thirty-one seconds.

"Thank you, Mr. Cruz," the proctor interjected as a new red light appeared behind the candidate directly center, "Mr. Cruz, my name is Ambra Collins, running for a first-term pillar. My followers are concerned with overpopulation and crowding in the districts. Past electees have combatted this with the argument of creating an eighth district solely for the Northern rebels; what are your thoughts on this?"

An eighth district? Overcrowding? "Ms. Ambra, I have seen dormant buildings and underpopulated classrooms, so I think the misconception of overcrowding is simply a stall tactic used to discourage the allegiance with the North and keep the South protected in this bubble, and I'm outraged at the insinuation that saving the lives of helpless human beings has been turned into such a political agenda for the elite!"

"Mr. Cruz, forty-five seconds remain. Do you have any final remarks for the viewers?"

The room swarmed around Issa and his blood boiled. He never had a chance; this was all just a political stunt for the districts.

He shook his head in dismay, "no, I have nothing further to say here." Turning hastily, Issa felt all eyes on him as he left the room. He'd worked so hard, but he'd failed. He never had the upper hand, he let them walk all over him.

Bounding through the doors, Rafi and Annette peered at the television, recalling Issa's final statement.

"Issa, wait!" Rafi called as Issa set off at a sprint. Pushing through the doors, he nearly mauled Kathreen. He hadn't seen her in two weeks, since the final exam, and his heart deflated, needing the comfort of her arms. But as he moved to hug her, the glimmer of silver caught his attention and he looked down. He knew she'd said yes, knew he no longer had any unspoken claim to her heart, but the evidence crushed him.

"Issa," she exhaled, reaching out to him, but he was already on the move again. He ran home, but stopped short of his doorstep. Nevaeh would be home, she would have seen the report, and he wasn't ready to face her. Turning around, he descended the stairway and stopped in his tracks, debating where to go. The lake would most likely be occupied and Issa wanted to be alone. Behind him, he opened the latch for the garage door and pulled it open, sliding in and closing the door behind him. Rafael's truck sat idle and he hopped into the bed, sitting on the edge as he recalled the meeting.

He was steamrolled. He hadn't even had a chance to present his ideas or methods for disguising the bands. He failed.

Issa sunk into the truck bed and felt the hard grooves of the flooring massage his back as he laid down. He couldn't face them. He couldn't admit defeat, not to Rafi, not to Annette or Nevaeh, certainly not to Kathreen, and not to himself. Even if it meant he had to climb over the wall alone and hunt down every last Revival member he could find, he'd do it. He couldn't let today's setback keep any more Northerners from knowing the safety and security of a warm bed, a hot meal, and the comradery of having real neighbors that weren't always on the move.

The sun outside crested and filtered in through glass panes above and Issa watched as the clouds moved and the shadows changed. The sky here was the same as the sky in the North. The birds here, while more abundant, were still birds. The ground under his feat still warmed as the sun lit the sky and cooled when the stars came out at night. But a thirty-foot brick wall guarded with sharp shooters and metal wiring kept the Southerners safe at night while Northerner's sleep in fear of a timid alarm bell that carried the weight of destruction and annihilation.

Issa jumped when the garage door creaked and slid open, sunlight pouring in as Rafael stepped inside. He didn't look surprised to see Issa, so Issa didn't feel the need to defend his hideout.

Resting his head on the gate, Rafi peered at Issa, but remained silent.

When the silence drug on too long, Issa shrugged, "What?" His friend pulled the gate down and hopped onto the edge, still silent. Issa sat up, his legs outstretched as he pushed back and leaned against the cab. "Aren't you going to say anything?" he asked.

Rafi reached into his pocket for a mint and popped it into his mouth. "I figured I'd just wait 'til you're ready to talk."

"I failed, what more is there to talk about?" Issa responded, the dramatic tone causing Rafi to laugh. "What the hell, man?" Issa chided, frowning.

"You know," Rafi sighed, "I remember this boy I knew once when I was up North. His sister and I were pretty close, some would even say possibly in love… And one day we were walking along a bridge, a pretty decrepit thing that should have capsized long before…" Issa remembered the bridge, the wooden frame creaking under it as he stepped onto the ledge.

"It spanned a good fifteen or twenty feet and really wasn't safe for anyone to walk on, but that little shit kid decided to play on the damn thing like it was a toy." Issa smiled, recalling how he'd bounced on the center to test his weight and Bethany nearly keeled over as she urged him to get down.

"The stream below was gentle and only a few feet drop, and although the girl was yelling for the boy to return, and I could see how fearful she was, I too jumped out on the bridge, testing its limits." Issa recalled her red face as shouted for them to stop being foolish. "And when the boy and I crossed the bridge, mocking her for her obvious lack of bravery, this bullheaded girl stomped forward onto the bridge, and what happened?"

Issa laughed, "the damn thing came tumbling down".

"Yeah it did. And God was I scared. That brief instant when I couldn't hear her yelling at us, I thought she'd been really hurt.," Rafi recalled somberly.

"But she wasn't," Issa recalled.

"Nope. She was muddy and wet, but she wasn't hurt. And good Lord was she angry," Rafi smiled.

Issa grabbed the necklace from his chest and held it up to the light, the gold metal shining in his hand. "I miss her," he admitted, and Rafi nodded.

"Not a day goes by that I don't think about her; what she would look like, what her adult voice would sound like, or what she'd think of all this," he gestured outwards.

"So, what's your point?" Issa asked, "with the whole bridge story thing?" He shuffled and scooted to the edge of the truck bed, nestled beside Rafi.

"I don't have one, just thought it was a fun memory," he lied, but sensing Issa's growing frustration, he continued, "my point is, that bridge was falling apart. I knew it, you knew it, and Bethany, she certainly knew it." He chuckled, "but it withstood your weight. You were maybe fifty pounds back then. And then I joined, a whopping hundred or so, and it still didn't cave. And then we got off and your sister, she couldn't have been more than eighty pounds, she comes barreling on there, and the whole thing comes crumbling down." Issa shook his head, still not connecting. "Sometimes it's not the pressure we put on it, but the timing of the pressure and the force with which it is delivered."

Issa hesitated. The story was cheesy, but that wasn't unusual when it came to Rafi. He tried to take Rafi's context and imagine what Bethany would say to him if she were there. He figured she'd scold him for being late, but then she'd tell him to dust himself off and try again.

"I need to go back," he admitted, "but I don't know what to say or where to start. They steamrolled me in there."

"So? Steamroll them right back," he nudged Issa, "this bridge isn't the same, man. It's strong and built of concrete. You have to pack more weight if you want to bring this one down."

"I don't know what to say," he announced, hopping down from the tailgate.

"That's a cop-out. You know what to say, you just have to say it so they understand. And just remember, whatever you do, I'm on your side man, no matter what." Issa thought about it carefully and looked out over the skyline. The sun was just beginning its descent, probably around 4 in the afternoon. "They're scheduled to finish around 5."

"And if we get in trouble? They could throw us out."

"Let them try, we'll bring one hell of a storm back with us when return. Either way, you and I are heading back North," Rafi exclaimed, jumping off the gate and slapping Issa on the shoulder.

"You have your keys?" Issa asked, and Rafi smiled.

The two men hopped into the truck and the engine roared to life. Rafi sped to the courthouse and Issa jumped out before the truck had fully stopped, running past Hunter as he ascended the courthouse steps and bounded through the front doors. Hunter turned and followed hot on Issa's heels.

"Issa, you can't go in there now, this isn't how it's done!" But Issa didn't listen, throwing back the last door and storming down the center aisle.

In front, the council sat just as Issa had left them, and errant reporters quickly chimed to life as their machines purred back to life.

"Excuse me, sir, but you can't just-" the Military pillar exclaimed, a finger outstretched towards Issa.

"No, you listen now, sir," Issa demanded, the microphone buzzing with his steep tone. "This time, I get to speak. Now, I have a plan if you'd all just stop talking and hear me out for a moment."

The silence surrounding him was deafening, and he took that as his sign to continue. He grabbed the gold chain, unlocking it from behind his neck. "This necklace belonged to my older sister, Bethany. She was the wise one of the group, and she adored this necklace," he began. His mind wandered to the vulnerable place that he hated, the place of blame and fear and sorrow as he touched the delicate gold.

She was safe when she wore this necklace, she knew God was protecting her, and the very day it was yanked from her neck, was the day her bad luck caught up with her.

To his right, he caught sight of Rafael and Hunter trudging into the empty auditorium. When no one interrupted, he trudged on. "When I was seven, the sirens went off in our neighborhood, indicating that the Troops were within sight," he recalled the moment vividly. "When it was time to hide, my sister chose to leave, hoping to help a friend, get home safely. And just as she turned to leave," tears pricked behind his eyes as he pushed back the need to cry, "I reached out to her, to try to keep her with me. I wanted her to hide with me, to stay safe. But she didn't," He cleared his throat, no longer able to hide his emotion as the tears graced his cheeks. "I used to blame myself. I sat up for countless hours thinking, if only she'd had this damn necklace. It was supposed to protect her, and I'd ripped it off her when she left me."

The proctor pushed some napkins in front of him as the political leader spoke up, "sir, this is very touching, and I can sense how much you loved your sister. But I don't see what this has to do with your petition."

As much as he may have wanted to blame Rafi or Malik or the Troops, a small secret part of Issa knew that he played just as large a part in Bethany's demise as they had. She'd known the power behind her necklace, knew it kept the darkness at bay, and he'd taken it from her when she needed it most, his hand grasping it and ripping it from her chest as she turned to follow Rafi. He may as well have ripped the heart from her very body, it would have all ended the same.

Issa wiped at his eyes, arched his back, and braced for impact. "I tried to keep Bethany safe, but couldn't. I tried to urge her to hide with me, but she refused. She refused because we're not supposed to hide. We're supposed to fight back, to step out of our comfort zones, and help others. And I'm here today, not to ask for you to help me, because you've already done that. You've given me a clean home, a safe place to sleep, a job, and food. And I am so very thankful."

He raised his arm, the golden chain tickling his wrist as it swayed, "but now it's time we take a lesson from Bethany, to stop thinking of our own safety, and start helping others. It's time for us to bring them here, to show them safety. So that no other child has to lose a sister," he turned to where Rafael now sat in the empty audience, "or a friend, or his parents."

The men shared a brief painful glance, and Issa turned back to the mic, his voice raising, "and we can't do that by hiding behind walls." His words rang out, the only sound a faint buzzing in the background.

"You have the floor, Mr. Cruz," the lead military pillar announced, "tell us, how do you envision this taking place?"

Success. His heart pounded with exaltation as he took a deep breath, organizing his thoughts.

"Well for starters," he began, "We are going to market to all the districts, asking for volunteers. If they pass basic training, they'll be permitted to join in the scout to the North. But the training won't be simple. It will consist of food deprivation so volunteers grow acclimated to the taste of what they'll find in the North."

"We'll structure the band just like the neighborhoods, with medics, hunters, gatherers, nurturers, and even Revival members; scouts, muscles, grunts, the whole nine yards. We will not utilize technology as doing so would raise suspicion in the North, and the goal is to blend in. Unlike the neighborhoods, all volunteers will be trained in basic combat skills so as to increase the likelihood of success."

"To begin, the band will go out for a month at a time, returning only for rest, medical attention, and to restock before heading back out. In the meantime, we'll have separate parties remaining here in training to switch out with the returning band, so we can keep a consistent presence in the North. If, after a few attempts, it is determined that a month is not sufficient, we will re-evaluate then."

Issa paused; the room warily silent around him as the political pillar spoke up. "And what will you do if we say no?"

Issa studied the man, his wiry glasses and round belly. Issa decided in that moment that he didn't care what the council decided. They would have to lock him up if they wanted him to stay in the South. If he had to do it alone, he would, and he'd bring back as many as he could.

"This isn't up for debate," he declared before he registered his words. "Whether you decide to throw us out because you're too complacent, or if you agree to these terms, either way, I'm heading North. I'd like your blessing because I know the support this court carries and the heightened capabilities a tribe would carry, but I'm ready to make the move alone should that be my only option." His voice grew, his pulse racing, as his passion pushed him onward.

"Yes, the Great War was terrible, it was awful and the inhumane losses were unforgivable. But those losses ended over a century ago for the South, and the North is still living it. And the people dying there? They don't know you! They don't understand the cause of the war or why the battles began; they don't have time to learn that stuff because they're too busy fighting for their lives. If you can't see that these innocent people need help and that you're in the position to do something about it, then you don't deserve to sit in those chairs," he yelled, his voice now a loud boom over the intercom.

"And if you can't see the opportunity you have to make a difference, then we'll find you a better pair of glasses. Because if not now, if not today, then when? If we don't, then who will?"

CHAPTER 11

SEVENTEEN YEARS OLD

Fear crept up his spine as he tried to ignore the doubt seeping into his mind. He'd done everything he could. He petitioned the council in the seventh district, gained the support of several of the newly promoted political pillar candidates, and the vote to send a tribe to the North had gone in his favor. But sticking to his agreement, he had nothing to bargain with, no monetary compensation or reward could be negotiated with the volunteers, and he needed at least fifty before they could travel beyond the gates.

Issa looked away from the door, kicking his feet on the slick gymnasium floor. He'd done everything to the best of his ability, he'd even asked Rafi and Nevaeh to pray with him, seeking a good turnout for sign-ups. He'd worked overtime in order to afford the meager spread of chips and deli sandwiches, used most of Rafi's savings printing the flyers and filming the thirty-second advertisement that circulated the television every evening before the district-wide updates. He'd gone to all of the campaigns and spoken to anyone willing to hear from him, and it would all boil down to this. He was given one year. Ten months to recruit, train, and prepare for the mission, sixty days exploration in the North, and then return to the South to sum up their experiences for the council. If it was a favorable end result, the council would consider making the venture a permanent mission. Although Issa hated waiting, knowing that thousands of lives could be lost in the span of those ten months, having already lost thirty days to marketing, he was growing apprehensive as to whether ten months would be enough time to execute their plan.

He looked at the door again, pleading the double-doors to open, but no one came. He glanced at his watch; eight o'clock on the dot. Had he posted the wrong time? Had the address been wrong? His neck began to sweat as he feared the worst. But Rafael wasn't here, nor Annette, and both had promised him their unwavering dedication to the mission. Pensive, Issa jumped down from the stage and bounded for the doors, his heart thumping with anticipation as he neared the entry and could hear faint voices on the other end. Taking a deep breath, he pulled the door open.

A crowd formed around him, some in a single-line formations and others standing idle in the lot. Rafi was the first at the doorway, Nevaeh beside him.

"We were beginning to wonder when you'd show up," Rafi teased, cupping Issa's shoulder with gentle reassurance. "Let's get this thing started, huh?" He pushed forward and Issa stepped back, allowing the crowd to enter.

He attempted to count, one, two, then eight, ten, twenty, but the number kept growing. Issa had posted the sign-up forms near the far side of the room and several had navigated there and grabbed a form, following Nevaeh's directions. Elated, he wanted to run to her and pull her into a hug, but he held back. Surely there were enough in attendance to reach the minimum fifty, even if they lost some through the training process.

Issa recognized some of the faces from throughout district seven, but most were foreign to him and he wondered how far they had travelled to join the cause. Among the strangers, he counted three others in full-length shirts and pants, and curiosity peaked at him, wondering if they were some of the fellow Northerners that had resettled in the South.

"Why don't you make your way to the front," Annette suggested as she came up behind Issa. "Welcome everyone and suggest they take some refreshments before getting seated."

He agreed, shaking his head and pushing forward to the stage. "Hi- ughh, hello-" he muttered as the shrill squawk of the microphone buzzed in the wide room. "I want to welcome you all here tonight and thank you for coming. We will get started here in roughly," he looked at this watch, "thirteen minutes. Please feel free to take some refreshments and snacks and please grab a sign-up packet from the table to follow along with today's presentation. I'll be back up here in just a few minutes to kick things off." He smiled awkwardly in an attempt to hide his uncertainty. Stepping to the side, he watched closely as the groups clustered around the snacks and then settled slowly into the open chairs in the middle of the room. His clock ticked by slowly as he watched each minute drift away, forcing himself to move forward when the time was up.

"Ughhh," he tapped the microphone again and looked at Rafi who was silently encouraging him, and dug his speech from his pocket. "If you're just coming in," he exclaimed as he opened his wadded notebook paper, "please be sure to grab a microphone and eat a sign-up form," he blushed, his words catching up in his brain as he faked a cough. "Excuse me. I meant, please take a sign-up form and feel free to grab a snack. I'm gonna go ahead and get this started this evening. For those who don't already know, my name is Issa Cruz. This gathering was put together by myself and several others who I would like to recognize. First, Rafael Sanchez," he pointed to Rafi who raised his arm in a casual wave, "Ms. Annette Gabriel," he paused again, directing attention to Annette, "Hunter Fox and Kathreen Bennett," Issa searched the crowd until he landed on Hunter and Kathreen sitting in the second row, "and many others whom were unable to attend today, including the current and newly elected members of council." He swallowed back a knot in his throat and continued, "I see several faces in the crowd today that share a history similar to mine and I'd like to open the floor to give any of these individuals a moment to share…" Issa waited, a long pause growing ominous in the room. "Please, feel free to tell us about yourselves, how you came to the South, your experience acclimating to the rules here, or your life in the North," he paused again, and panic set in when he realized no one was going to speak. He hadn't quite thought this through, hadn't anticipated the silence-

"I'm sure most of you heard Issa's speech during the council meeting the other night," Rafael interrupted as Issa searched the crowd for his friend who rose from his seat. "But I think now it's time for me to share my version of that night," he declared, shifting awkwardly. "I was actually a part of the same neighborhood as Issa and Nevaeh," he cleared his throat and Rafi silently thanked his friend for helping. "Our community was rather small, and getting smaller all the time. We had a band of Troops that stayed on our trail and made a game out of raiding our neighborhood. On the eve of my thirteenth birthday, when I would have to decide my path for my future, whether I wanted to be a hunter, gatherer, nurturer, or so on… We were raided again," He hesitated, looking up at Issa, pain shared in the look they exchanged. "I made- a choice. A choice that cost me the life of my best friend." Although feet away, Issa could see Rafi's lip tremble. "Except, calling her just a friend would be a disgrace to her memory. She was much more than that, she was, and probably always will be, the love of my life." He couldn't look at Issa and turned away, rogue tears staining his cheeks. "Bethany," the name fell softly from his lips. "She had this fire in her, this passion and energy that didn't belong in the North." Rafael wiped at his eyes, smudging the puddles of tears that clung to his eyes. "When she was taken, it was like I'd lost my fight, like I'd forgotten how to live without her, and it all happened so fast. One moment we're playing games and then running to safety and I was caught, and they doubled back for her and-" he hesitated, remorse befalling him as he cried out, "the fear in her eyes haunted me for years," he whispered, "I never thought I'd see those eyes again," He turned and looked back at Issa, "but I did, when I hugged her little brother three years ago." A silence ebbed between them as curious glances bounced between the two men. "I failed- I failed Bethany, I failed you, Issa, and I failed our neighborhood. And on behalf of the North, I'm done accepting failure. So, I'm here." He glanced back around the crowd, "And I hope you all are here to help us bring some power back to those we continue to fail in the North."

Issa nodded, moved by Rafael's words. He lifted the mic to speak, but another voice interrupted in the room. "You didn't fail," Nevaeh's soft words echoed. "You were of more use here, paving the way for others like us," she gestured towards Issa, "and I am certain that Bethany would be thankful for everything you've done to support us." She smiled weakly and let out an awkward chuckle as she continued, "hi- ughh, I'm Nevaeh, or Nay as some of you have come to know me. A lot of you know the story of how I got here. A ten-year-old girl riding on her brother's shoulders as he carried me to the South," she glanced up at Issa, confessing, "I owe everything to Issa, for taking the leap of faith that led us here, and I will be forever grateful, but-" she sighed, kicking her heels together, "there's a part of our story we haven't spoken about much." She cleared her throat, looking down at her feet. "You see, I didn't know Bethany really, I was too young to remember her once she'd been taken. But what I do know, is the hole that was left in our home once she was gone." She stopped, playing with the frayed end of her shirt, "Death is pretty common in the North, so losing someone isn't a big surprise when it happens. The real impact comes not in the actual loss, but in learning how to readjust your life without the person. My parents were suddenly busier; they didn't have Bethany around to help bring in the food or to watch us when they had to work extra. Then, Issa was asked to join the Revival, an honor at his age, but it was another loss that my parents had to figure out. Who was gonna take care of me, make sure I was fed, or that food was on the table when Dad would be called away to the Medic station?"

Issa listened intently, images of his parents running around flashing in his mind as he pictured their lives through Nevaeh's eyes.

"And with the added stress, came more disagreements, more fights, and although they both loved Issa and I, they had less tolerance for the day-to-day disruptions." She paused, silent cries emerging over the microphone sending goosebumps down Issa's arms. "Before we left, our neighborhood had suffered an unimaginable loss. And our dad was busier than ever as he tried to salvage the remnants of our neighborhood."

Issa remembered it clearly, the mall, the near-death experience, losing his friends and mentor, the sudden panic as the alarms blared and they had to pack up their lives again to run...

"I think their signals were crossed, because both mom and dad had showed up to make sure I was covered in my hiding hole, and they cracked; the anger, and frustration, and exhaustion finally overflowing."

Issa closed his eyes, willing his mind to conjure up the images from the basement. His dad was in the rocking chair and the gun was on the floor, three rounds discharged. His mom's hind legs perched on the mattress, her arms falling out from under her and a round hole exiting from her shoulder blades.

"Mom tried to calm him down, make him see clearly, but dad had snapped," she wasn't speaking to the crowd anymore, but directly to Issa, her voice heavy with remorse. "She died protecting me. The gun was aimed at me, and mom flew over the bed and grabbed it."

The room was dead silent, Issa standing on the stage in shock. The bullet in her chest, the stray bullet in the ceiling; the puzzle pieces coming together in his mind. The old Revival stories of killing your siblings, the girls first, then saving a bullet for yourself. His dad was trying to kill Nay, so she wouldn't end up like Bethany.

"And when he realized what he had done, that she was gone," Nevaeh continued, churning the knife in Issa's chest, "he turned the gun on himself. Our parents died as victims of the North, not the Troops."

The hole was at the back of his head, the gun most likely aimed through his lips before it fell to the ground. He remembered finding Nevaeh, shaking and scared, the hole slightly ajar allowing her to watch the entire scene unfold.

"There are countless stories like ours," Rafael's voice boomed though the vast room, drawing the attention away from Issa who stood motionless, his face pale and his breathing uneven. "So, we want to thank you all for showing up here today. We wouldn't dream of forcing anyone to join our tribe, but we are beyond thankful for those of you who are willing to risk your lives to save more of ours. Is there anyone else who'd like to speak before we continue?"

Hunter's voice boomed in the crowded room, recalling his time spent with Issa, Rafael, and other Northerners that he'd come across. He was a good salesman and took several minutes encouraging the volunteers to join the tribe. But Issa couldn't hear a single word.

Falling back behind a closed door, Issa fell to his knees. He couldn't move, couldn't breathe. He could feel eyes on him as the door propped open and footsteps fell in. Nevaeh approached him cautiously, her doe-eyes seeping past Issa's barricade.

"I'm sorry," she said tentatively, "I know I should have told you before." But his mind couldn't digest her words. He had known the added stress they were all under when Bethany was taken. He'd tried to help however he could, making sure to care for Nevaeh so his parents hadn't needed to. But when she was able to take care of herself; walk, talk, and eat, he'd thought it had all worked itself out. He hadn't meant to abandon his family, caused further tension.

"Did I cause this?" He asked, recalling how he'd skip school and stay out odd hours practicing drills.

"Everyone is here today because of you, Issa. We have a potential to help so many more by being here. We can't blame ourselves for the suffering we were forced to endure there."

"She's right," Issa turned to find Kathreen behind him and he felt the tension melt away. She looked amazing, long faded black pants and a dark teal tank top with matching gold and emerald earrings. He'd kept his distance from her since the engagement and could feel his body aching to pull her in, to hold her, but he didn't move.

Nevaeh left, giving Issa and Kathreen space as he attempted to reacclimate himself. He had a plan for this evening and nothing was panning out as he'd imagined. "You shouldn't be here," he shot out as he stood, moving further away from her as she reached out to him.

"I'm here for support," she argued as he continued, "you're distracting me."

They stood in silence for a moment until Kathreen reached down and grabbed the notepad with Issa's speech. "Hey!" he exclaimed, "stop, I need that."

She held it behind her, out of his grasp. "No, what you need is to relax. You're a great guy and this is a great cause, but you'll mess it up if you go back to reading off this script. You're better when you're off the cuff." His brows furled in confusion and she explained, "it means that you do better when you're put on the spot, when you don't have time to plan."

He rubbed his eyes, allowing the wall to support his weight as he leaning backward. "There's too much riding on this, on me."

"Issa," she exhaled, walking toward him and placing her body between his legs, running her hands through his long hair. "These people are here because they believe in this, they believe in you. Stop trying to convince them and start training them; tell them what they need to know to get out there and get started."

He pushed his head back and closed his eyes, allowing himself to feel her dainty hands curl through his hair, her scent wafting upwards and soothing him. He reached down to grab her free hand, but stopped when he felt the hard, cold band on her finger, and he leaned up, pushing her away. He had broken the moment and he considered apologizing, contemplated repairing the hole growing between them, but decided against it. "I should get back out there," he stated coldly.

He walked back out to the gym and onto the stage where he tapped on the microphone; a new energy pulsing through his veins.

"Alright, I want to thank you all again for joining us here today. And thank those of you who shared with us tonight. Now that we've taken a trip to the past, I want to take you all forward and share our plans with you. I've come to understand the history of out nations and the Great War, but while the war ended in the South approximately one-hundred and fifteen years ago, the war in the North has continued for over a century. The brief peace among our nations lasted a mere two years before the Troops took over in the North.

Those that started the war are long gone and those remaining don't have time to think of politics or religion or war, they're lives are fully engaged in trying to survive. That's where we come in. Our goal here is not to change the values of the South, but for all of us to learn the mistakes that were made before the Great War, and to share in the journey as we rebuild a nation stronger than the one that we outgrew."

Issa looked out among the crowd to ensure they were following along. All eyes were trained on him.

"The council has given us a trial period. We have one year before we have to address the courts again to determine whether this can be an ongoing, sustainable mission. Which means," he pushed away from the podium and walked forward, dropping down to sit on the edge of the stage as he ruffled through the pages of the sign-up packet, "if you will please turn to page two with me-"

He discussed the pages with enthusiasm, having memorized even the tiniest of details to the plan. They'd form a neighborhood just like the one he'd left. There would be hunters, gatherers, everything. They'd work with master craftsmen to create wagons to transport their belongings, just like in the North, and they'd be stripped of anything material that would rouse suspicions. Should they choose to volunteer, they'd be placed on an immediate diet consisting of foods found only in the North. This would not only help them lose the weight they'd need to resemble a true Northerner, but it would help them acclimate their taste before crossing the gates.

All attendees stayed throughout the duration of the meeting which lasted well past the anticipated conclusion, but Issa predicted several wouldn't return.

*   *   *   *   *

A week later, Issa walked to Rafael's truck where Nevaeh sat on the outstretched tailgate, her favorite hangout spot. She had recently acquired a radio gadget she referred to as an 'iPod' that blasted music from the spaghetti strings she attached to her ears. Issa hadn't seen the allure of the noise-makers, but Nevaeh hadn't been able to set the thing down after Annette gifted it to her.

"Whatcha listening to?" He pushed into her casually as he sat down beside her.

She pulled one of the bobs out of her ear and pushed it toward him. Eyeing it cautiously, he conceded and slid it into his ear. The ruckus was loud and she adjusted the volume to a more reasonable pitch. While he didn't understand all of the words, he enjoyed the beat and softly tapped his foot to the beat.

"What is it?" he asked Nevaeh as the song concluded.

"It's called 'Almost Heaven,'" she announced, running her fingers over the box as the continued to listen. When the song ended, Issa asked Nevaeh to replay the melody from the beginning, the words seizing him.

"What do you think it means?" Nevaeh asked, replaying the words in her head and watching Issa as he stared off in the distance.

'*What did it mean?*' Issa wondered. The beginning words brought him back to the North, back to the day of his first scout when he matched the gold necklace to the shape of the cross on the stained-glass window. And the ending? The words were like a knife to his heart.

"I think-" Neveah began to distract from Issa's silence, "it's a challenge."

171

"How so?" He pondered, replaying the words in his mind.

"Like, we have the Bible, but many people interpret it differently. And while we are all assuming we are staying true to God's words, that we're kind to our neighbors, good to our families, and hoping we're doing enough to earn our spot in Heaven…" she rambled, "but there's no guarantee."

Issa looked at her puzzled; not drawing the connection. She continued.

"Until we're truly in front of God, facing his judgement, there's no way for us to know whether what we're doing here is acceptable to him. And we also won't know the truth in our loved ones' hearts, not until they face judgement and stand beside us in Heaven, or not. So I think it's saying, when our time comes and we're judged for our actions here on Earth, will we receive the same judgement as our loved ones and be able to make a home together in Heaven?"

'She's thirteen! How could this young kid come up with such a deep connection? She's a child!' Issa wondered. If he'd asked the same question of any other Southerner at her age, would they be able to come up with a similar answer? Or was it because they were from the North and had been faced with mortality on a daily basis?

The sky above was just dark enough for the stars to appear as the sun kissed goodnight. Issa checked his watch, a solid forty-five minutes until he would need to be at the gym for the meeting, but as he saw Kathreen appear from around the corner, he considered getting a jump start on his walk.

Kathreen waved at the pair as Nevaeh jumped down from the tailgate, Issa eyeing her curiously. "I think it's time I head in," she lied, "lots to do."

"No, stay-" Issa protested as she galloped off and Kathreen took her place. They sat oddly silent and Issa checked his watch, certain that ten minutes had passed, but only two had ticked off his watch.

"What were you and Nay talking about?" She asked casually, severing the growing tension.

"Just some song she played on that box Annette gave her. I keep- I often forget how young she really is. She acts so much more mature and it scares me. I worry about how she's been affected and how she'll hold up when I leave," he explained, heaving his emotional baggage. If he could trust anyone to keep his secrets and provide insight, Kathreen was one of the few he trusted wholeheartedly.

"Yeah, she is a lot wiser than many in her age group, more perceptive. But if anything, I think it makes her stronger. And you know she'll have Annette and I keeping a watchful eye on her while you're away."

'Perceptive, huh?' Yeah, he could see that word being used to describe Nevaeh. "I don't know what to do with her sometimes," he announced. "I want to protect her, but she's so darn smart," he laughed timidly, "I think she might actually be the one watching over me." Kathreen nodded in understanding. "What will happen to her if we don't come back?" He asked bluntly.

"Issa-" she scolded, but he argued back.

"No, seriously, I've lost sleep over it. I'm terrified. She's lost so much already. I know I'm not the world's best brother, I won't win any awards for how well I care for her, but I'm the only constant thing she's had in her life. We moved from home to home, she lost all of her family and friends, couldn't even keep the toys she cultivated. She's all alone."

"She's not alone," Kathreen protested. "We'll each take care of her and support her however she needs." She studied him, reaching her arm over to him and pulling his head to face her. "You're her big brother, her protector. If anything happens to you, she will always have the memory of you carrying her through the toughest terrain and battles imaginable, and she will be stronger knowing everything you did for her." When Issa didn't respond, she continued. "This is the same girl who has overcome two very different worlds; she's faced the brutality of the North and combined it with the security and knowledge she's cultivated here in the South. Besides you, she's the strongest person I've met; the world had every opportunity to churn her up and tear her apart, instead she's come out stronger."

That thought intrigued Issa, his mind wandering back to the Revival and the prophesy of the Chosen One, of him. *A boy, raised among two identities, who would face an unspeakable loss and, with a stomach full of fire, would tear down the foundation that betrayed him, and lead the forsaken to destiny, freeing them from the pains of their century.* He was living the prophesy.

His heart hurt with the understanding, wishing he could tell Malik or his mom or dad, tell them that they had all been right.

"So, anything fun planned for tonight's swearing-in ceremony?" She nudged him, forcing his wandering mind back to the present.

"Well, first, it's not a swearing-in."

"Oh right," she smiled, "just a blood oath, then."

"Ha- ha," he choked, looking down at his watch. He only had thirty minutes left. "I actually should get going," he sighed, hopping down from the truck with Kathreen following closely behind.

"Issa," she called out, grabbing his hand before he could walk away. "Just promise me you'll keep yourself safe out there," she waivered, "you're not the only one losing sleep over this mission."

He turned back, grabbing both her hands gently in his and leaning close. He wanted to kiss her forehead, to breathe her in and never let her go.

"I'll do my best," he swore, "to keep Hunter out of trouble."

He closed his eyes, dropping her hands from his and turning away. He knew the words stung, they tasted vile as he said them. But he knew they both needed a firm dash of reality.

PART 3

CHAPTER 12

EIGHTEEN YEARS OLD

The darkness overwhelmed Issa as he sat idle. Hours had passed and he hadn't so much as dozed off, his mind conjuring up images that he wasn't ready to handle. It would only be another hour or so before the clock struck midnight and he would need to get up, leading fifty-two men and women beyond the safety of their Southern gates to the unknown of the North. *'What if the North had changed, what if they were caught, what if they couldn't find anyone to save...'* Thoughts of doubt and fear plagued his mind as he pushed up and navigated to the kitchen for a glass of water. They had trained. Nine months of energy, food rations, wrestling matches, bumps, bruises, and near starvation, all wasted if they quit now.

With a full glass of water in hand, he walked to the window and watched out. Tomorrow, he probably wouldn't have a window to look through, but if he did, it wouldn't be safe to stand idly in front of it.

Outside, he could see the movement of bare feet in Rafi's truck and could make out the waves of Nevaeh's hair. He hadn't heard her leave, but it didn't surprise him to find her awake on the eve of such an important day. Within the hour, he'd be grabbing the remains of his items and meeting the others at the Northernmost checkpoint. They'd prepared years for this moment and it seemed surreal to finally be headed back to the North. He'd asked for it. Heck, he'd begged for this. But leaving the security he'd come to enjoy was harder than he'd first thought. Plus leaving Nevaeh, he dreaded the thought. He knew she was safer in the South, helping prepare for newcomers that could arrive without a moment's notice, but being so far from her, without contact, for the first time since they had arrived, unnerved him.

He set his glass down and pushed towards the door, slumping down the steps as he rounded the corner to where he'd seen his sister perched.

"What do you see up there?" Issa asked as Nevaeh jumped, startled by her brother's sudden appearance. He hopped into the bed of the truck and his arms brushed hers as they laid together, staring up at the stars.

"Hmmmm-" she moaned lustfully. "I see... potential."

Issa's brows furrowed and he turned onto his side, eyeing his sister. "You're telling me, you look up at that sky and you see potential?"

"Yeah," she smirked, gazing off at the galaxy. "It's miraculous. God created the mountains that soar into infinity," her hands gestured to the sky above her head, "and the caverns that rip holes through the land we walk on," her hands lowered to her side, "and he created the stars as a map to remind us..."

"Of what?" Issa questioned when she was silent.

"To remind us of where we've been, and where we're headed."

Issa pushed back down onto his back, following her gaze. "That's all bullshit, you know."

Nevaeh snickered. "No, you're wrong. God didn't create that masterpiece for us to simply gawk at. He made flowers beautiful, but they also provide nutrition. Waterfalls, not just to watch or bathe in, but to provide clean water to sustain us. Everything he has given us has had more purpose than just to be an attractive painting or landscape, I believe he fully intends for us to join up there in the sky one day and make something of the universe."

Issa watched her amazed. How had the little girl he saved turned into this adult who could say things like 'nutrition' and 'attractive landscape'. She had always been so fragile and small, it was hard to see the same girl now strong and vibrant, a thirteen-year-old with her own opinions and thoughts on life. "Then why would he make it impossible to breathe?" Issa challenged.

Nevaeh hesitated, pondering his question, and smiled. "Some flowers are poisonous, but their poison, when made properly, can provide a cure to illnesses. God's handiwork didn't come with instructions, he challenged us to figure it out."

She was satisfied with her answer, a large grin settling into her timid features. But Issa wasn't as optimistic as his sister.

"And what did he want us to conclude from the Great War?" He asked with a tssk. "Or what about Bethany's death? What did he want to come from that?" He questioned as he reached around his neck for the gold cross.

"What makes you really think Bethany's gone?" Nevaeh asked, turning to her side as Issa had done. Issa met her with a sigh.

179

"It's better than the alternative."

"I disagree," she stuttered, seeing Issa tense as he turned toward her.

"Oh really? You think it's better that she be alive and tortured by the Troops?"

"No," Nevaeh shook her head instantly, eyes meeting Issa's, "I just don't think she's really gone. I think she exists in the world around us." She raised her side arm. "Ms. Gabriel said that, 'when someone dies at a young age, they were really an Angel who had a greater purpose here on Earth; that they're here to teach us something and then to watch over us when they leave their physical form'."

"And what lesson did Bethany teach us?"

Nevaeh smiled, "well for one, she taught you about being an older sibling. You might even argue she taught you to love. And I think we'd both agree that we wouldn't be here today without her."

Issa blinked back his frustration. While he thought of Nevaeh as naïve, he couldn't argue with her. He was terrified of the Revival as a boy, constantly had nightmares. He never thought to join them until he lost Bethany. And now, planning a resurgence to avenge the North? He couldn't refute the logic. Maybe she was right, that is was all 'meant to be' somehow.

"What do you think you'll find out there?" Nevaeh asked, interrupting the prolonged silence.

Issa hefted out a sigh, his entire body deflating. "I'm not sure. I-" his voice croaked, "I hope that maybe there are some trails I can pick up on, maybe find a small neighborhood to start. We don't need a large crowd yet. Just few enough to bring back and show the South that there are still good people worth fighting for, and large enough that we can convince some more volunteers to join the tribe and go back out again. And the better maps we can get started to retrace our steps and plan for the future, the better off we'll be next time."

"You think they'll let you go again?"

"That's the point, isn't it? A scouting expedition now with hopes of doing more runs, rescuing more Northerners, and spreading word about the alliance…"

Nevaeh leaned over and pressed her free hand against Issa's cheek, softly rubbing with her thumb. "I'm proud of you. Bethany would be, too."

He smiled and his watch rang out like fifty-two matching alarms across the South. They had been urged to go to bed early in hopes of getting rest before their first walk, but Issa had failed like he presumed many others had. He was certain he wasn't the only one with anxiety and fear building in his chest, and he had a lot less to lose than some of them had; families, kids, jobs…

He hopped out of the truck bed and watch Nevaeh follow. "So, are we doing this now?" He asked, hoping she'd agree. He didn't want the added pressure of seeing her as he turned to leave, his new tribe following his lead.

"If you'd prefer," she hesitated as he held out his hand for her to jump down and he placed his hands over her shoulders.

"You listen to Annette, I want a good report when I get back. Our plan is only sixty days to start, but it could be longer or shorter depending on what we find out there."

Nevaeh pushed his hands off as she lifted her arms up and mimicked his stance by placing her hands over his tall shoulders. "I know the plan. You just watch your six and be safe, you're no good to anyone if you're hurt."

Above them, they could hear Rafael's door closing as he came thundering down the steps. Issa eyed him, this being the first time he'd seen Rafi's bare skin since his family was sequestered into the opposite neighborhood so many years ago. His skin was lighter than Issa had remembered, a juxtaposition to his dark hands, face, and feet which continued to face the elements on a continuous basis. Since Rafi joined the tribe, he'd been allowed to grow his facial hair and mane out to add to his camouflaged appearance. Issa still had to do a double-take occasionally when he'd hear the husky tone coming from his childhood friend.

Turning back to Nevaeh, he surprised her by leaning over and pulling her upwards, into his arms, as he swirled her around in a weightless hug. His face tinged as tears surged forward, but he refused to let Nevaeh see them. Slowly dropping her to her feet, he kissed her forehead and turned away with Rafi in tow.

CHAPTER 13

EIGHTEEN YEARS OLD

Xavier limped forward, his crutch barely supporting him as pushed through the crowd. "Move," he seethed, his bloodshot eyes like a snake.

Issa hesitated, but slumped aside as the serpent stood at the pulpit.

"You jealoussssss, Chosen One?" He slithered, "Is this a game to you, boyssss," he taunted, his forked tongue whipping insults. "Your stupid bitch sister couldn't follow the rulessss, and she paid for it with her life," he continued, pushing the pulpit over as he loomed over Issa, his green body slithering into the abyss.

"Fucking Bastard!" Issa yelled as he fought against the snake, the serpent tightening his hold on his body.

"I bet the Chosen One can't even kill," Xavier's voice teased, but it didn't come from the serpent's mouth anymore and Issa looked over to where Xavier now stood, hovering over his sister's lifeless body.

"No!" Issa called out, fighting harder to free himself.

"Ne-vay-ugh" he called out in a sing-song voice. "Not so brave now, huh?"

If We Don't

The snakes hold grew tighter, cutting off circulation in his arms and legs. He only had a few moments left. "Wake up!" he yelled with the little oxygen he could muster, "please, Nay, wake up!"

"I could blow you away right now," Xavier exclaimed, leaning in toward Nevaeh and whispering in her ear. "Could you do it, Issa?"

"Please," he begged, his face red.

Xavier cocked the gun and pointed it towards Nevaeh who was starting to come around.

"Nay, wake up!" He yelled fervently. She stirred and turned to look at him, her head turning as she saw him, but it wasn't Nevaeh's eyes that peered back at him.

"Issa, help me!" Bethany's voice called out as two soldiers appeared and grabbed her by the arms, pulling her away.

"Bethany!" Issa screamed. The serpent was gone and Issa leapt forward, charging toward Bethany, but stopped when Xavier turned the gun on him. "Please," he pled.

"If a Troop member had your sister in his arms now, knowing the fate that beholds her if he gets his hands on her, that young, sweet pussy-"

"Stop!" Issa screamed, wrapping his arms around Xavier's neck and pushing him against the wall. He knew he could do it, could snap Xavier's neck, or simply wait until the boy was deprived of oxygen.

"Issa," Nevaeh's sweet voice sang out from behind him. "What are you doing?"

"Look away," he demanded, his grip on Xavier tightening as he faced his sister.

"You're hurting him," she cried, pointing toward Xavier who was becoming limp in Issa's arms. Issa turned back around to see the light fade from his commander's eyes, but when he turned back, he saw his father's body fall lifelessly to the ground, red fingerprints marking his neck.

"No-" Issa bellowed, stepping back as Nevaeh rushed toward their father.

"Issa, help!" Bethany's voice rang out in the distance and Issa hesitated. The room was empty with the exception of Nevaeh, surely she would be safe there Turning towards the door, Issa bolted down the hallway, following the sound of Bethany's cries.

"I'm coming!" He yelled as he ran through the tunnel. The hall was dark and filled with doorways, each locked as he tested them. "Keep yelling, Bethany!" He called, hoping her voice could guide his path. But all at once, both Bethany and Nevaeh's screams filled the space, and he turned back to see the doorway closed where he'd left Nevaeh. "No!" he roared, pacing back as the room extended, the doorway sliding further and further away from him.

"Issa!" Nevaeh's tiny voice rang out.

"Nay! Where are you! Come to the door!" He instructed as he ran.

"Help me!" Bethany's voice thundered as he turned toward the closest door to test the knob. Taking another step, Issa fell to the ground, his feet seized as he tried to inch toward another door. Looking down at his feet, the serpent clung to him, coiling its body around his feet and nailing him to the ground. He tried to kick, but his feet were bound tightly together as both Nevaeh and Bethany's voices screamed out.

"Help us, Issa!"

*   *   *   *   *

"Issa- Issa!" He shuddered, hands pushing at his shoulders as he blinked awake. "It's just a nightmare," Nevaeh's soothing voice clarified, "you're having a bad dream".

His chest heaved as he caught his breath. "Did anyone hear?" he asked as he leaned over and grabbed a bottle of water from his sister, forgetting momentarily that he was mad at her.

Her lack of response was all the answer he needed. Placing the cap back on the water, he threw it down, dirt exploding around the bottle as it landed on the tent floor. He felt gritty; sweat and dirt clinging to his back, feet, neck, and hands. Attempting to brush some off, he recalled how much he always hated the filth in the North.

Issa looked over at Nevaeh, wearing only a thin white t-shirt that was purposely aged with holes and mud to look more convincing. Her hair was tied back in a thick braid, loose ends fraying from the edges adding to the authenticity of her appearance.

"What shift are you on?" He growled, making eye contact with her for the first time in almost a month.

"I'm off now… was just about to hit the sack." He looked down at the raw scratches on her feet and knees.

He hadn't planned for her to join and was livid when he heard she'd been found hiding out in one of the storage wagons three days after they had left the South. The plan had been for her to stay behind with Annette, help prepare rooms and gather essentials for any newcomers they might send back from the North. He'd said his goodbyes to her, waived at her as he ran to the checkpoint. But he hadn't imagined she had devised an alternative plan, a plan that included leaving behind a note for Annette and hiding out in a covered wagon until they had traveled too far to justify turning back. He about killed her when Rafi brought her to Issa's tent and he fully intended on forcing her to return. But there weren't any souls he trusted to keep her safe for a three-day hike backwards in Troop territory, and he couldn't be seen abandoning his tribe. So instead, he was plagued with worry and fear with each passing moment, knowing he was risking not only his life and his tribe's, but also Nevaeh's.

But since she was here, lucky number fifty-four in his tribe, he figured he needed to put her to work. So far, they hadn't come across the need for any nurturers, so he assigned her duty as a gatherer; responsible for searching the land for fruits and vegetables, or any remnants of food that was left behind from former tenants.

When they first set out, they were pleased to find stock piles of canned goods in the border towns. Issa figured Northerners were too afraid of stepping on Southern territory, the land surrounding the wall was practically thriving with edibles. But having been on the road for twenty-nine days, they had far passed the land of luxury and were now running low on essentials. Nearing the half-way point and having not come across a single neighborhood or wanderer, Issa was about convinced to call it quits and return to the South with his tail between his legs.

"We're packing to leave at nightfall," he declared, "you should get some rest while you can."

She hesitated, hoping he'd say more, but his agitated scowl told her it was wiser to move along and not tempt him. Nevaeh knew he'd be angry with her, she even anticipated him making her return to the safety of the South, but she was a force to be reckoned with. She hadn't spent nights hiding in the rafters of the gymnasium, watching the drills from overhead, to be pushed away at the first sign of trouble. She was only surprised that he hadn't caught on sooner, she was his sister after all. He'd done practically the same thing with the Revival.

"Issa," she sighed, dragging her feet as she neared the edge of the tent.

"What?" he hissed as he rummaged through his tent, avoiding eye contact. They had been on rocky terms and she couldn't quite figure out how to repair the damage she had done.

"Nothing," she sighed, heading toward the tent she shared with three other women. She had just stepped outside when she glanced at two men and Rafael pacing toward her, presumably to speak to Issa. Turning the corner of the tent, she hid outside and waited, slowing her breathing as she listened intently.

"What is it?" Issa's voice was easy to understand, his anger toward Nevaeh causing a heightened volume.

"We've found some tracks," Rafi announced, and Nevaeh's stomach flipped. This is it! This is what they had come here for! She did a dance outside the tent, jumping up and down and screaming inside her head.

Doubt was beginning to plague her mind as they continued further North without sight of another soul, and this is exactly what they needed. They could follow the tracks and find a neighborhood, convince them to head South, and all of this would be worth it!

When she calmed down and nestled beside the tent, her heart sunk when she heard the negative remarks that pursued. "I want all guards on alert now, send a signal," Issa demanded. The skin on her arms rose as fear spiked up her back. She remembered the god-awful sounds of the alarms, knew what they meant.

She stumbled as she ran toward her tent, wondering how they could be certain they'd found Troops instead of a neighborhood? She had just crossed into the tight quarters, surprising her roommates, when the alarms sounded. The three women hesitated, frozen in their spots.

"It's okay," Nevaeh coached, she wasn't new to the sighting of Troops, just out of practice. "Just take it slow," she exhaled as the girls all watched her. She found her sleeping bag and began to fold and roll it, wrapping the cord over it to secure the bond she'd created. The other women mimicked Nevaeh's actions as they disassembled their tent and joined the tribe in their formation at the predesignated checkpoint. Issa was at the lead.

"The scouts have confirmed that we've stumbled upon a bank of Troops. We've followed them West and found a much larger camp about three miles from us. We don't believe they have spotted us, but it is far too dangerous to settle this close to a camp, so we're going to head due East a few miles."

A hand shot out of the crowd and Issa nodded for Hunter to speak.

"If we've found a camp, wouldn't they probably have Northern slaves? Should we attempt a rescue mission?"

Issa's head hung low and Nevaeh's heart seized. "Unfortunately, no. You're right, they do probably have several Northerners locked up. Camps stay idle for quite a while, they let the smaller bands travel in and out to raid and bring supplies back. But that also means they're well-stocked. They prepare for an ambush and they have gear that outweighs what we have. If we had travelled longer, had more experience, we could maybe entertain the idea, but we..."

"We came here to make a difference," Hunter interrupted. "We've travelled almost an entire month and are on the verge of turning back and haven't done a single thing that we set out to do."

"That's not true," Issa exclaimed, "we've plotted the land. We've gained real exposure and experience which is something most of you haven't had before now. Even if we go back empty hand-"

"We *are* going back empty handed, and we don't *have* to!" A voice Nevaeh couldn't recognize yelled from the crowd. She could feel the tribe unravelling. In a real neighborhood, this sort of insubordination wouldn't be allowed, but these people grew up with different rules than she had, they didn't have to listen to their commander the way she was trained.

"There are fifty of us; there's probably hundreds of them..." Issa countered.

"We don't know unless we go and look!" Someone else, a woman, exclaimed as Issa's eyes met Nevaeh's. She swallowed back the lump in her throat, curious as to whether her presence here was clouding Issa's judgement. She didn't want to leave the North empty handed, but a one-on-one battle with the Troops didn't sound promising either.

"I say we send another scout team, just to size up the competition," a man announced, and several heads nodded in the crowd.

"It isn't about competition," Issa argued, "this is about survival."

"If we wanted to survive, we would have stayed in our cozy beds in the South," Hunter glared, challenging Issa.

Nevaeh felt like she could see the visible wheels turning in her brother's head. He was responsible for this tribe; their success and their failure. If they returned with nothing, he'd face blame from the current tribe, and possibly their families and friends, ruining potential recruits for a future mission. If they returned with tales of provoking the Troops, the council would eat him alive and potentially shut the whole thing down. It was a lose-lose situation.

"Okay," he hesitated, bowing his head. "I'm not promising a rescue mission, but I will agree to send a scout team to further investigate." A perfect mediation. A scout team would appease the tribe, feeling like they didn't abandon the enslaved campers, but it could also be seen as tactical to ensure the security of their tribe if brought up to the council.

Looking among the crowd, Issa singled out six people; two scouts, three muscles, and Rafael as the leading commander. Nevaeh pushed forward, attempting to hear the instructions. From what she could make out, Issa was going to lead the tribe due East two miles, a solid five miles from the camp. One scout and one muscle would stay at their current checkpoint while the remaining four would head the three miles West to find the camp and assess the situation. If any trouble should arise, they should notify the remaining two who could locate the tribe and warn them of any potential dangers.

In agreement, they all watched as four of their tribe set off in the direction of the setting sun.

"We're going to head East for two miles," he announced to the remaining forty-nine tribe members. "Two members are remaining here," now forty-seven, "to keep watch and provide warning to us should any trouble arise."

Issa looked out among them, his eyes landing on Nevaeh again, knowing he should have pushed her back to the South when he had the chance. He was too on-edge with her there. "I'm also going to send two scouts out East ahead of us to ensure safe passage," he indicated, pulling two more of the tribe towards him and relaying instructions.

Heading towards a blackened sky, the two scouts took off at a sprint, leaving only forty-five behind, all looking to Issa for guidance. Issa circled the crowd as the group turned toward the sky that promised rain, leading the pack as the wheels slowly churned on the wagons. They had walked a mere ten minutes when a mist softened their hair and water dripped from their ragged clothes, several members sticking out their tongues for a drop of the liquid gold.

"Let's stop," Issa exclaimed when the rain picked up, lifting his cup to signal that they all fill their bottles with the falling rain.

Nevaeh looked at one of the members beside her, watching the water bead on his skin and glide over the dark etchings, no smudging fading the fake tattoos.

That was probably one of the hardest battles she heard Issa fight. Southerners didn't have tattoos, their political and religious stance on the matter resolute following the war. Since their arrival, Issa had to remain completely covered to conceal his heritage, but Nevaeh had it easier since her markings were easily disguised with Band-Aids and bracelets. But when she jumped in the lake and a bandage softened and fell off her wrist, her closest friend in the South pushed her away, treating the darkened skin like a disease or rash. Nevaeh had quickly run to the shore, grabbing an arm band that covered the colored skin, but it didn't matter. Her friend had already spread the word to others and they huddled in a group pointing and laughing at her. It didn't matter to them that her skin was the same as theirs, the same color and texture; her tattoos were evidence that she was a foreigner, an enemy.

Out here though, roaming the land where she was born and raised, tattoos and brandings were allowed, encouraged even; a clear sign to any onlookers that the tribe didn't reign from the South.

But convincing the other tribe members to adorn such markings was a battle that Issa hadn't prepared for. And it was a tough mediation here in the North, costing hours of essential daylight to repair and reapply the henna markings.

With full bottles and reserves, the tribe set foot again, seeking cover under trees and around buildings, to avoid the harsh wind and pelting rain. Nevaeh's heart sank when she looked up, and she stopped, causing a domino effect.

"What are you-" Issa grunted when he saw his sister pause, and he turned, following her gaze. Jacob was ahead of them, running towards him with hand covering over his arm, red streaks pulsing from the open wound. Issa could feel the tribe step backwards as he surged forward. The boy was fast and Issa met him just as the boy fell toward the ground, heaving as a medic joined them and helped wrap the hole in his arm. "What happened?" Issa demanded, "where's Eu-"

"Eugene's dead," the man exclaimed, testing the strength in his legs as he attempted to push onward with the tribe, the medic still attached to his arm. "There's a band due Southeast of here, we need to press on."

Issa conjured a map in his mind. If a band was Southeast, they needed to head Northwest, the complete opposite of their original plan. Add the camp that is stationed due directly West with at least four of their strongest men, and Issa had landed his tribe in the perfect shit storm.

"Fuck," he growled as they pushed backward, "Head Northwest," he yelled to his scouts as they turned the tribe in the opposing direction.

'This is exactly how neighborhoods die', Issa thought, *'trapped on each end by Troops'*. He also considered the fact that the band to the Southeast could have already phone their camp in the West, and his friends may have already lost a battle they didn't even know was coming. *'Shit, shit, shit!'*

Logic told him to head North, but that would mean losing contact with those in the West. He needed to send a team to meet them, hoping they haven't been captured. But what if there was another camp in the North? Heading to un-explored land could be just as dangerous.

"How big was the band?" He asked Jacob as they continued in the opposing direction.

"What?" The man asked, fear and bewilderment evident in his eyes.

"How big was it? Could we fight them?"

He shook his head, visibly shaking off the fear that paralyzed his mind and dulled his senses. "It wasn't large, I only- maybe four or five men, but they're armed."

Issa knew immediately they needed to stand their ground. Five men was no match for the tribe and their odds could be worse if they headed further North.

"Stop!" He yelled, his voice booming over the thundering steps and creaky wheels. "Stop moving and prepare for combat!" The tribe came to a slow stop, glancing around at each other for reassurance. "Damn it, I'm in charge here, so do what I say! Drop your load in a circle barricade, grab your weapons, and stand ready!"

Nevaeh was the first one to follow orders, dropping her bags at her feet and throwing their extra loads down to form a barricade. Hunter joined her quickly and the rest followed suit. When the barricade was as strong as it would get, they dropped low and grabbed weapons. Nevaeh watched as one of the women fearfully lowered her weapon and she seized it from her. "Just stay low," she instructed as she peered out towards the vacant land.

She heard them before she could see them, horses' feet were hard to disguise even on a rainy night.

"Don't shoot until I say," Issa instructed, "We can't afford to lose ammo and we want to draw them close. Try not to hit the horses if we can spare them."

The horses wandered aimlessly; the men appeared to be heavily soiled and wasted on booze. They didn't even notice the barricade until they were within a block, which made their guarded stance easy.

They took the camp out with ease, bullets ringing through the air as they made their assault. Besides Eugene, the tribe took no casualties, and Jacob was their only wounded.

"Do you think they heard the shots?" Hunter questioned as the tribe began to reassemble their load.

Issa blinked, pondering the question. "We're roughly four miles from the camp, I doubt they could have heard, but the storm should have deterred any suspicions."

"What about the radios, would they have called it in?" Nevaeh asked. Following Issa's lead, they wandered over to the bodies of the deceased. There was only one radio among them and the sound on the other end was silent.

"I'm going to take a guess and say they were too drunk to call it in."

"So, we're safe?" Hunter exclaimed, exhaling loudly along with half of the tribe as they sang quiet cheers.

"No, we're not." Issa countered, drawing silence. "We don't know when this tribe was due back to the camp."

"They were sitting around a fire when we saw them," Jacob informed.

"So... best case they just left camp and won't be missed until their scheduled radio check-in. We have their radio, so we could possibly intercept that call and, if we're lucky, hold off on alerting the camp another day or two. Worst case, this band was returning from a raid and they're expected back at camp any moment, in which case they'll be sending teams out to search in the next few hours."

Issa spelled it out point blank, not caring who he might offend.

"What do we do?" One of the other men asked. They all looked to Issa who started to walk in circles, contemplating their options.

He still had six members unaccounted for due West. But the forty-something here were his priority. He had no way to contact the others, to let Rafi know of the change in plans. He either needed to send a rescue team, or count them all for dead. But Rafi. If he abandoned the six, he'd lose Rafi. If he risked the tribe, Nevaeh would be in danger.

"Well?" the man pushed.

"Would you give me just one goddamn minute to think?!" Issa yelled, saliva spewing from his mouth and red veins etching his face.

There was still no chatter on the radio which was a good sign. If they could get to the West before any alarm was raised, they could find their men and head home. Issa looked at the dead soldiers. They looked well-fed, clearly had a full bottle of booze, all signs they had just left the safety of camp. It was only four miles; they could cover the terrain in a matter of a few hours and then they could be on their way.

But the rain! Their tracks would be evident. If, or rather when, the camp realized their friends were missing, they would send out a search and evidence of their tribe would be written all over the freshly muddied terrain. They passed some concrete roads in the West that were easy to navigate. They'd need to go back there first to throw off the trail, then they could split into two teams; one spearheading the trip South with the heavy load, and a smaller team heading due West to grab the others.

Issa shared the plan and was not surprised when Nevaeh fussed at being forced to join the South-bound team.

"I need to focus, and I don't need to be worried about you while there are lives on the line," Issa dead-panned.

His eyes were bloodshot and she thought she could see tears brimming, so she caved and joined the larger team heading South. Both teams continued West until they reached the city limits, shaking off the mud and grass from the wagon wheels and attempting to brush off any evidence from their feet, before they departed.

Issa watched his sister walk away, this time making sure she followed his directions and asking Hunter to watch over her. He didn't quite like the guy, having fallen for the man's fiancé, but he did trust him to take care of Nevaeh. Hunter wanted to get back safely to Kathreen, so he wasn't likely to risk their safety with any risky moves now that he'd seen the reality of the dangers in the North.

When the Southbound team was out of sight, Issa finally relaxed. They were jogging at a mild pace without the weight of the wagon slowing them down, so he anticipated they'd be on the camp's doorstep in less than thirty minutes. At roughly ten minutes, they ran into the scout and muscle he'd left behind. The two men were unprepared and nearly set off a round when the team came up from behind.

Issa gave a brief rundown of the current situation, and their team grew heavy by two as they made the jaunt to the West. When thirty minutes passed, he encouraged the team to slow and to stay alert of movement, reminding them that they had friendly fire out there. Luckily, the newly added scout was part of the team that discovered the camp earlier that day, and was able to direct them through the outskirts of the city.

Issa could tell when they were close, bright lights lit up the sky like a beacon, and music echoed through the empty streets. Using hand signals only, they team skillfully navigated around buildings and through the streets toward the camp. With each step they advanced, Issa's concern grew. He'd instructed the team to survey, not to advance into the camp, but there was no sign of his men.

The camp was nested in the middle of the city, tents and awnings lining the streets like a carnival intertwined within the heart of the dilapidated skyscrapers. He had pushed as far inward as he could without drawing attention, and was about to turn his men around when two lonely uniforms appeared from around the corner. The men swayed when they walked and were, to Issa's surprise and amaze, heavily drunk. He eyed them cautiously as they continued to saunter towards the outer streets.

Turning to one of the muscles, Issa and the man shared an idea, and they raised their weapons.

CHAPTER 14

EIGHTEEN YEARS OLD

The clothes were stiff as he brushed off his pants and straightened the collar. Luckily the sleeves were long enough to hide his tattoos, but Issa feared his lack of recent hygiene would be a giveaway if anyone got too close.

"You ready?" Winston asked, walking confidently into the room. The uniform fit him better and his smug demeanor would blend in perfectly with the Troops. Issa checked himself in the mirror again, trying to forget the mannerisms he'd just spent seven months training the other Southerners to portray. In his short eighteen years, he'd been a starving Northerner, a skilled Revival leader, a humble Southerner, an instructor and guide, and now a Soldier. With each new title, he'd had to learn and adjust his attitude to fit the situation, but this task would prove to be the toughest. He'd hated the Troops, despised them. And now, looking at his reflection, he couldn't see the difference between the men he sought to destroy and the ones he called his allies.

Issa slid off the cap and tied his hair back, brushing through the waves, but there was only so much he could do to tame the long, dark mane.

"It's not too late to switch with someone," the man indicated as Issa grabbed his cap back.

"No, we're doing this," Issa demanded, stalking off towards the room where he'd left the remainder of his team. "You all know the plan?" He asked, turning to the muscle he'd left in charge.

"We wait two hours. If you're not back, we leave. If we stumble upon the others in that time, we leave, we don't wait for your return." He recited the plan verbatim. "If we sense danger, we leave. If we're caught, we are on our own, no indication of the South."

Issa's heart thundered. He'd known some neighborhoods to take risks, but he'd never heard of anyone impersonating the Troops. This was unfamiliar territory and he had no idea what to expect. He could count on one hand the number of times he'd come into direct contact with a Soldier. He didn't know if there was a pecking order, any formal or informal rules; he was walking in blind.

"Watch your six," he exclaimed as he had often during training, and he tapped the muscle on the shoulder, surveying the others for any signs of doubt. Knowing he had prepared them to the best of his ability, he stepped outside the room and felt the brush of the other man following him. "What's your name?" He asked, pausing in the open doorway to the outside world.

"Karter," he announced, as they both stepped into the swampy post-rain dew.

Issa's steps were quick, too quick he noted, slowing down as they rounded a corner and entered the camp. His pulse was throbbing, his eyes adjusting to the bright lights cast overhead from the lamps. The camp was buzzing with noise; soldiers on patrol walking the grounds, drunken laughter coming from a partially covered tent, the clattering of chains dragging along the concrete floor as they dangled from women's feet.

He watched them closely. The women weren't fighting back, but they were clearly dissatisfied. The two women closest in view wore dainty black carved outfits, barely enough fabric to cover their intimate parts, black chokers with metal spikes slicing their skin if the ropes that dragged down their backs and to their ankles were pulled ever so slightly. Issa felt an urge to save them, to tear apart the fabric that bound the women as they waited upon their captors. One leaned over, pressing a slice of meat to the Soldier's lips as he snarled and grabbed her bare bottom. The girl couldn't have been older than sixteen and images of Bethany, stripped of her dignity, chained at the waist and feet with metal spikes scarring her perfect skin, popped into his head. *'How long had she suffered?'* He wondered. *'How long had they all suffered?'*

"Let's keep moving," Karter snarled, following Issa's gaze to the women. "Let's see if there is a shelter or cage where they're kept."

Although it haunted him, Issa knew that he was right. They were too public, to exposed, to do anything. If he attempted to save those two girls, they probably wouldn't make it a quarter mile before they were captured or shot. He was on a reconnaissance mission; he needed to gather intel.

He pushed forward, further into the center of the camp. It was evident to Issa that the camp was surrounding a large city park, their tents and awnings scattered around erratically, some serving food and beverages, one a booth offering free exploits with slaves, another area cornered off for target practice, though there weren't any dead corpses tied to the barrels as he had been led to believe.

"What do you think of that?" Karter asked, and Issa turned. About two yards away, tucked away in the darkest corner, he could see five rows of 18-wheeler trucks with two or three identical vehicles stacked behind. From what he could see, there were chains on the doors, but none were currently locked. Only one guard was posted, sitting at the bottom of the dilapidated wooden stairs in a rickety lawn chair, his cap pushed over his eyes until another soldier called out to him.

Issa moved, hiding under a tree as he watched the second soldier approach the cargo. The guard lifted his cap momentarily and then resumed his slumber while the new soldier galloped up the steps, fiddled with the handle, and then slipped inside. Issa clicked his watch, starting the timer. One minute, three minutes, seven minutes….

"Hey man, we're starting to draw attention," Karter whispered to Issa as he stepped closer. Issa's eyes wandered. To his right, two soldiers were sitting eating and pinned them down with stares. The younger one, a black-skinned boy with curly hair, caught Issa's attention, the softness in his cheeks oddly familiar, but Issa blinked the thought away to deal with more pressing concerns. To their left, another soldier had pushed his seat out from under him and was heading towards them. Issa looked down at his watch. Eight minutes.

A new face approached the cargo and Issa hesitated, trying to play it cool.

"Don't speak," he warned Karter.

Jordie Cole

"What are you two up to?" The man slowly approaching called, his posture still relaxed as he slid his hands into his pockets.

Nine minutes. The guard nodded to him and the man tucked into the third cargo door.

The men at the eatery were watching the exchange as the muscular giant drew near. "You deaf?"

Issa was out of time and turned to face the man. "Nah man, just minding our own."

The soldier was clearly skeptical, but he nodded anyways. "You could just go in if you're that curious," he tilted his head toward the eighteen wheelers they'd been watching. "They don't bite," he smirked, "unless you ask," he chuckled. Issa wanted to pummel him, kick in the side of the guy's face, but he remained still.

Finding it acceptable, Issa turned back to the cargo and watched as the third man slid out the door he'd just entered, towing a young blonde girl behind him, the same weaponized choker dangling from the girl's neck and feet as the soldier tugged the tail. The girl whimpered as she followed in tow, probably no more than twelve years old. Issa's stomach clenched and he held back the vomit churning up his throat.

"You a gimp or something?" The man asked, "can't get it up?"

This caused Karter to stir as he stepped beside Issa, but Issa held his arm out in warning.

"Nah man," Issa faked a chuckle, trying to find a plausible excuse that would appease the guy without hiving much away, "I prefer to watch," he lied. The soldiers' lips tilted up and he let out a small groan.

"I don't think we've had the pleasure," he extended his hand toward Issa, "I'm Owen."

"Issa," he exclaimed, shaking the guy's hand, "and this is Karter", he gestured over to his comrade who remained silent.

"You two come in with the ninth division?" Issa panicked, not wanting to confirm or deny anything that could come back to hurt them.

The first cargo door squawked open and Issa turned back, watching as the original solider slid out the door, adjusting his belt as the door closed behind him.

"I think that's our queue," Karter intruded, cutting off Owen's question and pushing Issa toward the 18-wheelers.

"You boys have fun," Owen called out, and Issa debated cutting the guy's throat.

"What do we do now?" Karter asked under his breath, continuing toward the cargo with Issa on his heels.

"Just keep walking and play it cool," Issa sighed. He knew they had limited options. They didn't know the rules for going inside, didn't know quite what they would find, but it was too late to turn back as he continued to feel Owen's eyes on their six.

When they closed in on the cargo, the guard was motionless and both men paused. Issa cleared his throat, causing the soldier to stir.

"They're all pretty full, take your pick, last one's reserved for senior officers only" the soldier declared, pushing back in his chair and ignoring their presence. Issa looked at Karter who shrugged, and they pushed forward to the second to the last door and climbed the steps.

Inside it was dark, small yellow light fixtures placed every few feet providing dim lighting. It smelled foul; Issa equated it to the pile of dead bodies the Revival would stack up after a raid. They stepped inside, closing the heavy door behind them. A long walking corridor stretched forward all the way to the back, and wrought iron bars divided the left side of the space into prison cells. As they walked, some ignored their presence, while others cowered into corners, but no soldiers were present. Three- six- ten cells in total. Most cages carried only one prisoner, but Issa noticed a handful with children crammed together.

Karter jangled keys that were on the wall behind them, drawing Issa's attention. "For the locks," he indicated, gesturing toward the padlock on each cage.

"And the shackles," Issa acknowledged, counting three keys on the wall outside of the first cell, just outside of the prisoner's reach. The two men continued down the corridor, Issa pushing Karter to the end where he played with the handle to the next opening. When the bolt wriggled free, the next door opened and Issa stepped into what he imagined was a second eighteen-wheeler with an identical setup, luckily still no sign of a Solider presence.

He stopped in his place, doing the math. If there were ten cells per truck and one prisoner in each cell, and about fifteen trucks, that meant they'd stumbled upon roughly one-hundred and fifteen slaves.

Issa looked up and back down the corridor. The binding on some individuals were different. Some had the shackles that cupped their ankles with the rope that tied to their neck. Others had shackled around their ankles that connected to a metal pole separating their feet, and some even had cannon ball ties weighing them down at the ankles. Among the imprisoned, most were female, but he caught sight of two boys in the mix as well, not a single prisoner looking older than thirty.

Karter walked further back, moving to the third truck, and Issa watched as his partner continued and moved on to a fourth cell. That meant the trailers went further back than Issa had originally thought.

"Stop!" Issa called before Karter opened the next set of doors. "We don't know how far this goes, and there could be guards at the other end to keep them from escaping," Issa explained. He imagined if the soliders had gone through this much trouble to imprison the slaves, surely it wouldn't be that easy to rescue them. "We need to see what's waiting on the other side before we keep going."

Karter agreed, closing the door to the fourth and returning to Issa. "So, what next? Even if we brought reinforcements, it would probably take an hour to try and unlock the cells and the shackles."

"No, we have to go back. Regroup and come up with some sort of plan. This is still too exposed, someone could come in at any time," Issa assumed, though he wasn't sure the rules for privacy. Even if they caught up with the rest of their team and doubled their efforts, they still wouldn't be able to save all of them without being caught.

They closed the doors to the third truck and were almost back to the first when the door opened, light from a nearby street lamp cascading into the room as the younger black boy pushed into the space. Issa's heart constricted, fear churning in his stomach. They were trapped, but they still had the upper hand.

"Is it really you?" The boy's gaze searched past Karter to Issa. "I knew you looked familiar, but when Owen said your name-" the boy shook his head in disbelief, slowly stepping closer to them. Issa eyed him cautiously, noticing that he hadn't drawn a weapon. "Christ, it's really you," he exclaimed in a hushed exaltation. Making quick steps to close the distance, Karter moved aside and allowed the solder to approach Issa. "We all thought you died, that you wouldn't make it to the South-"

"I'm sorry, I think you're confus-" Issa attempted, but was cut off by the Solider.

"Benji," was all the boy said, and realization dawned on him. Benji. Nevaeh's friend from the neighborhood. The boy he'd saved in the mall, his fellow Revival member.

Confusion racked Issa's mind. It wasn't possible. Benji had been in the Revival. If he had been seized by the Troops, he would have been murdered instantly. Now in touching distance, Issa sprang to life, grabbing onto Benji's arm and lifting the edge of his uniform, tearing the fabric away from his dark skin.

It was there. The raised edges of skin, the lightning bolt, the 'R'. It was really Benji! He glanced up at the kid as if seeing him for the first time. He was older, some of the boyish chubbiness gone, but it was him.

Issa's gaze drifted as his mind plagued him with memories. He was their leader. Malik died in the mall, he killed Xavier, and then he turned down the role as First-In-Command and headed for the South with Nevaeh. Zenhara died and all structure was gone, Issa hadn't known who'd taken command in his absence, but he'd hoped his old allies had survived since they refused to join his expedition to the South. But if Benji was in the neighborhood, in the Revival, and now standing before him as a Soldier… how was that possible? Had their entire neighborhood fallen siege to the Troops? Were they all dead or slaves or, worse, Soldiers?

Reading his thoughts, Benji reached out to him, "we need to get out of here, they'll get suspicious. If you come with me, I can get us somewhere safe," he announced. Issa looked to Karter who exchanged an apprehensive glance. "I could have raised an alarm twenty minutes ago and I haven't, that should earn me some trust."

He was right, unless an army awaited them on the outside of the truck, Benji had kept their identity a secret. And if he hadn't, they would face death regardless. Issa shook his head, and piled out of the truck, sans army, and followed Benji across the courtyard to one of the skyscrapers lining the park. Issa glanced at his watch, they were at fifty minutes, time was slipping by and, to his dismay, he was no closer to finding Rafael or the others.

The trio settled into a small apartment that seemed organized and homely. "Take a seat," Benji offered as the door locked behind them.

"Are these quarters private?" Issa inquired, seeing several closed doorways protruding off the main living space.

"For now," Benji declared, "I just moved up here and haven't been assigned new roommates yet," he clarified.

Issa sat and bent over, resting his shoulders on his knees and rubbing his temple. He desperately wanted to ask Benji about the neighborhood, to know what led him here, but he couldn't find the right words and he let Benji take the lead.

"Where's Nevaeh, is she safe?" He extended a chair and sat across from Issa. Karter took a seat beside them and exchanged a cautious glance with Issa.

"I need to know that we're safe here, Benji. That you're not going to turn us in." He sat back, conspicuously fingering his gun.

Benji watched him intently, sorrow filling his eyes. "When you left," he sighed, ignoring the question, "they appointed me Third-In-Command," he chuckled. "There were so few of us left and no one had leadership experience," he recalled. "The elders tried to teach us," he shook his head, "but they were out of practice and we had Troops hot on our tail." He stared off at the wall, the memory playing like a movie on the clean surface. "Within a week, we were decimated down to less than a handful of people, and when the final raid came, I hid behind a little boy in a dumpster, waiting for them to come for us. But they never found us," he groaned. "At the time, I didn't know if we were the only ones to survive or if we were left behind, but the kid and I walked on for four more days before the Troops caught us…" he trailed off.

"And the others?" Issa asked, his chest tight.

Benji shook his head, tears brimming. "Three of the young girls were in the kennels, but they're all gone now."

Issa's hand dropped from his gun, the weight of the news crashing in on him. His neighborhood was gone. Dead. Deceased. Caput. A neighborhood that was soaring and thriving, now ceased to exist.

"They didn't search me when they found me. I've hidden my scar from the very beginning and haven't given them any cause to doubt me, but-" he choked.

"What about the boy that you were with?"

His gaze froze over. "He's here, but he's- he's just as rotten as they are; finds joy in the torture."

After a long silence, Issa glanced back at his watch. It was ten past the hour. If he had any chance of making a plan, of saving any of the slaves they'd found, he'd have to move quick and warn his team.

He pushed forward, crossing his hands as he leaned on the table. "Benji," strength filled his voice as he spoke with renewed hope, "I made it to the South." Karter's face shot up with the announcement and they watched as Benji's features flicked from confusion to shock and then his brows furled back to dismay. "Nevaeh and I have lived in the safety of the South for the past three years. And we brought a team with us back here, in hopes of bringing people back with us."

Benji's expression was blank, astonishment seizing him.

"We have a team not far from here, but they have orders to leave us soon if we don't come back. We lost a few of our team and think they might have been captured-"

"We seized a small brigade earlier. Four people?"

Issa nodded in confirmation, closing his eyes. "We have a solid month trek back and I can't promise it will be easy, but you can come with us. We'll gather with our team and strategize, we'll come up with a plan to rescue-"

"You can't," Benji shook his head, "you don't have time." Issa sat still, his lungs begging for breath as he waited for Benji to say the words he dreaded. "They're scheduled for the firing squad at noon."

CHAPTER 15

EIGHTEEN YEARS OLD

I ssa looked out over the courtyard, the leaves just beginning to redden with the hint of fall; it was almost peaceful if you could look past the murder and prolonged torture that befell the camp. Turning back to the apartment, Issa watched as his team assembled the finishing touches on their wardrobes. With Benji's assistance, they managed to scrounge up enough uniforms for each of them and maneuver past the guards to the safety of the secluded apartment where Benji provided instructions for blending in amongst the soldiers.

Dawn came like an unwelcome guest at a dinner party, and unease fell among the men as they ran through their plan. It was unwise of Issa not to reach out for the remainder of the tribe, but he refused to endanger Nevaeh and their window of opportunity was narrowing.

"The new guards should be taking post in about ten minutes," Benji declared as he strapped his rifle to his chest. Looking around the room, Issa was impressed with his team. These men that lived safe lives and slept in comfortable beds with wives and children and no fear of what the next day would bring, they'd stepped out of their secure world to help save the lives of people they'd never met, and today, they'd be putting their training to the ultimate test.

"You can still back out," he reminded them, the fresh memory of losing Eugene causing him pause. "If you want to leave and join the rest of the tribe, now is probably your last chance."

He looked among them, but none of them faltered, and his chest heaved with pride. There were too many in the kennels, he knew they wouldn't save everyone, but he felt an unwavering need to try. And although he wouldn't admit it to his team, he couldn't live with himself if he abandoned Rafael.

"Just remember," Benji announced, the room falling silent with his authoritative tone, "it's not a matter of if the Troops find out, but when. As soon as you hear those alarms, split into your teams and run. They're not prepared for a long hunt right now, all the bands are out, so as long as we divide their resources, we'll stand a better chance of surviving."

Everyone nodded in agreement and divided into their respective groups. Benji provided inside knowledge on the Kennels. There would be no way to get all the cages unlocked in time, but there was a trigger at the end of each of the trucks that would simultaneously unlock all cages within one truck at once. There were five rows of trucks, four deep with the exception of the last row, the officer row, which consisted of only three trucks. The last truck in each row was attached to a cab, but the keys were under tight surveillance.

Issa and Benji would go for the keys while the others went in pairs to the kennels. The morning guard would be starting his shift and was known for abandoning his post first thing in the morning to visit the coffee hut at the far end of the block. As long as they didn't draw attention, that would be Karter's opportunity to lead the others to the trucks and get inside. Because they had odd numbers, Karter would help the first line, where Rafael and the others were held, until they could release them and increase their numbers. From there, Karter would bring help with him to tackle the officer kennel and begin unlocking the cages. The plan was to hit the trigger at the back of the trucks to unlock the cages, then assist with unlocking the individual restraints and move all prisoners to the furthest truck in each row. Issa and Benji should have retrieved the cab keys from the lieutenant's office by then and would deliver these to the trucks where they could, in theory, drive safely out of the city.

Now the drawbacks. There was no way to predict whether there would be any lingering soliders inside the trucks to offer opposition. Then, the plan rested on the ability of Issa and Benji to get past the guards in the lieutenant's office to get the cab keys and then somehow also manage to get back across the square to the trucks without being stopped. That also assumed the trucks had enough gas in them to get enough of a head start out of the city where they would divide their efforts and fan out, compelling the Troops to either split their forces or choose a single team to chase. So, the strategy had flaws, but they each agreed to the terms.

"Ready?" Benji asked, turning to Issa who shook his head.

"I have," his voice croaked, "one last thought to share," he hesitated. "Growing up in the North, we're taught one really vital thing; to save a bullet for yourself," he groaned. "If you- if you don't see a way out, but you have a shot, I encourage you to take it. I say this, not just because I want your suffering to end, but if you're captured and tortured, they'll try to get you to talk," he stopped to allow his words to penetrate. "I want you all to think about the South. Think about your families, your wives, children, parents, and grandparents. If you talk, you're not just hurting the rest of us here in this room, and you're not adding any new pain to those in the cages, you're adding a new danger to your friends and family." He looked up at the men expecting to see fear, but met instead with a resounding confidence. He took a deep breath. "I want to thank you all for coming here with me, for believing in me and this plan, and for risking your lives. And hopefully we'll meet up on the other side."

"We need to go," Karter announced, glancing at his watch.

The men silently shuffled out of the room, Issa and Benji at the rear. The group divided, hiding in plain sight as they spread out across the courtyard.

"We're headed this way," Benji informed Issa as he took off to the East, the kennels in the opposite direction.

Issa remained silent as he followed Benji's direction, not hesitating until they approached a security checkpoint. He checked his watch, 7:59 AM.

"Just do as I do," Benji instructed.

"Who's the newbie?" A soldier asked as Benji was pulled forward in the line and was patted down.

"Didn't Offerman tell you? He's doubling detail, this guy's just the latest in a swarm of potential recruits." They both laughed and Issa scowled.

"Serious one, ain't he?" The soldier chuckled as he called Issa forward.

"Nah, just ain't had his morning dumps yet, he'll chill out once he can pinch one off," they both snickered and the guard pushed Issa through, not bothering to check him.

They entered a tall building with flawless windows, almost as if it had remained untouched by the casualties of the Great War. Inside, the walls and floors were sleek, a white and black cascading river glimmering on the floor and walls. They entered a smaller section and sleek silver doors parted, surprising Issa. They walked into the confined box and the doors closed behind them.

"We're being lifted to the tenth floor." Benji announced as the box shifted and the walls shook. Issa reached out for the walls, holding tight on the rail and glancing at his watch. 8:02 AM. The guard would just be arriving. The team had about five to ten minutes left before he'd vacate his post.

The door beeped as they stepped out and Benji nodded at the guard they passed. Unease crept up Issa's spine as he wondered how they were able to bypass the security efforts so easily. "We need into the box," he announced as they approached a long desk with an un-shackled female behind the podium. She wore a suit similar to theirs, but the jacket was open and she wore a tight-fit tank top underneath, accentuating her curves. Her hair was black with a white streak down the center, tied tightly back into a bun, and she pursed her pouty red lips. Issa figured her to be around twenty, maybe thirty years of age.

"Not even a hello this morning?" She groaned, ignoring his request as she fiddled with trinkets on the other side of the counter.

"Hello," he deadpanned. "We need into the box."

"Can't help you," she grinned. "Did you hear we lost contact with Brady's team?" She asked, leaning over the counter, enjoying the latest gossip.

Issa's breath halted; fearful they'd been caught before even getting started.

"They're probably just drunk," he placated, walking down the corridor and crossing the desk, "sleeping it off".

"I don't know, dad seems pretty disturbed. Sounds like they might be sending a search party, or engaging a practice drill to keep everyone on alert."

'Shit'. Issa thought, glancing at the time; 8:04 AM. *'They didn't have time for small talk!'*

"You gonna offer to join the hunt?"

"Didn't Offerman call this morning?" Benji asked, changing the topic. "I'm here for the keys."

"I didn't get a call," she growled, her tone changing as she retreated, "and I'm not delivering the keys if they're calling an alarm this morning."

Panic tugged at Issa's heart as he stood helpless, they didn't plan for this.

"Fine," Benji played coolly, "but it's your ass on the line if he jumps me, I was here on time, I'm not taking the hit," he turned, side-eyeing Issa.

"Fuck you!" she exclaimed, slamming her hands down over a key ring that clattered against the desk. "Fine, but you better bring them straight back if the alarm sounds."

Benji didn't justify her with a response, but simply turned the corner of the desk and followed her to a panel on the wall that opened when she pressed it.

8:07 AM.

She dangled the keys tauntingly in front of Benji who snatched them a bit too quickly, and she grimaced when he turned without a word.

Issa turned, walking back the way they'd come in, Benji hot on his heels silently cheering himself. Issa was impressed with this old friend. He'd imagined a harder battle being fought, but they were in and out of the room without hesitation. That is, until the doors slid open to the moving box-thing.

"Benji!" A voice bellowed in the room as Issa moved aside, allowing the trio to exit from the box. "What are you doing here, man?!" The voice sounded enthusiastic, not alarmed, but Benji's expression was foreboding as he slipped on a fake smile.

Two men continued down the corridor, ignoring them, but the animated one stopped to talk as Benji avoided contact and joined Issa along the side of the room.

"I'd love to chat, but we have to get-" Benji excused, but was interrupted with the skunk-striped woman came rushing out, her feet tapping on the floor, "Offerman, what a pleasure to see you today!" Offerman, Issa replayed the name in his head. That's the lieutenant that Benji worked for, the very ruse they'd used to gain access to the building, to the keys.

"Benji didn't say you'd be coming in," she glared as Benji pushed Issa closer to the box, pushing his hand inside to stop the progression of the closing doors. "Had I known," Benji pushed the number 'one' and the circle turned red, "I would have just given the keys to you," the doors closed as Issa heard the man begin his protest.

"Fuck!" Benji shouted as the box moved. They descended four floors when the alarms sounded and Issa knew their gig was up, but Benji reacted quickly, pressing the dial for number 'three' and rushing out of the metal box when the doors slid open.

Issa didn't argue or waver when Benji pulled at his gun, running into the stairwell and continuing their descent to the first floor. The slid down the stairs with grace, the alarms flashing a bright light in the space as they continued.

"What are we going to do?" Issa asked as he readied his weapon.

Benji burst through the doors on the ground level, but the commotion surrounding them wasn't directed towards them.

"Have you seen them?" Benji asked the same guard he'd been joking with only moments before, slowly making his way towards the exit with his gun poised.

"No," the guard confessed, his pistol raised, "haven't heard what we're looking for". Benji's shoulders relaxed, but he remained stoic.

"The two men with Offerman, heard they jumped him," Issa lied, a new story forming as they created an escape plan.

"Shit," the guard yelled as he turned toward the magic box, Benji yelling, "we're going to check outside!" as the guard waved them on and entered the box.

The alarm continued outside and several soldiers approached, looking to Benji for direction. "Two perpetrators on the loose, male, last seen on ten. Heard they're trying to get the keys, we're going to secure the kennels," he informed the men as he pushed against the crowd. Once the majority were gone, Benji turned West at a full sprint and Issa followed.

The courtyard was lined with soldiers headed due East towards the alarms and they made it about half way before eyes turned on the men headed in the opposite direction.

They'd crossed nearly two-thirds before the sounds of gunfire rang out, dirt exploding from the ground at their feet.

Issa pushed harder, his legs on fire as he pushed faster. The sound of bullets pierced the air, but Issa was determined to continue. He'd was only yards away when realization settled and he noticed the opposing fire from the West. *'Had he run into an ambush?'* But no, when he looked up at the barricade, familiar faces greeted him. Blinking back his confusion, he searched the firing line and his heart sank when he saw the disheveled dark brown braid disappear into one of the trucks.

"Nevaeh!" He yelled as he sought coverage beyond the line, following her path to the third kennel.

"Issa!" Benji yelled, pulling apart one of the keys and handing it to him, "go to five!" he demanded as he turned and headed for the first line of trucks.

The barricade his tribe had created was holding strong, but the members were starting to fold backwards as the onslaught drew closer.

"Head for the back rows!" a voice rang out as Issa pushed past the third row where he'd last seen Nevaeh, wavering as he ignored his instincts to protect her.

"Issa! Issa!" Rafi's voice penetrated the chorus and Issa turned at the fourth row to find his old friend. "Issa, she's here, we have to get her!"

"I know," Issa chimed, I just saw her running through three," he exclaimed as he continued for the last row.

"No, man! She's in the officer cage!" Issa stopped dead in his tracks, turning to Rafi, images of Nevaeh trapped in a cage plaguing his mind.

"No, no, Nay's fine, she's-" he argued, clawing at his eyes to remove the haunting images.

"Issa," Rafael grabbed his hands, pushing them down as he forced Issa to make eye contact with him, "Bethany's here. She's alive."

The world stopped. Bullets flying suddenly halted, voices ceased, bodies froze. Issa pictured the kennels, dark and dirty, the smell of rotten flesh and piss, and barely dressed women cowering in corners of cages with blood stains around their feet and hands while sharp spikes carved scars into their weak skin; and Bethany's tortured eyes peering back at him. His skin prickled as he knelt over, vomit rising from the pits of his stomach.

"She's- no, she can't-" the words fumbled as he wiped the saliva from his cheek.

"She's here, Issa. They're in the last row!"

Issa didn't waver, pushing past the bodies of fallen comrades and weaving through the array of bullets, his mission set for the fifth row. He yanked open the door, a solider-dressed tribe member assisting the last woman with her shackles.

"Keep moving," he barely heard the words as he maneuvered past them, tripping over a dead body, landing with his face next to Karter's. He pushed off his friend, noticing a bullet wound to his torso and a matching lesion on the body that lay beside him.

He checked the lifeless body for a pulse, the cab key slipping from his grip as he dragged himself off of his friend's corpse. "Shit," he exclaimed, tightening his grasp on the key as he turned and shoved it into Rafael's hand. "Go!" he yelled as his friend's hand curled around the brass ring, "It's for the cab, we need a driver!"

Rafael turned back as Issa continued to the next truck. As he entered, he registered the scene. Women were fumbling with key rings, attempting to aide their caged allies. Seeing him, several ran toward the back, pushing the last doors open and revealing the last truck where all slaves were still locked tight in their cages. Issa ran past them, not bothering to explain his motives as he searched the back of the truck for the trigger. Grasping the metal handle and shoving it down, the cage doors swung open and he ushered the women to the back.

"No time!" he yelled, as the women fumbled with their locks. "Take your keys with you and run to the back! We have to go now!" he shepherded them to the last truck, surveying each face as they steered past him. But his eyes caught hold of one in particular, a pale, round-faced woman who looked to be in her early twenties, with a young boy tied to her waist.

He approached her timidly, watched in horror as she covered her son with her body, fear coursing through her as she protected her young.

"Bethany?" He whispered, and cries stilled as she slowly peeled back to look at him. "Bethany," he cried again, falling to his knees beside her as her eyes registered recognition.

"Issa?" She lifted a hand to his face, "please tell me this is a dream," she whimpered, "that you're not-" he followed her gaze to his uniform.

"It's a disguise," he confessed, "a costume." She slowly nodded her understanding. "You've been here this whole time," he murmured, unsure if it was a question or simply a statement.

The roaring of the engine behind him penetrated the cloud of emotions that paralyzed him. The truck was gearing up and they weren't on it.

"Move!" he yelled, pulling her thin frame with him as he stood. He forced open the final door and pushed Bethany and the boy past the final gap.

The truck surged forward, light pouring into the newly open space. To his right, Issa could see the four other trucks that had separated from their columns and Nevaeh's braid floating behind the trucks as she sealed the doors shut. The first three were already on the move and she tapped the door to the fourth truck, signaling for the driver to leave.

She ran to the final truck, closing the left door. Securing her grip, she leaned forward to grab the second door, but Bethany's voice rang out, "Issa!"

Nevaeh paused, looking at Bethany and then turning back to Issa. Noticing him for the first time, panic crossed her face as she screamed, "behind you!"

CHAPTER 16

THIRTEEN YEARS OLD

The sounds of bullets hitting metal surrounded me as I watched soldiers enclose on his position. Hot metal ricocheted and I leaned forward to close the door to the last truck. I could see my getaway truck rounding the edges of the columns as I slid the final latch into place, jumping down and running to the side of the eighteen-wheeler to escape the onslaught.

The red truck emerged and I waved, flagging it down. "Issa!" I yelled as the truck careened past him and he caught sight of it. He soared to the ground and ran from the opposing direction as I grabbed hold of the rim, landed my foot on the runners and catapulted over the side. My body burned as my bare flesh collided with the rough texture in the bed, but I didn't have time to complain, lifting myself up to check on my brother. The ground began to pulse beneath me and fear seized my chest as Issa threw himself at the gate.

Shots rang out in the distance and dirt flew up from where they buried themselves into the ground I reached for him as he struggled to climb aboard the moving vehicle, but his footing on the tailgate was strong as he pulled himself over.

A loud bang rang out and he toppled backwards, losing his grip and crashing his torso into the tailgate as he held onto the edge. I surged forward on my knees, grabbing his hand as his grip faltered. The ground beneath moving too quickly for him to gain traction, he screamed in agony as he balanced his weight against the truck.

If I dropped him, it would be over. We couldn't turn back, we were already too close to the Troops for comfort, the red truck surging ahead of the pack.

"Don't- let- go!" I pulled, pushing my weight backwards as I carried his weight forward into the truck bed. When he was a solid two-thirds into the bed, I dropped his weight, my abs screaming from the impact of slamming into the truck. When air returned to my lungs, I turned to Issa, placing my hand against the raw texture of the bed and pulling it up to inspect the slick moisture that coated my arm and fingers; blood.

I quickly examined my body for any life-altering wounds, but aside from some scrapes and pending bruises, the growing pool of blood wasn't coming from my body. Realization settling, I looked toward Issa who had pushed himself against the opposite edge of the truck. Testing my footing, I ambled over to him, pulling his limp body close to inspect the damage.

The green uniform was soiled in red and I tore at the fabric, peeling it off without any assistance from Issa. I felt for his neck, his eyes barely registering my presence. "You stay with me, Issa, you hear me," my voice was weak and shaky as I spoke. The wound pierced his lower abdomen and I turned his body to search for an exit wound that didn't exist. "He's hurt!" I yelled to the driver, banging on the window to the cab, smearing blood. "Hurry, he's hurt!"

I pushed down on the open wound, applying pressure as I remembered my dad telling me to do. "Issa, keep your eyes on me," I demanded, wrapping my free arm around his head. "You stay with me!"

The truck continued forward for what felt like an eternity. When the remainder of the tribe decided to turn back to the camp, against Issa's wishes, we sent several members ahead, beyond the hills to set up a camp. That's where the truck was heading, along with at least one of the eighteen-wheelers from what I could see. The other large convoys must have flanked out, because they weren't around when we finally joined the tribe.

"Set up a barricade," Rafael yelled as he hopped from the eighteen-wheeler, shouting demands at the tribe in quick succession.

"Help!" I cried out as soon as the truck stopped, "we need help! Please!" Rafi stormed toward us, his poker face sliding into position when he saw the pool of blood. "You have to help him!" I sobbed as several medics approached and moved Issa onto the wagon.

"No, you have to get cleaned up," Rafael demanded, holding me back when I attempted to follow Issa.

"Stop," I fought against him, "let me go!" I argued, but his grip was iron, and I caved. "You have to help him," I demanded, pulling on Rafi's arm as I fell to my knees, Issa's blood smearing on his arm.

"Navaeh!" A foreign voice called out to me and both Rafi and I turned to face the man who was running toward us. "Are you injured?" he stopped short, seeing the blood staining my skin.

The man was tall, sharp cheek bones cresting below his soft eyes, his short black hair curled and the light dusting of a mustache forming on his upper lip. But his eyes! There was something familiar to them. Images of a heavyset boy flash through my mind as I peer at him to get a better look. He was lean and muscled, but the soft circles below his eyes were unmistakable.

"Benji?" I exclaimed, lifting to my feet mere inches from him. He wore a soldier uniform, but so did half of their tribe as part of their disguise. Has Benji been with us the whole time, had I missed him? Surely not, I'd watched the drills intently. Sure, I was focused on the skills, the maneuvers, not their faces, but I'd have known if Benji had made it to the South.

Rafi raised his gun, training in on Benji. "Stand back!" He demanded.

"Rafi, what are you doing?" I countered, moving between the men and sliding the end of the shotgun away.

"He's not one of us," Rafi yelled, a crowd of onlookers forming around us. "What's your intention here?" He demanded.

"Stop!" One of the scouts, dressed in a soldier uniform, yelled, pushing through the wall of bodies, "he's the one that helped us. He's good!"

Rafi faltered, the crowd silencing, concern echoing throughout the group as he lowered the gun.

"Are you hurt?" Benji asked, turning to me, but keeping an eye on Rafael as he closed the distance, his arms caressing my waist as if no time had passed. My heart raced. How had he managed to find us? Why was he with the Troops? "Nay, are you injured?" He repeated and I shook my head, crying out.

"Issa! Where'd they take Issa?!"

Rafael moved in closer, placing a hand on my shoulder. "The medics are working on him, they'll help him, but we need to get you cleaned up." He pushed me aside, out of the center of the circle. "The Troops won't give up that easily, make a barricade!" He yelled behind him, the crowd scurrying.

Melissa ran over to me, leading me away from the tribe, away from Rafi who continued to holler out demands to the tribe. She had stayed behind when I joined the team heading back to the camp, and she'd already setup our tent. Pulling out partially filled bottles of water, we ran the water over my skin, scrubbing at the blood that had already started to dry and crackle on my bare arms. "Have you seen him?" I hiccupped, "Issa, did you see him?"

"No," she stuttered, "they needed the space, so I came to find you." We emptied all the bottles and my arms and torso clung to the red hue. "There's a pond down the hill, we're not making much progress here," she sighed as she stood, reaching for my hand.

"We need to check on him first, I can't leave-" I argued, but she didn't listen, pushing me away from the tents. The tribe had settled in a wooded area, tree limbs lurking from above provided shade and a dense forest to the rear hid the trucks and campsite. I reluctantly followed, falling to my knees when my feet hit the soft mud. "He can't die," I cried, my body weak as I toppled over, murky water splashing my face as I collapsed. Issa was all I had.

We'd barely spoken since one of the medics found me in the wagon on that third day. When they forced me to confront him, Issa's face was a shade of red that I hadn't known existed, spit spewing from his mouth as he screamed at me. He'd instructed them to take me back, but no one was willing to go. They'd all trained for the mission, spent countless hours practicing drills, depriving their bodies of the nutrition they craved; no one was ready to go back after such a short journey. And he certainly couldn't abandon his post, not after months of convincing the tribe of the importance of their mission, he'd look like a hypocrite. So he was forced to let me stay, split the rations, and increase the headcount by one soul.

The first day he spoke to me, it was by mistake. He hadn't realized that it was me that had foraged for his meal that night, and he spoke before confirming my identity. Since then, the few words we had shared, were mostly out of anger. I defied his wishes by returning to the Troop camp, and I couldn't allow that last moment, fear and panic as I pulled him into the truck bed, be my last memory of him, our last words.

Melissa sat beside me, brushing my hair in the water as I floated in the pond, a nearby waterfall drowning out the world. The sun was piercing, breaking through the trees like a fire tearing through a wooden house, warming my skin and the water that sloshed at my sides. Mel was humming something, but I didn't recognize the tune, choosing to focus on the sounds of the crashing water as I dipped my head below the surface.

Issa had provided for me to the best of his ability, choosing me over anything else. He'd fed me when mom wasn't home, rocked me to sleep when dad would leave for an emergency, carried me when we searched for a new home. And when the floor fell out from below our feet, the entire neighborhood relying on a fifteen-year-old orphan boy, he'd still chosen to protect me above all else. And at the first chance I got, I defied him.

Crackling of leaves warned Mel of a visitor and she turned, causing me to stir and lookup. Benji pensively approached.

"Is Issa okay?" I asked, slipping as I pushed myself up to face him.

He gave a slight nod. "The medics have controlled the bleeding for now, I don't think they found the bullet yet, though."

"Any sign of the Troops?" Mel asked, diverting the conversation.

"Not yet, but we're not staying here long. Rafael wants to put more distance between us."

"Is it safe for Issa to travel?" I questioned, not caring about a status update on the Troops. If they approached us, I wouldn't hesitate to show them the pain that they so willingly inflict.

Benji glanced at Mel and neither one bothered to answer me. We all knew it wouldn't be in Issa's best interest, but they didn't add salt to my wounded ego.

"The barricade is armed and strong, we won't head out until nightfall. You two should try to get some sleep."

Sleep seemed like a foreign concept, like a hot bath and warm roast dinner in the North; highly unlikely. When we returned to the tribe, I fell into my sleep sack, but remained alert, listening for Issa's cries above the hustle. When Rafael appeared to inform us of the timeline, I rushed through the packing process, rolling up my bag and disassembling the tent in record time.

With my belongings holstered over my shoulder, I ran to the wagons in search of Issa. I didn't wait for permission, pushing aside the draping of the first tent and luckily, or not so luckily, finding my pot of gold. Issa lay unconscious, the wooden walls of the wagon damp with his blood, a nurse cautiously pressing a rag over his chest, avoiding the taped bandage on his torso. His face was cast aside, blood congealed in the curls of his dark hair and crusted around his neck. He'd never looked so frail, and my heart sank as tears crested in my eyes.

"No one will tell me the truth," I announced, my stomach gutted as I forced my eyes away from Issa and toward the medic. "Please?" The question was assumed, my words limited for fear that I'd lose my willpower and cave to sorrow.

The medic heaved, looking mournfully at Issa. "He is very weak," she admitted, her tone ominous. "He appears to have several broken ribs and his breathing," she wavered, "there's indication that he's pierced a lung-" She continued, but the words didn't penetrate, something about infection and the bullet, but I couldn't hear it. I pushed away from the wagon, the curtain falling back and concealing Issa from view. Movement around me indicated we were leaving and I fell into step alongside the others, the world around me a blur. We were twenty-some odd days from the safety of the South. Even at full speed, there wasn't much hope that Issa could hold on that long, that his body could fight the infection, his heart endure the pain...

At some point the sun rose, heating the earth beneath our bare feet, but we kept walking. I couldn't be certain how long, or how far, we had travelled, but we stopped within the confines of a small city; the tall buildings providing shade and shelter, as well as a defendable perimeter as a new barricade was erected.

Most of the others were busy finding a place to rest their heads, a home to sleep in while we restocked, but I couldn't muster the energy and planted myself on a street corner.

"Nevaeh," a woman's voice called out to me as I untied my pack and grabbed my bottle. I looked up at the lady, using her body to block the sun that peered from behind her. Her body was frail and she hunched, huddled over a little boy that clung to her legs. "Are you Nevaeh?" she asked, her voice sounding stronger than she looked capable of. I raised my eyebrows, too numb to respond, but when she didn't get the hint, I gave a curt nod.

"Do you know who I am?" her eyes squinted, her brows furrowing together. I lifted my hand over my eyes, shading them from the sun that escaped as she swayed, and tried to get a better look at her. She wore a long brown sleeveless gown with buttons tied down the length of the front. Unlike most of the women they rescued, her attire was more conservative, but the loose material didn't offer much support and her breast were exposed with the simple shift of the breeze.

The boy, no older than five, was more familiar; his gentle curls reminding me of a young Issa. He watched me intently, the same brown hue as our dad. Lifting my gaze back to the woman, my breath caught as an image of my mother faded away, replaced by the girl.

"You were so little," she exclaimed, her gaze drifting as she remembered the toddler that she'd cradled to sleep every night. "My name's Bethany," she announced, reaching out for the boy, "and this is my son Joseph, named after our dad. I-" she faltered, "I'm your sister."

Sister. Bethany. I could hear the words, but couldn't put the pieces together. My sister was dead, abducted and killed by the soldiers when I was two. I didn't know her, couldn't conjure up a memory of her, for all I knew, my sister may as well have never existed.

And now? To come back to us now? When my brother's life hung in the balance? Surely this was some sort of cosmic joke, an unbalanced woman grasping for ties to give her life meaning. Or perhaps a mirage, a hallucination from the dehydration, physical exertion, and lack of sleep. It had to be. The idea of Bethany reappearing now, it was absurd.

"Excuse me," I cut, abruptly standing and grabbing my pack. The delusion called out to me, but I ignored it as I floundered through the city. Seeing Melissa, I jogged over to her and she grabbed my pack.

"We're setting up in the far building," she pointed to a corner brick building with holes where the windows had once been. "The checkpoint is due South, so we'll be the first out in an emergency," she clarified.

"I'm gonna find Issa first, then I'll be in," I informed, sweeping the streets for signs of the wagon.

"They're tucked into one of the garages," she announced, pointing toward a large open space in the middle of the street.

I muttered a 'thanks' and ran toward the opening, colliding with Rafi when I turned the corner in the garage. I slowed to a walk, cautiously avoiding the medics that lingered around, and approached the back of the wagon. The same nurse was tending to him, along with another who perched over him, stitching the hole where the bullet entered.

"We got the bullet out," the first nurse broadcast when she saw me approach, "the hard part is behind him," she soothed, sharing a menacing glance with the other medic.

"Has he regained consciousness?" I asked, delicately hopping onto the cart. Neither responded, but the male shook his head tentatively.

Not much had changed since I'd last seen him, but his olive skin was a shade paler than I remembered. Attributing this to the loss of blood, I ignored it.

"Issa," I said as I knelt beside him, opposite the medics, "I need you to stay strong for me," I demanded. "Just, sleep. Give your body time to rest," tears slid down my cheek, the salty liquid painting the floor. "And don't worry about us, Rafi's taken lead and moved us further South. We've got a good head start." But we're still a month away from the hospital, I shut my eyes as I forced out the thought. "We've got a strong group with us. I- I don't know how many were in the other trucks, but we're heavy maybe twenty or so heads," I wiped my cheek and took a deep breath in, calming my nerves. "The council won't believe it when we get back. They'll be ready to send us right back out again."

"You should get some rest," Rafi interjected, "I'll let you know if anything changes here."

I looked over at him, his eyes bloodshot, dark circles like a raccoon clouding his sockets. "Shouldn't you be the one to catch up on some sleep?" I argued playfully,

"I'm good 'til nightfall, then Armon's taking over. I'll make sure he's briefed of the situation." I nodded, grabbing Issa's hand. He was right. If I was having visions, I surely needed to catch up on sleep.

"I'm in the brownstone closest to the checkpoint," I recited, "if anything-"

"I'll find you," he promised.

I pumped Issa's hand twice, but he remained still and cold. "I'll be back in a bit to check in on you," I informed him, dropping his hand and hopping down from the wagon. I hesitated before turning the corner, seeing Rafi bow his head toward me as the concrete wall cut off my view.

The walk was short. Few people meddled in the streets, most probably already huddled in their sleep sacks or tents, exhausted from the latest events. Surprisingly, the tribe was holding up well. Given their posh upbringing, Nevaeh imagined there would have been more injuries or complaints, but their leader had prepped them well.

Melissa had set up my sack on the third floor, predicting my need for privacy and seclusion. Slipping into my sack beside the exterior wall, a soft breeze filtering in through the broken windowsills, I made a mental note to make it up to her later.

When I woke up, the sky promised rain and a heavy dew clung to my skin; it was as melancholy a painting as I could ever conjure up, and a punch to my stomach when my mind recalled our current status. Pressure behind my eyes reminded me of the tears I'd shed, my body fighting against the efforts to hide my emotions.

I figured it was time I get up, check on Issa, grab some food, but my body resisted; it was thoroughly exhausted. Turning to my side, I watched the dark clouds as they moved in, the earth blissfully unaware of the turmoil of its tenants.

When thunder roared, I reached under my headrest for my iPod. I wasn't supposed to have this. Issa banned all Southern technology from the mission, for safety precautions, but just as he had failed to re-check the wagon for any stowaways, he'd missed the palm-sized square that I'd hidden below the stockpile of grits.

I shoved one headphone into my ear, letting the other dangle down as I turned on my music; thunder and Skylar

Grey's 'I'm Coming Home' soothing me momentarily. But I hear the footsteps climbing the stairs below, and I hear the dark husky tone clashing with the soft treble of female voices.

The hairs on my arms raise, goosebumps forming as a shiver runs down my spine. I sing along, pushing out the sounds of the stairwell creaking.

The footsteps stop in the landing, fresh tears clouding my vision as the first drops of rain splatter against the floor.

'The music! Pay attention to the music!' I command my brain, but I still hear the creaking of the steps as he draws near.

"Nevaeh-"

'No, no, no!' I scream internally, my body tightening into a ball as tears escape and my breathing shakes. *'Please, God, no!'*

Rafael sighs, his voice cracking. "I'm so sorry."

I force the lyrics out, a hiccupped version of a once melodious song. I don't want to hear him; I don't want to face the words. I don't want to think how, unlike the song foretells, Issa won't be making the trip home with us.

"He's gone."

The music fades and my world goes black.

CHAPTER 17

I don't hear his words. I don't hear the creaks when he walks away. I don't feel the rain as it soils my sack or the tremble in my gut as my stomach growls. I don't see Melissa when she packs up my stuff, and I don't feel Benji as he carries me down the foyer.

I'm numb.

Issa's body is buried at the Southern checkpoint, a ritual burial in the North. My nerves as dull and lifeless as Issa's body while small pebbles of dirt tickle his arms, suffocating him as the tiny nuggets filter into his nostrils and smother his mouth.

Issa is dead.

Rafael memorializes him, but I don't listen; can't understand the words. Someone touches my shoulder and caresses my back, places Issa's golden cross chain in my hand, but I don't see who they are.

Issa is dead.

We walk South, one foot in front of the other. Issa isn't with us because he died. He survived the trip to the South, he studied their religion and history, he passed the exit exam, and was celebrated as a fully capable member of the Southern society. He was safe!

But now, Issa is dead.

I don't know how many days pass. I don't recognize when two trucks intersect the tribe, increasing the headcount. I don't eat when Melissa pushes a plate of food in front of me. I don't swim in the pond when the others wash up, and I don't sleep when my sack is set out.

But I do see the grey brick wall when we cross the border. I see the final two eighteen-wheelers that managed to surpass our arrival. I see the faces of friends and families reuniting, hugging, laughing and crying as the gates close behind us. I see Kathreen and Annette searching the crowd for us. And I see their features change when they don't spot Issa.

Because Issa is dead. His body buried in the North, decaying under the ground that robbed us of our childhood, our freedom, and now Issa's last breath.

I cry when Annette hugs me, her grip tightening as our bodies succumb to the pain. Beside us, Kathreen hides her tears, hugging Hunter. She doesn't cover it well, neither of them were very good at concealing their affection for one another. One only had to watch them to see it; the late-night walks, afternoon soirees at the lake, and the occasional longing glance while the other wasn't watching. But now it wouldn't matter, she was free to marry Hunter, because Issa is dead.

The days following our return are busy, or at least they were for the others. The council granted me a pardon, allowing me a temporary pass to mourn my loss before dissecting my memory for the small details they deemed valuable for planning future missions. Future missions, of which the council fully supported following the momentous success of the first trial. Four casualties were nothing compared to the nearly two-hundred souls that were saved during the mission.

As it turns out, Bethany wasn't a mirage. She was real. So was her son, my nephew, who now sleeps in Issa's bed with his mother. The council loved that turn of events; the long-lost sister returned. Issa's death avenged by the rescue and survival of his treasured sister and nephew. They'd even asked her to lead the next tribe North, a symbol of sorts, to show her appreciation for being rescued and remind others of the loss that occurs daily in the North; a reminder of Issa's sacrifice.

She asked for my opinion, but I didn't give it to her; she declined the offer of her own volition. We may share blood, but Bethany is a stranger to me. And instead of living in a house with a stranger, Annette graciously spared me her guest room to move into when we returned.

Rafael followed Bethany's example and also turned down the council's request to lead the next mission North. He hadn't overtly said it, but now that Bethany was back, he didn't have any more debts to settle up there. Their relationship wasn't immediate, he kept his distance and allowed her to gain solid footing, but it was less than six months when he boxed up his apartment and moved in with Bethany and Joseph.

I wasn't given the option to return to the North, not right away anyhow. The council didn't pay me much attention, probably not wanting the bad image of the dead leader's baby sister leading the revolution. I was told that I could return, if I wanted, following my successful completion of the exit exam. And while I wasn't certain I ever wanted to cross the border wall again, I finished my exit exam in record-breaking time. When the time came, I enrolled in college, figuring it prudent to be as educated as the South could allow.

I had hoped graduation would be enlightening, help me determine my future plan. Suffice it to say, it wasn't. But the answer I was searching for soon followed.

Rafael was out of town the day of my graduation. He had a last-minute council meeting in the Third district that was unavoidable. He dreaded missing it, but he sent Bethany, Joseph, Gabrielle, and their newest addition Issa Jr. in his place. We had a large celebration brunch, hosted by Annette, and I was sent away as the non-honoree women cleaned the dishes.

It was a calm autumn day, red and orange leaves blanketing the ground and a crisp chill promising of a frosty winter. The sun was beginning its descent, painting orange and purple stripes across the sky. I jumped up on the tailgate of Rafi's old blue truck and watched, enjoying the fresh air and sounds of children giggling in the background.

"You missing out on all the hoopla?" Rafi asked as he approached, returning from his trip.

I laughed, but didn't respond as he sat beside me.

"It's so beautiful here," I chimed, "Issa would have loved this."

He smiled. He was the only one who openly talked of Issa with me since his passing. "Yeah, he would," he pointed towards a pile of leaves under one of the large trees, "he would have raked the yards clean, making one giant pile, only to jump in and send them scattering all around again."

I pictured his vision and chuckled, agreeing that it sounded exactly like something Issa would have done.

"He'd also have been immensely proud of you," he announced as I blushed.

A silence grew between us as my thoughts wandered. Bethany and I had talked a lot about religion and what 'was meant to be'. I'd thought losing her was what God had intended since it created a ripple effect that led us to the South. But after losing Issa, it was hard to accept that God could have planned it all; losing Bethany, Issa joining the Revival, our parents' death, the journey South, the journey North, Bethany's reappearance, and Issa's death, all just to save one-hundred and eighty-eight Northerners.

"I guess he wasn't the Chosen One after all," I admitted aloud.

Rafi turned to me; his brows furrowed. "What do you mean?"

"The Chosen One," I clarified, but he shook his head in bewilderment. "The prophesy? A boy, raised among two identities, who will face an unspeakable loss and, with a stomach full of fire, will tear down the foundation that betrayed him, and lead the forsaken to destiny, freeing them from the pains of the century."

"Yeah, yeah, I know it. But what made you think it was Issa?" he asked, astonished.

"The whole neighborhood thought it. That's why the elders let him join the Revival early. At first, we thought the two identities meant the neighborhood and the Revival, but when we came South, I figured it meant the North and the South."

"Okay, and?"

"Then, Issa was born exactly one century following the start of the Great War, so that made sense."

"Hmmm-" he interjected doubtfully.

"What?" I chimed, my voice rising with the challenge.

"He was born a century after the *start* of the Great War."

"Yeah, so?"

"So, the North won the war. The real pain didn't start then. It started years later, when the Troops arrived."

He was right. The war lasted for three years, then the time of peace when the wall was resurrected, dividing the nations. It wasn't until two years later that the soldiers arrived and the North fell to the Troops.

"There's one other problem with your recitation," he declared, kicking off of the truck, gravel smashing under his feet.

"And what's that?" I challenged, hopping off the ledge and following him.

"You said the prophesy spoke of a boy," he turned, shoving the tailgate shut, and resting his elbow on the top.

"Yesss-" I bellowed, urging him to continue, my heart throbbing in my chest.

"The prophesy spoke of a 'child raised among two identities," he recalled, "it never mentioned it had to be a boy."